Imogen's Chance

PAULA VINCE

Endorsements

I would like to commend the author for the very clear Biblically correct way she has described one of the ways that God supernaturally heals people. She has revealed exactly the incredible power that is in the words of the Bible when they are treated as they were designed to be treated.

God's provision is in the promises He makes in the Bible. When we have a need then we have to find the promise relating to the answer, meditate on it, meet the conditions, allow the faith to develop and believe and claim it.

This word has to be meditated on so that it becomes part of us, so that our thinking automatically agrees with the Lord's thoughts. As this happens our minds are renewed, our heart is changed and it becomes simple to obey and this in turn supernaturally releases God's 'health' power into our lives.

As a person who has spent the last 35 years ministering the healing power of God to sick people and having approximately 1000 confirmed testimonies of people who have been healed, including terminally and medically incurable people, I know full well that Jesus is the same yesterday, today and forever.

He is also healing people through His believers today the same as He did when He was here on earth.

My prayer is that many people who read this book will be encouraged to seek God with all their heart and come to the point where, through receiving His word, they will be able to believe and receive their healing.

Weston Carryer, Evangelist, Tauranga, New Zealand

Imogen's Chance is a gripping, fast paced book full of the suspense, intrigue, romance and great characterisation that I have come to love and expect from Paula Vince. Through the lives of Asher, Imogen, Robbie and the other characters, it thoughtfully and provocatively presents the power of faith in the face of cancer. This powerful and moving drama raises important questions and possibilities and is well worth reading.

Jeanette O'Hagan (former) GP, theologian, and writer.

Imogen's Chance

Published by Even Before Publishing, a division of Wombat Books

PO Box 1519, Capalaba Qld 4157

www.wombatbooks.com.au

www.evenbeforepublishing.com

Copyright Paula Vince 2014

Cover Design by Wombat Books

National Library of Australia Cataloguing-in-Publication entry

Author: Vince, Paula, 1969- author.
Title: Imogen's chance / Paula Vince.
ISBN: 9781922074881 (paperback)
Subjects: Australian fiction.
Dewey Number: A823.4

Acknowledgements

I am grateful to those who worked enthusiastically on this story with me, particularly my editor, Iola Goulton, and my publisher, Rochelle Manners. I thank you, ladies, for all your hard work and encouragement. I also appreciate the support of my family, Andrew, Logan, Emma and Blake.

Prologue

Ginny squirmed, turned her pillow over and sighed. The worst part of staying with the Dorazio family was being sent to bed by Mrs Dorazio—Aunt Marian—at nine o'clock, even though there was still a tinge of daylight visible through the chinks in the blind. Becky's breathing was already even, and the usual few hours of boredom and homesickness stretched ahead of Ginny.

Humping her back beneath the covers, she pressed her face into the pillow, trying to smother her thoughts. It never worked. They just got shaken up a little, and then jostled each other through her head. Her mind insisted on reviewing each day before she could sleep.

At least I might get to see The Twelve Dancing Princesses tomorrow. Seth Dorazio had offered to take Ginny and the twins to the movies, but they couldn't agree on which to see. Seth had ripped a piece of shiny, gold construction cardboard into fifty tokens which he'd hidden all around the house, and the person who found the most would get to choose the movie.

So far, Ginny and Becky had pooled together their eighteen tokens while Asher had discovered twelve. Twenty tokens were still concealed but Aunt Marian had announced it was bedtime, and she never listened to protests. Ginny and Becky would have to find the others in the morning. They just had to. There was no way Ginny would sit through the silly movie Asher wanted to see, about racing cars and basketball players. She and Becky hadn't thought of checking the back of the laundry cupboard yet. Or behind the dishwasher, or under the plastic thingy in the cutlery drawer.... *If I was Seth, where would I choose to hide tokens?* That was a challenge, to imagine the way a cute fourteen-year-old boy would think.

Movement along the passage caught her eye. Uncle Hayden sometimes crept past to whisper goodnight to whoever was still awake, but not this time. The shadow that darted across the wall past the girls' open bedroom door was too short and furtive. It was Asher, and over his wrist dangled his plastic bag of gold tokens.

Rolling out of bed, she tiptoed after him. 'Hey, you're cheating.'

He jumped out of his skin. 'I am not.' He tried to hide the bag behind his back.

'Yes, you are. You're snooping around looking for tokens without us.'

'Well, you two girls were cheating even more.'

'We aren't cheating.' It was hard to keep her voice soft. How could he make such a groundless accusation with his sister sound asleep in the bedroom behind them?

'You are. Of course you'll find more tokens than me if you team up. That's not fair.'

'Yes it is, because Becky and I want to see the same movie.'

Asher glared at her. 'So what? You should be playing just for yourselves. Then I might have a fair chance of winning. But I won't if you add your tokens together. Can't you see how unfair that is?' Even in the dim passage, his eyes blazed.

She understood his logic but pretended not to. She wanted to choose the movie too much. 'I heard you tell your mum, and she said it was okay for us to team up.'

His scowl darkened his fair features. 'Yeah, she wasn't really listening. Nobody listens to me. That's why I'm making things even.' With a tilt of his chin, he was off. Ginny scampered after him.

'Hey, go away.'

'No!'

They ended up outside in the patio. It was the most refreshing time of a summer night when Uncle Hayden's drip hose moistened the creepers in the garden bed, making everything spring to life and smell fantastic. There was enough light coming from the kitchen window for Ginny to spot a token poking up over the top of Aunt Marian's peg basket. She swooped on it.

'Hey, stop finding 'em,' Asher said. 'I'm not watching any princess movie.'

She pressed her hand against her mouth to smother a grin and watched Asher, clad in Spiderman pyjamas, crawl behind a lavender bush in search of more gold. A glimmer high in the hollow of a gum tree near the gate caught her eye. Ginny glanced at Asher, who was still digging around near the fence, and then searched for something to retrieve the token. Seth was really crafty, and there was a lot at stake. Not only would she win the competition to choose the movie, but she'd also be the one who'd boast to Seth that she'd discovered one of his trickiest spots.

There was a broom beside the kitchen door. She raised the handle high to poke into the tree hollow, trying to dislodge the gold paper. It barely moved but she couldn't get a good angle. *How does Seth expect us to get this one?*

'Hey, what are you doing?' Asher backed out of the lavender.

'Mind your business.'

He squinted up where she'd been prodding. When a grin spread across his elfin face, she knew he'd seen the token.

'It's mine. I'm getting the ladder.' He bounded across the patio to a stepladder set up beside the house.

'No, I saw it first.' She took off after him. It was getting harder to keep her voice low.

Asher tugged one side of the ladder just as Ginny grasped the other. It wobbled between them and crashed to the pavers. Something above their heads caught Asher's attention and his eyes widened with horror.

Ginny followed his gaze and gasped. A pair of legs was sliding over the side of the house. Someone had been placing their foot on the ladder the moment it toppled and they hadn't even noticed. It was Aunt Marian. For some reason, she was up on the roof. Her comfy, round-the-house shoes dangled off her feet. One slid off and fell down on the pavers, then the other. Aunt Marian screamed, hands clutching at the gutter as she tried to stop the momentum of her fall.

With a lurch of the heart, Ginny bent to raise the ladder again. Snap! Before she had time, the echo of broken tin filled the patio. Aunt Marian was hanging by one hand, groping for another hold.

'Mum! I'll catch you.' Asher was beneath Aunt Marian, his spindly arms stretched high. Ginny's eyes turned fuzzy and then refocused.

Aunt Marian fell hard on Asher and knocked him backward, where his elbow hit the pavers with a smash. His face turned grey and he whimpered with pain. Aunt Marian lay, half on him and half on the ground.

'I can't move!' she groaned. 'I can't roll off you.'

It was clear that both mother and son were seriously hurt. Ginny's heart thumped so hard, it sounded like a drumbeat in her ears and she could barely hear herself scream.

Imogen's hammering heart woke her, as it had many other nights. Her tight chest meant it would take a moment before she could draw a breath deep enough to calm her spinning head. Perspiration had trickled down the sides of her temples, sticking her hair against her face. The pillow was damp, too. Even though the last part of the dream was just a few seconds long, her memory had been putting her body through that same re-enactment for so long, her sweat glands knew just what to do.

Not this again! Please not this again. God, please make it stop. I went to a therapist to try to end the nightmares. What more can I do? Any normal recurrent dream would be hard enough to deal with but this event had really happened. It had been partly her fault for helping knock over the ladder and the more she relived it, the more everything else played through her mind too.

Some things simply got worse with time.

Chapter 1

Imogen could do nothing to ease the sinking weight in the pit of her stomach. The closer the plane got to Australia, the more her stomach churned too deep to touch. She'd already felt queasy when the plane took off from LaGuardia in New York. Since then, she'd changed flights once and still had one more ahead of her. Saying goodbye to her parents at the airport had been hard. The concern creasing her mother's face and regret tugging the lines of her father's forehead down into a frown almost swayed her to abort the whole plan.

She'd seen a similar droop in Dad's brow whenever he'd been called out to a sudden emergency. It matched the expression on his mouth. The double frown usually meant another patient, often a small child, was gravely ill, causing her dear dad pain—pain Imogen always longed to heal, but never could. Several hours ago, in the airport terminal, she'd experienced regret, knowing that this time she had the power to erase his distress but wouldn't. Although changing her mind was possible, she'd set her heart on leaving.

'Stay home,' Dad had pleaded. 'After all this time, there's nothing you can do for the Dorazios. They've had years to come to terms with what happened. Your racing over to Australia won't make things easier for them.'

But Dad only knew about her part in Aunt Marian's accident. Marian had been on the roof, trying to coax down the family kitten, and hadn't expected the ladder to shift as she placed her foot on it. It turned out the gold glimmer up the gum tree hadn't been a token. It was a piece of foil chocolate bar wrapper blown up by the wind. Seth said he'd never have chosen such a dangerous spot to hide tokens. Imogen had misread the

5

situation, just as she'd done the last time she'd been in Australia, far more recently. She never told her family what had happened then either. *I've brought heartache to that family twice now.*

If it hadn't been for the promise she'd made when she had a ruptured appendix, she'd never have considered flying back. And if she'd made it to anybody else, she still might have tried to reason her way out of keeping it, but she'd promised the one person who wouldn't buy her flimsy excuses. She'd promised God.

Her mind drifted back to that time in the hospital. Pain had attacked her in unrelenting waves. Until they worked out a cause, the incessant agony was enough to prevent her moving or drawing a deep breath. Knife-like swells of sharpness tore into her, while perspiration trickled down into her hair. Imogen clamped her teeth, wondering why her belly appeared flat and smooth. She would have expected it to roil and heave with the war that raged within. If death had crept up at that moment and stolen her away, she would have welcomed the relief.

A nurse had mopped her forehead every so often, as if that gesture would soothe the torture ripping her grip on reality to shreds. It was then that Imogen pleaded inside her head, *if there's anything I can do to end this, I promise I'll do it.*

And right there on the hospital bed, three words filled her mind. The Dorazio family.

Okay, you got it. God, you take this horrible pain away, and I promise I'll go back to Australia. I'll make it up to the Dorazio family.

Soon the obliteration of general anaesthetic followed. She woke feeling woozy but wonderfully calm deep in her midriff beneath the new stitches. The promise stuck in her exhausted mind. The Dorazios. Since that day, not going to Australia was out of the question.

She'd spoken to Aunt Marian over the phone. She had to remind her about the nine-year-old girl who'd spent three months with them fifteen years ago. When she mentioned wanting to spend time working in Australia, Marian insisted on letting her board with them for old times' sake. Imogen's heart had thumped with misgivings. Reminiscing about the past with Becky and Asher was almost more than she could bear the thought of, but of course she could face it. One of Marian's remarks had helped set her mind at ease.

'They don't bear any grudges against you. Everyone knows you were just a child. And Asher had been disobedient too. Anyway, it was such a long time ago.'

I wonder if fifteen years has changed me enough. Hopefully using her full name would help them bury the past. They would remember her as little Ginny. Such a lot of time had passed and they would see that she was different now. The only thing she didn't tell Marian was the real intention for her trip, which was to bless them however she could.

She pressed her cheek against the window but wouldn't let herself drift off to sleep because it would bring the touchdown in Australia too close. But her eyelids insisted on drooping. They felt like sandpaper over her eyes, whether from fatigue, stress or recycled air-conditioning, she couldn't tell. She gave in and tilted her head back against the headrest to try and relax.

Memories of the first time she'd met the Dorazio family filtered through her mind; the time her parents and brother visited Australia's Northern Territory as missionaries for three months but left Imogen with her father's old pen pal, the man she called Uncle Hayden, and his family. Knowing that her parents wanted to take Scotty with them, but not her, had long since receded as a lesser pain. Not only had they thought the scorching outback too much for a little girl, they'd assumed she might have more fun with Uncle Hayden's kids.

They could have at least left me with Auntie Ally. If only they had, Aunt Marian might still be whole. But her parents had decided it would be unfair to leave Imogen with her mother's unmarried sister for so long. She'd never figured out whether they meant it was unfair to her or Aunt Ally. Anyway, the Dorazios had offered to have her, so the decision was made.

She had to think of each of them sometime so it might as well be now. Uncle Hayden, Aunt Marian, Seth and the twins, Becky and Asher. The twins were her age. Like many adults, her parents hadn't realised that just because children were the same age didn't necessarily mean they had anything else in common. Imogen had asked her father, 'Would you hang around with a group of other forty-year-olds just because they're the same age as you?' but he didn't really get her point.

Drawing a breath of stuffy air to calm her thumping eardrums, she wondered how she would greet them all. It was only a matter of hours now.

'I'll be a grandmother soon.' Marian's warm voice had poured into

7

her ear over the phone. 'Do you remember Seth? His wife is pregnant.'

So that brilliant, handsome boy was going to be a father. He had been fourteen years old when Imogen had known him. She used to concoct ways to impress him because Seth Dorazio was the sort of person whose approval boosted a little girl's self-esteem. If the twins were around to witness the flash of his admiring smile or hear his affirming words, so much the better.

Come to think of it, Seth's smile probably hadn't been admiring so much as amused; the way a clever, teenage boy looked at a bashful nine-year-old girl. Back then, she hadn't recognised patronising kindness when she saw it, and lapped up any attention he threw her.

Seth was always the person they'd seek to umpire their disputes. 'I'll ask Seth, then,' was the retort that would clinch it all.

Once, she and Becky had been ganging up against Asher, as usual. It was over a crazy subject that was probably long forgotten by the Dorazio twins, but Imogen remembered it. It was strange, how the memory worked. Things she tried hard to recall often receded into haze while weird, random things stuck like glue.

On this occasion, Asher had been trying to convince the girls that raining animals was a true phenomenon. Becky had taunted him for saying 'raining cats and dogs' because it was so ridiculous. Asher took that as a cue to ramble on about how certain parts of the world actually did rain animals such as frogs and fish, some on a regular basis.

Becky laughed at him. 'If you really believe that, you're dumber than I thought.'

Asher kept insisting he was right. The conversation grew more heated, ending with the inevitable, 'Let's ask Seth.'

Seth had howled with laughter. 'Of course animals don't fall out of the sky.'

'Ha!' Becky shot her twin a triumphant glare.

Asher's face got the scrunched up expression that meant he would start talking so fast, they'd be unable to understand what he said. 'It's true!' His voice grew high-pitched. 'I can show you where I found it. It even has a name.'

'Asher, drop it,' Uncle Hayden called from the lounge room. 'Nobody wants to hear your nonsense. Learn to concede defeat and admit when you're wrong.'

'But I'm not wrong.' He'd fallen into one of his door-slamming, head-banging, screaming moods. Uncle Hayden stalked in to seize Asher's arm and yank him out to the kitchen to roar at him.

Seth had made both girls giggle for days to come. 'Hey, Ash, look at those dark clouds. Is that a hippo I can see? Run for it!'

Shifting on her seat, Imogen looked at the tiny, perfect condensation drops caught in a vacuum between the plane's double windows, never being able to drip. That was another reason she'd tried to earn Seth's approval—simply to avoid his ridicule. She had been determined never to make herself appear stupid in front of him.

But just last month she'd been flicking around the television stations and come across a documentary about raining animals. The 'Rain of Fish' festival in Honduras was a regular event, said to be the miracle of an old saint's faith in God's provision to feed the hungry villagers. So, Asher had been right after all.

The suddenness of the pilot's voice broke into Imogen's thoughts. 'Ladies and gentlemen, we're approaching the coast of Australia.'

She gazed down at the scattered early lights of towns illuminating the rugged coastline at the edge of the inky Pacific Ocean. The water was a sheet of blue and the land was a similar canvas of red and brown. The dim sky would probably be pitch-black by the time her next flight touched down in Adelaide.

Chapter 2

'Everybody is waiting to meet you.' Marian Dorazio hobbled into the house and Imogen wheeled her suitcases over the threshold bump. 'Here's Becky, Asher, Kaitlyn, Seth and his wife, Jodie.'

Marian's inclusive hand gesture didn't reveal which was which. Three pretty young women were sitting in the lounge room with the two guys. Imogen would have to figure out which was Becky, her old friend and confidante.

'Hi, Imogen. It's been quite a while. I hope you'll like Australia.' That was Seth, the darker-haired and slightly sturdier of the two young men. His smile was reminiscent of the fourteen-year-old boy's. She'd expected Seth to be friendly and pleasant, and she was right.

'You forgot to introduce the little one in here.' One of the girls patted her stomach bulge.

Okay, so that one isn't Becky. 'Congratulations. You look as if you're glowing.' Imogen said what she hoped a pregnant woman would appreciate, but the girl heaved a sigh.

'I'm well into my second trimester now. I felt sick as a dog at the start, didn't I, Seth?'

'Keep up the complaints, Jodie.' One of the other girls patted her arm and hitched a foot over her opposite knee, revealing one of the sharpest points Imogen had seen on the heel of a shoe. 'You're a great source of inspiration. I'm going to audition for a pregnant woman next week.'

'Are you an actress?' Imogen probably sounded foolishly slow.

She flashed her green eyes and nodded.

'In film or on the stage?'

'The stage. I sing and act in musicals.'

Just like Uncle Hayden used to.

'She does a fantastic job.' The third girl's hair stood out from her head in a bright, frizzy crown.

High-heels' smile seemed forced. 'Well, as you have the lead role in *Much Ado about Nothing*, you must be super-fantastic.'

Okay, so they both act on the stage, but which is Becky?

'Here's a review about you.' The other young man raised a newspaper and began to read. 'Kaitlyn Peters brought Shakespeare's feisty Beatrice to life and Rebecca Dorazio shone in her role as the loyal and hard-done-by Hero. Their antics had me glued to my seat, relishing every moment.'

Imogen found herself trying not to stare at him. It was Asher, but who would believe he'd be so handsome? Loose, wavy-blond curls, firm jawline, broad shoulders. What happened to the pixie-faced, skinny-legged little stick she remembered from her dreams about that horrible night?

He went on, 'I'll surely follow the career of Miss Dorazio with interest, as it's rare for an actress to take on a character with such gusto and conviction.'

'Which paper is that in?' High-heels snatched it from his hands and scanned her eyes down the open page. 'I can't find it.'

A grin spread across his face. 'I tricked you.'

Frizzy-hair punched his arm and he winced.

'I can't believe you did it again. How do you keep fooling us?'

'It's pretty easy. I thought I'd give you a good review this time, instead of a bad one.'

'That was worse than all the bad ones you've ever made up. Asher, you're a jerk.' High-heels' voice wavered.

He had the grace to look contrite. 'Sorry, it was just a joke.'

'I thought it was for real. How do you think it makes me feel to be let down?' She appeared ready to cry.

'Let's make him write it out and we'll put it on your website. It sounded real.' It seemed Jodie was a peace-maker.

'That wouldn't be the same. People check these things.' High-heels got up and strode away.

Asher shrugged at Imogen and smiled. 'Welcome back. You can see I've still got a big mouth.'

'I don't think she needs to be told.' Frizzy-hair wriggled closer to him and kissed his cheek. As he linked his fingers through hers, she leaned her head on his shoulder.

Imogen knew the answers now. If Frizzy-hair was Asher's girlfriend, High-heels must be Becky. Of course, it was obvious now that her bright eyes were identical to Asher's.

Seth stood and arched his back. 'We have a table tennis match to head off to. Imogen, would you be interested in joining us some time? I know you'll be too tired tonight. I'm the captain and these guys are all in my team.'

'Well, I'm not.' Marian laughed.

'Everyone except Mum. So would you be interested?'

'Sure, I'd love to.' She'd played enough table tennis with her parents' foster children to feel confident.

'Hey, Seth, I might give it a miss tonight,' Asher said.

'You can't. Without Jodie, we'll be two players down if you sit out. She has the best excuse not to play.'

'Aren't I allowed to just be tired?'

'Not unless you're pregnant or have jet lag. All you've been doing is sitting around designing computer software.'

'That's hard work.'

'Don't complain. You get too well paid.' Seth stretched a hand to help Jodie to her feet. 'He earns more than the rest of us put together,' he told Imogen.

Asher shook his head. 'I don't think so.'

'Hey, what have you done to your arm?' Marian pointed to a purple-black bruise beneath Asher's t-shirt sleeve.

He looked and shrugged. 'Dunno. Kaitlyn just hit me there.'

'That little punch wouldn't cause a bruise like that,' Frizzy-hair said.

'Did you get in a fight at the office?' Seth gave his brother a wry smile.

'Sometimes I wish someone would pick a fight with me, just to break the boredom.'

'Let's go.' Becky reappeared from another room, wearing flat shoes now. 'See you, Mum. Bye, Imogen.'

As they left, Imogen felt the effects of jet lag sweep over her. Marian's cheerful voice seemed to come in waves that fazed in and out from miles away as she was shown to the guest bedroom. As soon as the door closed behind her, she opened the curtains a crack. Years ago, Uncle Hayden had taught her and the twins to identify the Southern Cross and she could still discern its square angles. She saw the Milky Way, a path of smudged light in the darkness. There was another path beneath her, a narrow lane that ran in a dip below the fence. Footsteps crunched along the gravel and moonlight poured onto the bald head of a passer-by. She would sit by the window and linger in the mellow darkness another day, but for now, it was a relief to slide between fresh sheets.

I think the Dorazios have got their normal lives back. They're probably happier than I am. Imogen's head was spinning. *And Becky's an actress, just what she always said she wanted to be. Uncle Hayden would've been proud.* A pang of pain pierced her armour.

It was all back to front. She'd flown half way around the world especially to make amends, yet not only were the Dorazios coping better than her, but Marian was the one helping Imogen, by offering her accommodation until she could find work in Australia.

How on earth am I supposed to help by being helped?

The pillow was soft and snug. Now that she was back with the family whose lives were shattered, she dreaded the return of her nightmare. *God, if I find ways to help the Dorazio family, won't you please make it stop for good?*

His usual habit of twirling one thumb around the other set off the burning, stabbing pain in his left shoulder, so he wriggled his toes inside his shoes instead to try and allay the boredom. Asher was in the last place he'd ever intended to find himself. Exhaustion alone would have kept him away from the doctor but the pain proved far greater.

Why am I still this tired? He'd attributed it to being a leader at the youth camp, but Seth had reminded him that had been well over a month ago, and he couldn't use it as an excuse any more. For once, Seth was right.

Doctors' waiting rooms hadn't changed much over fifteen years. A suffocating shroud hovered almost visibly from the ceiling, or were his eyes turning hazy and playing tricks on him?

I'm being a wimp. Tiny children were having fun around a toy box. They were waiting to see doctors too, and they weren't terrified. A Lego car rolled beneath his chair, and a beaming toddler lumbered after it on dimpled legs. Leaning down to retrieve it, Asher was almost blinded by a bolt of red-hot pain shooting from his shoulder. Clamping his lips to prevent crying out, he twisted around to lift the car with his right arm instead.

'Here you are, mate.' He even sounded breathless.

It had been the same playing table tennis last night. Even though he swung the bat with his right arm, the jerk to his left shoulder made his head swim every time. He'd lost the match for them, to Seth's annoyance, but Asher hadn't mentioned his shoulder. He'd never spoken of that to his family since three months after the accident, when he was still nine years old.

But now it had grown worse. It was nothing like the sporadic, dull ache he'd been dealing with for fifteen years. A few weeks ago he'd still been able to lift his arm gradually and carefully, but today just raising it a millimetre was a major event.

A doctor called his name. At least now he'd get it over with, but once in the consulting room, he struggled to remove his shirt.

As Doctor Mason poked the swollen flesh around his shoulder, then raised his arm to prod beneath the murky armpit, Asher gritted his teeth. He focused on the doctor's eyes, watching for a sign, but those watery grey pools revealed nothing.

'How would you rate this pain on a scale from one to ten?' the doctor asked at last.

'Twenty.' Asher tried to laugh.

'It's obviously been like this for some time. Why have you waited until now to come?'

'I started off thinking it was just normal for me. I've had a bit of pain in that shoulder for fifteen years.' Asher moistened his lips. Having to talk about it was part of the reason he hadn't wanted to come.

'What happened fifteen years ago?'

'I broke my shoulder joint.'

The doctor winced. 'How did you do that?'

'I was trying to save my mum from falling off the roof. She'd been up there trying to rescue our cat, and we didn't know. The ladder got knocked over just as she started stepping down. It was mostly my fault. I shouldn't have even been out there. When I saw her falling, I tried to catch her but she was heavier than I expected. I fell backwards really hard onto my left elbow.' Speaking about it brought the memory flooding back and he closed his eyes. At the time, the doctor who had treated Asher said that if only he'd landed on his hand instead of his elbow, the injury might not have been as serious. As it was, the elbow's horrific impact with the patio pavers had provided no give to shield his shoulder joint.

'Did you have proper treatment at the time?'

'Yeah, it healed, but it was never as good as before.'

It seemed the doctor was in no hurry to say anything else so Asher rushed on to fill the gap. 'What happened to Mum was worse. She really hurt her spine and neck. For months, nobody thought she was going to be able to walk again. Then she was in a really tight traction brace for ages.' He was doing it again. Rambling on with details nobody had asked for. 'I got used to my shoulder twinges. They were no big deal.'

'Do you see these red streaks running out from the swelling?'

Asher hadn't before, because he'd been too sore to twist his arm around that far, but now that the doctor had done it for him, he could. The streaks looked like an angry rainstorm beneath his skin. 'Yeah.'

'They concern me a lot.'

Fear began prickling Asher's skin, creeping over the base of his skull. 'Why? Do you reckon it might be blood poisoning or something?'

The doctor's pause didn't bode well.

'There's a hard lump beneath your armpit.' His gusty sigh hit the side of Asher's face like breeze from a crypt. 'I'm going to take some blood tests. I want to organise an ultrasound and X-ray too.'

Asher's heart sank. He'd been optimistic enough to hope the ordeal would be over that same day. 'When?'

Doctor Mason was at the sink, washing his hands. 'I'll try to organise them for this afternoon. You can't go on like this. Now, where do you work?'

'At a company called Lewis and Thorne.'

'What do you do there?'

'I'm a computer software engineer.'

'Well, they'll have to do without you for awhile.'

'That won't be easy to organise.' It would be impossible. Nobody else would want to work on his three projects. Mr Thorne would be seething mad because one was already overdue—it had been Kelly Finlay's assignment before Thorne had taken it back in disgust and given it to Asher instead. The client was already irritated because of the extra time it had taken to fill Asher in on the details.

Thorne should have given it to Asher in the first place and he wouldn't take kindly to the idea of explaining the intricacies to yet another person. Who else would Thorne ask, anyway? Apart from Asher there was only Kelly, and she had already messed it up. There was Tom, but he couldn't handle the JavaScript component. Thorne would have no choice but to take it on himself and he couldn't spare the time. Asher wasn't convinced that his boss had the technical skill to do it. Asher had a sore shoulder, but John Thorne was going to have a heart-attack. *Maybe I'll be able to work on it from home.*

On top of aggravating the people at work, Asher would have to explain to his family why he wasn't going to work. They would start asking questions and he'd have to tell them it was his shoulder. That would dredge up all the old guilt. He should have ignored the pain. Maybe he wouldn't tell them it was his shoulder.

'If you'd come in a few weeks ago, it would have been better for everyone.'

'Well, at least I'm doing something about it now. Nobody will blame you.' Perhaps he should have thought before he spoke, but the doctor's deadpan way of doling out veiled reproaches was growing really depressing. 'If you'll just do the blood tests now, I'll get out of your hair.'

Chapter 3

Imogen walked up and down the plush theatre foyer with Seth and Jodie, who had taken her to see Becky's performance.

Sipping his coke, Seth cleared his throat and leaned closer to talk. 'She's performing just as she used to when we were kids, all intense and serious. The techniques that used to work for Dad just seem over the top from her. It looks like she's performing at the audience, demanding that we like her.' He ruefully shook his head.

'We're too familiar with her to judge fairly,' Jodie said. 'What do you think, Imogen?'

'Her character is meant to be serious.' Imogen tried to come up with more good things to say about Becky's acting. 'Maybe it's just because Kaitlyn's such a contrast, having the time of her life.'

The tinkle of a bell filled the foyer, summoning the audience back to the auditorium. As they sank into the softness of their seats, Jodie whispered to Imogen, 'Poor Becky gets tired of Kaitlyn always getting the lead roles, but they're best friends, so it's hard for her to let off steam.'

The lights dimmed and a hush filled the theatre. Imogen watched Seth stretch his arm to wrap around Jodie, who melted into it. The curtain swished up to reveal Kaitlyn, smiling widely.

She was like an exotic bird with gorgeous plumage. Her bright physical features matched her flamboyant personality. She was the sort of girl who made Imogen feel a little dowdy, as if any colour she might have had was being drained. Most of the time, being quiet and reserved wasn't a problem—well, not much of one—but being around Kaitlyn felt like a perpetual reproach.

I'll bet if she'd been their daughter, Mum and Dad would've taken

Kaitlyn with them on more mission trips. That was just a silly thought.

Anyway, Kaitlyn was the sort of uninhibited girl she might have expected the gregarious Asher to fall for, if she'd given it any thought. Come to think of it, Asher hadn't been as talkative as she'd expected to find him. He had moments of sitting around brooding, which made her stomach coil whenever she let herself dwell on it. That guy made her plain nervous.

When she allowed herself to think about it, he was probably the person she had wronged most of all on her most recent trip to Australia, by not speaking up at the time. *I could tell him now. I could tell them all. After all, I did nothing officially wrong.* The thought of opening her mouth made her heart accelerate.

No, there are so many problems with that idea. The time to speak has passed. The family seems happy now. If I mention anything, it might drag them right back to their grief. They wouldn't want me living with them any more, even though it wasn't my fault. Keeping quiet is the best way to handle it.

Imogen couldn't deny that silence would be the easiest choice, although she hated to think she was talking herself into a cop-out. And she couldn't help feeling that Asher, at least, might not agree with her reasoning.

I wish he didn't still live at home with his mother. I feel as if I'm treading on eggshells whenever I see him. Whether or not she decided to be forthcoming about certain things, she was there to bless his family and make amends. He would prove the biggest challenge, as he obviously didn't need any good she had to offer. Asher had the girl of his dreams in Kaitlyn, a job anybody would kill for and the sort of looks to turn any woman's head.

She would focus on her plan and start by blessing Becky, who might be easiest. Perhaps she would post Becky an anonymous gift from an appreciative fan. Back when they were little, Becky loved white chocolate. Imogen would choose a huge box of white truffles and send it to the theatre's address. That might show Becky that she was appreciated for herself, and not eclipsed by Kaitlyn.

But does she still like white chocolate? And if she did, would she suspect that the gift had been sent by somebody who knew that? It was probably a small, pathetic gesture anyway. Her genuine desire to make a difference, when it seemed there was little she could really do, was beginning to seem as silly as she suspected her parents thought she was.

Imogen set her mind back to the play, where Becky, as Hero, was trying to plead her innocence to a furious and inexorable Claudio, who refused to listen. He insisted on his right to keep believing that she'd had affairs. Guilt prickled over Imogen's flesh. Watching an innocent girl blamed for something she didn't do sickened her. Anyone who knew the truth and wanted to look at her in the most severe light might claim that her story was quite the opposite from Hero's. Imogen should never have got away, scot-free, with what had happened five years ago. *Even though I still believe I was innocent, I can see how I might look guilty.* Coming to Australia just kept the whole mix-up playing through her head. *Should I just say my piece and go home?*

Was flying across the globe to make amends really enough? She'd thought it would help. But maybe God was parading *Much Ado About Nothing* past her eyes to convict her that nothing would ever fix what she'd done. Maybe it was his way of reminding Imogen that her personal story could easily be called *No Ado About Something.* There had been no ado at all about something terrible. Not as far as she was concerned, anyway.

'The results of your tests are back. Doctor Mason was wondering if it would be possible to consult with you within the next hour.'

The receptionist's non-committal tone was enough to ignite the fear he thought he'd squelched. Asher felt it set his head spinning. They weren't supposed to call him, were they? He thought he was supposed to take the initiative and he'd almost decided not to bother. The shoulder pain was only slightly worse than this mental angst.

'Well, yeah. Sure.' He supposed he'd have to go through with it.

'The doctor suggests that you bring a support person along.'

'Hey?' It was getting increasingly worse. 'I don't have a support person.'

'A friend or family member will be fine. Because if you don't, we may have to consider rescheduling to…'

'Okay, I'll bring someone.' He supposed he shouldn't have cut her off. His earliest memories included getting in trouble for interrupting people. 'Why do I need a support person?'

'I can't answer that question. That's for Doctor Mason to…'

'Yeah, okay.' This time he cut her off on purpose, but didn't care. The exchange reminded him of the silly mental games medical staff used to play fifteen years ago when Mum was going through her grueling recovery. They'd say, 'Mr Dorazio, your wife's injuries are so extensive, I'd suggest you look out for some permanent household help.' Dad's weary, red-rimmed eyes would cloud over with a film of hurt. 'Are you telling me she'll never walk again?' The staff would respond, 'You'll have to speak to the surgeon. We're not suggesting that.' Well, if they weren't suggesting it, then why did they say it?

Mum would be left lying on her bed, trying to give them a twisted smile while the catches in her breath betrayed her intense pain. At home, Dad would sit for hours staring into the glass of port or whisky in front of him, letting out occasional sighs. And he wouldn't go to bed. He'd slump over, sleeping with his forehead on the table. Asher had never seen strength literally drain out of a person. Dad would sometimes lash out, kicking doors and smashing ornaments.

And the times when he broke down in tears were even worse.

It was during those days that Asher made to the decision to keep quiet about his ongoing shoulder pain. He didn't want to think about what had happened when he had tried to tell someone.

'We'll see you soon.' The receptionist's receiver clicked in his ear.

Unfortunately, yes. Now for a support person. Did they think people were waiting around to perform his bidding? Mum and Becky were both at work. *I don't think I'll bother.* But what if they wanted to check? They might have their reasons. Perhaps they were going to inject something into his arm to relieve the agony that might make him drowsy and prevent him from driving. He wanted it over and done with. And he wanted the pain gone. It had dragged on for long enough.

He tapped the door of the guest room with his good arm and opened it a crack. 'Hey Imogen, have you got a moment?'

Her newspaper rustled as she spun around from the window. 'Oh, hi. Sure.'

'Would you have time for a drive to the doctor's surgery with me? They won't tell me what's wrong with me unless I have a support person.'

'Wow,' she said as she folded her paper. 'Health care in Australia must be pretty thorough.'

'I don't know if they do this often. I haven't been to the doctor for years.'

She seemed to be thinking it over. 'Okay, but I don't know how good I'll be at being supportive.'

'It's just a formal thing. You won't have to do anything. It's ridiculous really. I've never had a support person in my life, except for me.'

Asking her had been a good idea. He was grateful to have somebody neutral to call on, somebody he hadn't seen for years.

Flashy sports cars were very compact. She could smell the spicy aroma of Asher's aftershave as she climbed into the BMW beside him. He let the engine idle, waiting for a bald-headed guy to pass before backing out of the driveway.

'Nice car.' She wanted to distract him enough to keep him from asking questions about her.

'Would you like to drive it home, in case they give me a shot in the arm and I can't?'

'What's wrong with your arm, anyway?'

'Do you remember that accident when my mum fell on me? My shoulder's been playing up ever since.'

'Oh.' Her stomach coiled. Even though it was so long ago, she'd been afraid he was going to say that. 'I'd love to but I'm not sure I'm confident to drive on the right side of the car yet. It feels weird just sitting here.'

'Don't worry, then. I'm sure I'll be able to drive.'

She shot him a sidelong glance. 'But what if they do give you a shot?'

Asher shrugged. She noticed that he had a unique, lopsided shrug, tilting only one shoulder.

'I guess I could phone Seth. His school isn't far away and it'll be after home time by then. He always likes a chance to drive this car.'

'Seth would love a car like this.' She'd already heard him say so often.

Asher laughed. 'But he'll need a family car soon. School chaplains are supposed to drive old rust-buckets anyway, so the students don't think they're too worldly.'

'So you don't mind being perceived as worldly?'

'Hey, you wouldn't believe how boring it is where I work. I might as well get some benefits.'

'It's pretty exciting that you're going to be an uncle.'

'Yeah, it'll be great.' He pulled into a driveway on the left and parked the car. They were at the doctor's surgery.

'Would it be okay if I wait here in the car?'

'Sure. I doubt if they'll come out to check my support person. Listen to some music, if you like. And Kaitlyn usually leaves some nibbles in the glove box. If you find any, feel free to help yourself.'

She found it easy to imagine Kaitlyn's bright hair leaning against the sleek black upholstery. And she couldn't help thinking of something Becky had said. *'You should hear people carry on whenever they turn up anywhere in his BMW. "Kaity and Ash are here. Now the party can start!" Show ponies, the pair of them.*

Some people fell on their feet all right. She didn't need to speak up about that other matter. He was okay.

In a short time, he returned and slid into the driver's seat.

'So are you fit to drive?'

He let out a breath and nodded. 'They didn't give me any shots.'

Only then did she notice how pale he'd turned, and that his hands around the steering wheel were trembling.

'Are you okay?'

Without turning to look at her, he nodded as the car's engine purred to life. He was chewing on his lip, his chest rising and falling.

'Did they tell you some… news?' She bit off the word 'bad' just in time.

'Well, it was sort of unexpected.' As he cleared his throat, her heart began pattering hard.

'I think in the back of my mind, I was scared I was going to hear something like this. I just hoped that if I didn't think about it, it wouldn't turn out to be true.'

Chapter 4

At least he wasn't going to burst into tears. His eyes were completely dry. Waiting for an opening to tell them his news was a challenge. Seth and Jodie were over to share dinner, and Jodie's appetite was the best it had been for weeks. Becky was talking about how she'd been out with other cast members celebrating the final performance of Much Ado. Then everyone started joking about the way Jodie shovelled down Marian's beef stroganoff, and nobody noticed that Asher merely pushed his around on his plate.

Maybe I won't bother telling them yet. But waiting too long had brought this horrible thing upon him in the first place. Imogen was watching him across the table with a questioning expression in her hazel eyes. Since their houseguest knew, he had to tell his family. They'd only feel hurt if he postponed it.

When Seth began piling up plates to take to the kitchen, Asher knew he had to say something.

'I have something I need to tell you all.' His heart pounded as if it wanted to burst from his chest. 'I've been feeling a lot of pain in my shoulder lately, so I went to a doctor and he made me have some tests. Turns out I have cancer and it's spread to my lymph nodes.' Slowly, he released the rest of the breath he'd been holding.

Except for Imogen, who gazed down at her plate, the others were all watching him.

'So what's the punch line?' Seth asked at last.

'Huh?'

'Come on, out with it,' Becky demanded.

'You think I'm joking?' Somehow, he'd stuffed it up. A horrible feeling spread from his stomach to his fingertips

'You can't fool us every time. If you weren't joking, you wouldn't have left the big announcement until right before dessert. And you wouldn't be so matter-of-fact about it. So what's the joke?'

What do I say now? Perhaps he would have done better if he could have shed a few tears after all. Imogen raised her head to look at him and her face was pale. Perhaps they should have looked at her while he talked.

'It's true. The doctor even had some long, weird name for it.' It was written on a scrap of paper in his wallet. 'If this was a joke, you would've fallen for it. You always fall for my jokes. So the fact that you're suspicious proves it's true.'

'Nice try, Ash.' Seth was arranging cutlery so it wouldn't all tumble off the top plate.

He guessed he could probably cry now but it was too late for tears. No point in making them feel guiltier than they already would when the truth sunk in. 'If you don't believe me, why don't you phone the doctor's surgery and find out?' He pushed back his chair and headed for his bedroom.

Silence fell behind him, far louder than any noise. He couldn't bring himself to turn around and face them now. Tears were arriving but it was too late. Being too late was his pattern. Too late not to crash down on his elbow, too late to tell his father how he felt about everything, too late to visit a doctor in time to save his own life. He closed his bedroom door and swiped his right sleeve across his eyes, because his left arm was far too sore to lift.

The soft knock came far sooner than he was ready. His door opened, and there they all stood. Asher raised his eyes and scanned their faces, then glanced down again. It was too painful to witness their raw sorrow, but those few seconds were enough to print the scene on his memory. He would probably remember their united front of grief the moment before he died.

Jodie's eyes were filling with tears while Becky's were saucer-round, glassy with fear. Seth's complexion was pasty-grey and he squinted as if the dim light was too bright. At the end of the row, his mother's lip was trembling. It was a sign that she was going to cry and he had to do something. Trying to deflect his mother's tears had become second nature, ever since the accident when Dad told them to do all they could to boost her spirits. That was why he had to talk before any of the others got a chance.

'Hey, I don't want you all to feel bad for not believing me. I know it did sound sort of funny.'

'Hey, little bro, you know I'll be there for you. Whatever you need, I'll do it. Bone marrow transplants, blood transfusions… whatever. I'm your man.' Seth's voice was shaky.

'Hey bro, thanks.' Asher felt his throat clamp tight. 'You won't need to. They told me what they're going to do. They're giving me an operation, to see if they can cut some of it out, then several months of chemotherapy. Nine treatments, I think he said, with three week intervals in between '

Marian sank onto Asher's desk chair with her face in her hands. Poor Mum. She'd been through far too much in her life already.

Jodie stood on tiptoe to wrap an arm around Seth's shaking shoulders. 'Asher, did they tell you how successful all that will be?'

'Depends on how far it's gone.' He licked his dry lips. 'He reckons I have a thirty per cent chance to survive five years.'

Another silence fell, like the one behind him in the dining room, but this time he could see their devastated faces. Jodie's head drooped onto Seth's shoulder.

'Hey, I'm really sorry to dump this on you guys now, with the baby coming, and all.' He made an involuntary apologetic gesture which set off the sharp twinge in his shoulder that felt as if his flesh was being ripped raw from the inside. The pain bursting from his heart was even worse. He would never get to know his nephew or niece, possibly wouldn't even get to see them. Jodie's belly was rounding into a nice-sized little bulge but she still had almost four months to go.

'We'll start praying for a miracle.' She raised her damp face.

Marian heaved herself off the desk seat, hobbled to her daughter-in-law and rested a hand on Jodie's head. 'Of course we will. We can't stop hoping and praying that God will hear us and have mercy. I had a miraculous recovery, after all. We never expected I'd be able to walk again. God can provide a miracle for Asher too, if he wants to.'

He didn't feel better. Sure, Mum could shuffle around, but hadn't they all stormed heaven's gates, week after week and month after month, pleading for a full recovery for her? Her progress probably never had anything to do with God at all. Otherwise, why wouldn't he heal her completely?

'This time, it's life or death. We have to do whatever it will take.' Seth was striding up and down the carpet square. 'We can take you some place where miracles happen... Lourdes or somewhere. Hey Ash, surely you have plenty of savings tucked away, you can afford it. You could even sell your BMW. It's your life at stake here. We've got to do something. Are you sure some sort of transfusion wouldn't help? If you need blood, I'd give you every drop of mine.'

'Hey, Seth.' Asher waited until he was sure he had his brother's attention. 'I know you would. I'm really grateful, but it wouldn't work. And all that miracle stuff... well, I don't think it happens very often. If it worked all the time for everything, nobody would ever die.' The sooner they all came to terms with that, the better. He couldn't put his family through the ordeal they'd faced during Mum's long illness, and then just die at the end.

'Does this run in families?' Becky's husky voice spoke up from near the door.

'Hey?' Careful not to move his shoulder, he twisted his head to look at her.

'Well, I'm your twin.' Her fists were clenched tight by her sides.

'Oh.' Understanding flooded through him. 'No, no, I'm sure it's not a genetic thing.' At least he was able to raise his good right hand to touch his left shoulder. 'If I hadn't got used to this shoulder hurting all these years, I might have noticed something else was wrong or gone to the doctor sooner.'

His mother let out a cry. 'Is it the same shoulder you hurt when you tried to catch me?'

'Well, yeah.' He had a sinking feeling he was going to hate what was coming.

'Did this cancer come because of the accident?'

'No, they said it's not related. Accidents don't cause cancer. Just a horrible coincidence that it had to be the same shoulder.'

'Why didn't you tell us before?' Tears trickled down her cheeks.

He tried to shrug but caught himself. Old habits lingered. No, it seemed he was too late again. A wave of pain surged through him as the inflamed ligaments in his shoulder must have stretched just enough. 'I got used to it. It wasn't so bad… until now.'

Jodie was rubbing her belly. 'If this baby's a boy, we're going to name him after you.'

Although she was talking as if he was already dead, her words made Asher feel strangely better. The baby would have to ask how he got his name and they would tell him about his uncle.

No, come to think of it, it wasn't making him feel better at all. What would they have to say? That he went down in family history as the gasbag who made the hugest mistakes? His mother's condition was his fault. His father's death was too. It was probably fitting that his own demise would prove to be his fault too.

Seth was still sniffing hard. 'Why do things turn out the way they do? Why not me instead of you? I can't understand how fate makes these decisions.'

'Well, why shouldn't it be me and not you?' Asher felt exhaustion creep over his body.

'Just look at you.' Seth sniffed hard. 'Look how far you've come, how hard you've worked to get where you are. Think of the future you should have ahead of you. I can't stand thinking it'll all be wasted. I've got to do something. It should be me and not you. I'm not the successful, smart son.'

Asher heaved a sigh. Since his boyhood, he'd longed to hear his older brother praise him, but the price was too high. 'Well, don't worry. You soon will be.'

With a sob, Seth was on the bed beside him, hugging him, rumpling his hair and hurting his shoulder, although Asher didn't mention that. He patted his brother's back with his right hand. Out in the passage, he caught sight of Imogen. Her face was pale, her eyes dark and hollow. The poor girl hadn't known what she'd got herself in for when he asked if she'd come for a drive to the doctor's surgery with him.

Patti Browne

That's very sad. A diagnosis of cancer is always tragic but especially for someone as young as Asher.

Imogen Browne

I know.

She had more of her mother's undivided attention over Facebook live chat than she had for months.

Patti Browne

I can clearly remember what Asher was like as a little boy. When we dropped you off with Hayden and Marian, you went outside to play with Becky, but he stayed at the table with the adults, always wanting to dominate the conversation. He was the sort of child who had something to say about everything.

Imogen Browne

I know.

Online chat with her mother turned out to be the same as physically talking. She could get by on one phrase for a long time.

Patti Browne

Your dad and I were relieved to escape from the chatterbox. Our heads were spinning after an hour sitting there. And I remember Scotty said he felt like clawing the wall.

Imogen thought of something she could have typed. 'You had no qualms about leaving me there for three months.' No, some things were better left unsaid.

Imogen Browne

Yeah, that's no surprise.

Patti Browne

How did poor Marian take it?

Imogen Browne

She's very upset, of course.

Patti Browne

No wonder. First her horrible accident, then she lost Hayden, and now Asher. God seems to give some people more than their fair share of grief.

Imogen Browne

Could you and Dad please pray that Asher's operation and all the chemotherapy treatments will go well?

Patti Browne

Of course we will, but you must prepare yourself for the worst. When I described his condition to your father, he said he didn't have much hope for him.

Her mother's bleak words seemed to sway on the screen as Imogen's eyes clouded. Her dad had seen too much of all kinds of illness. If anybody knew what they were talking about, it was him.

Imogen Browne

I wish I was home. I feel terrible whenever I look at him, knowing he's probably going to die.

Patti Browne

There's nothing to stop you coming back. But at least you have the chance to help, as you said you wanted to. You can make life easier for Marian by helping around the house.

Imogen Browne

I know. But anything I can do seems so small. How are you and Dad going, anyway?

Patti Browne

Good. We're taking the girls to Disney World next week. Now that only Ruthie and Sue are still with us, we thought we'd give them a special treat.

An old familiar prickle was back. Imogen had to be careful what she typed.

Imogen Browne
They'll love that. Wish I could've come.

Patti Browne
Honey, are you feeling bad?

Imogen sat there, blinking. The screen was waiting for an answer.

Imogen Browne
Well, yeah, I am a bit. You know I've never been to Disney World.

Patti Browne
Come on, Hon, don't be like that. These foster girls have come from broken, traumatized homes. They've seen worse sights than you ever dreamed of.

Imogen wriggled her laptop to a more comfortable position on her knees. It was guilt trip time. There was no point in reminding her mother that Ruthie and Sue had both been lighthearted and even a bit cheeky for several months now.

Imogen Browne
That's beside the point, Mom. I'm just commenting that I wish I'd been to Disney World.

Patti Browne
Oh, Imogen, you have to remember how lucky you were to be born into a stable home with all the love we could possibly give you.

She arched her back and flexed her fingers. It really wasn't worth saying anything. She'd said it before but Mom and Dad never got it. That 'stable home' had included surreptitious teasing, pinches and pokes from rough foster kids for as long as she could remember. Arielle and Cara had been the worst, but at least they had moved out long ago. Ruthie and Sue merely huddled together whispering, shooting her saucy glances and breaking into smothered giggles whenever she came within earshot. They invented their own in-jokes with Mom and Dad, making her feel left out, even though she was twenty-four years old.

The screen was still filling.

Besides, you can't claim that you haven't had a chance to travel. Look where you are right now. In Australia.

Imogen Browne
Yes, but what have we just finished talking about? I'm not enjoying myself at fantastic theme parks. I'm sharing a house with a poor guy who's just found out he's dying of cancer.

Oops, instead of just thinking that, she'd actually typed it. There were the truculent words on the screen before her. Although thousands of miles separated them, she could easily imagine her mother's rolling of the eyes and whiny, 'This girl is unbelievable.'

Patti Browne
Now, listen to me, young woman! Let me remind you that flying to Australia was your idea. Dad and I tried to talk you out of it but you went off and refused to listen to us so don't get all bitter just because we're going to...

Imogen snapped the laptop shut on her knees. Her mother was surely still busy typing reproaches but her heart was beating too hard, and tears were streaming down her cheeks. She was in no mood for a pep talk. The words would still be there next time she logged on to have a look. Probably whole pages of them.

Chapter 5

Imogen tiptoed out of her room to stack the dishwasher so Marian wouldn't have to give it a thought. Moonlight spilled over the cushions on the kitchen window seat. She remembered a night when she'd sat wedged in there with Becky and Asher, watching Uncle Hayden perform magic tricks. That window seat was the perfect fit for three nine-year-olds.

She'd been mesmerised by the way he shuffled his deck of cards so fast. His clever hands flew. Looking forward to his cheerful presence each evening had been the highlight of her days. She used to peep at the clock–that same kitchen clock with the quirky, jagged hands–feeling more effervescent the closer it got to five fifteen. After all these years, she could still remember the exact time he used to arrive home.

'Voila!' Uncle Hayden had beamed. 'Ginny, I'll bet that was the card you were thinking of.' He seemed to understand the depth of her secret loneliness and managed to make her feel better for brief periods of time. While her attention was focused on his droll antics, she had no room in her heart to pine for Mom, Dad and Scotty.

'I know how you did that.' Asher chipped in. 'It's called sleight of hand. You tucked a card of the same suit up your sleeve and now you're going to ... '

'Shush, I haven't finished yet.'

'But I've worked it out! That's why I've never seen you do it wearing a t-shirt. It has to be long sleeves.' Asher's voice made her head throb. Sharp, loud and piercing, it jangled her brains. 'You put the cards in four even piles and then...'

'For the love of Mike, can't you shut that cake-hole for just two minutes until I finish the trick?'

Asher drew a deep breath.

'Hey, no you don't!' Uncle Hayden pounced on him with a pointing finger. 'I said shut it. Maybe it's too loose. Ginny, do you think we ought to take him to have his mouth wired so it can't open so wide, or so often?'

Ginny and Becky giggled. Asher leaned, scowling, against the pane of glass behind him.

Becky nudged Ginny's ribs. 'Our ears need a break. Mine are bleeding inside.'

'I'm sure it's a huge strain on him.' Uncle Hayden grinned. 'He won't manage to hold it in for more than thirty seconds so I'd better hurry and finish the trick.'

Asher scrambled out of the window seat mumbling something rude, and edged past his father. He shut the door hard behind him. The girls moved further apart to fill the gap he left.

'Ginny, talking about ears, look behind yours,' Uncle Hayden said.

She reached behind the ear closest to Becky.

'No, the left one.'

She still got right and left mixed up sometimes, but in this case it was easy. He meant the opposite one. She raised her hand to feel something pleasantly crisp and starchy nestling in her hair. It turned out to be a small black and white polka-dotted bow on a bed of lace, all connected to a hair clip. Ginny felt a smile spread across her face.

'Aha, I caught another one for my good luck jar.' Uncle Hayden used to joke about catching her smiles as if they were butterflies.

'Dad, show us your good luck jar.' Becky kicked her feet against the wooden panels of the window seat.

'If I do, all you'll see is an empty jar. It's full of my favourite things but they're invisible to everyone else. Smiles from Ginny, hugs from Becky, silence from Asher.'

'Uncle Hayden, how did you get this clip in my hair without me feeling it?'

His shaggy blond eyebrows waggled in a comical way. 'A good magician never tells his tricks.'

'I can tell you how he does it,' a muffled voice called from behind the door.

In two strides, Uncle Hayden was over there to open it. 'Come back in, now. I know you're dying to tell them how I do those tricks.' He ruffled

Asher's hair. 'You get why I was cross, don't you? Your biggest problem is not knowing when to hold your tongue. You're too quick to show off. You need to pause to consider other peoples' feelings before you shoot off your mouth. Trying to deflate someone's ego while he's in the middle of performing a magic trick is just very bad taste.' Uncle Hayden sucked his cheeks between his teeth and wrinkled his nose as if somebody had poked a lemon into his mouth. Ginny and Becky burst into peals of laughter, and even Asher couldn't help a grudging smile.

'Aha! Got it.' Uncle Hayden pointed at Ginny's laughing face. 'The best treasure of all for my jar. An outright laugh. That'll bring me very good luck tomorrow. You're the sweetest little luck token to have around here, my pen pal's little girl all the way from America.'

Oh, Uncle Hayden, you were wrong. Imogen finished wiping down the bench and sank into the window seat. *I know neither was my fault, but I always show up when your family are going through terrible times.*

Was there such a thing as a human jinx? She didn't want to be one, but surely the timing was strange and frightening. No, that was just silly. Her pastor from back home in New York assured his congregation that such superstitions didn't bear thinking about. *As a forgiven Christian, I couldn't be a jinx. Could I?*

A knock on the front door made her jump. Judging by the shuffling sound along the passage, Marian was the one to answer it.

'Hey, Mrs D, where's Ash?' It was Kaitlyn's bright voice.

Imogen was up, pulling the plug from the sink so she didn't have to overhear but they were standing by the kitchen door where she could see them. Becky was there too.

'Kaitlyn, love.' Marian's voice was low. 'There's something you need to know.'

'What happened?'

'No, Mum, we shouldn't be the ones to tell her,' Becky cried. 'Ash needs to do it himself.'

Marian swept back a wing of hair as grey as her face. 'He's been through so much today already.'

'What happened?' Kaitlyn's voice was rising with panic.

'Ssh, don't let him hear you,' Marian pleaded.

Kaitlyn swept into the kitchen. 'Has Asher been hurt?' A furrow had appeared between her carefully sculpted eyebrows. 'Imogen, you're not family. What happened to Asher? Tell me.'

Marian and Becky were looking at her too, as though they were begging her to break the news. Imogen's mouth turned dry as cotton wool. She opened her it to speak, not sure what would come out.

Asher's bedroom door creaked open and Kaitlyn's beautiful face peered inside, streaked with tears and an expression of grief he'd never seen from her before.

He stretched his good arm. 'Come in.'

Seth and Jodie shuffled to their feet. 'We'll be out of here, to give you some privacy.'

Before the door clicked behind them, she was on the bed beside him in a storm of tears.

'You can't die. How will I live without you?'

He used his good hand to stroke the glorious mass of golden hair he loved. They hadn't been going out for very long and he'd dreamed of having her lying beside him but never under these circumstances. 'So they told you?'

Her head nodded against his chest. 'Couldn't you have gone to the doctor in time for them to do something?'

Postponed tears began to drip down his cheeks. She wouldn't see them because her face was buried in his shirt. And she wouldn't feel them because they'd be lost in all that wonderful hair. 'I didn't know what they'd say. I didn't think for a moment it'd be anything like... like this.'

'It's breaking my heart.'

His own heart was aching. He wanted to live, not die. Nuzzling his chin over her silky head was supposed to be a wonderful precursor of times to come, pleasures he was supposed to enjoy until he was an old man. It wasn't meant to hold the painful knowledge that his chances to hold her were slipping through his fingers. He didn't want heaven yet. He wanted his own experience of heaven on earth, the dream of every man. It was supposed to include waking up to her softness and warmth for a limitless number of mornings. It was killing him that he had her now but wouldn't for much longer. No, it wasn't killing him because cancer had got him first.

If only I'd gone a few months sooner, they might have been able to save me before it spread. Why am I such an idiot?

As Kaitlyn cried beside him, he knew the answer. What goes around sure does come around. He and his big mouth had been the catalyst to kill his father, and he could never forgive himself for that. Now something Dad had spoken many years ago turned out to be part of the reason why Asher hadn't been to the doctor in time. *Touché.*

He remembered a night he'd been wearing a t-shirt and old pair of school shorts, because his pyjamas were all in the wash. Since the evening Mum had been rushed to hospital, nobody had been around to tackle the overflowing mound in the laundry. Dad spent every spare moment at the hospital, hunched beside Mum's bed, often leaving Seth in charge of the twins until late at night.

Asher had found his father gazing into the depths of a wine glass. From time to time, he'd swirl the last few centimetres around as if he was contemplating one of his old magic tricks, but he never smiled any more. He'd skull the remainder of each glass and pour himself more. After enough wine to lubricate his tear ducts, he'd weep the silent tears that made Asher feel as if his insides were caving in.

'Eh, what do you want?'

Tonight, Dad was talking. It was surely a good sign. When his American pen pal's family had come to take their daughter home, he had no word of farewell for the little girl he'd been besotted with for all that time. Ginny used to irritate Asher because she'd agree with every crazy thing Becky said just for the sake of ganging up on him. But he'd felt very sorry to see her face crumple when her beloved Uncle Hayden brushed her off without a word as she left. The accident in the patio hadn't been her fault. She wouldn't have been out there if she hadn't followed him. Everyone knew that.

'My shoulder is still sore.' Asher's voice seemed to echo in the quiet room.

Dad turned as if he was about to give him some undivided attention. 'Well, just stop to think, your poor mother is in far worse shape than you are. We don't even know if she'll ever be able to get out of her bed again. It's killing me to watch her, knowing I can do nothing to make her better.'

He turned away, but not before Asher noticed the sick sheen in his eyes, as if the liquid from all the bottles had started at his toes and made it all the way up there.

'Your shoulder has been fixed,' Dad went on. 'They told us you'll get better. It'll just take time. And I've seen you move your arm and pick things up. I don't ever want to hear another word about it.' His tone was final.

As Asher approached his bedroom, Seth stood waiting in the shadows near the door. He reached out to pull Asher close to him and rumpled his hair in a regretful way that told Asher he'd overheard.

'Dad's not himself right now,' Seth mumbled. 'We've got to give him lots of space. He's used to seeing Mum healthy, and now to have her lying on her back in bed not able to move… well, it's tearing him apart.'

Asher couldn't help snuffling a bit. He was careful to use the hem of his own t-shirt to wipe his face, not his brother's school uniform shirt. It was the only clean one Seth had left. Asher didn't know what would happen when they ran out of clothes, but he didn't want to be the one to set Dad off when he found out. His stomach began to cramp just thinking about it. He needed the toilet. Again. There were a lot of sudden trips to the loo.

Seth bent his knees into a squat so he was on enough of a level to look into Asher's eyes. 'If your shoulder still hurts a bit, do you reckon you can just be brave and put up with it?' His brown eyes were deep with sympathy.

Asher tightened his lips and nodded. He wanted his mother. He wanted her to give him a hug and tell him they'd both be okay. He would have even welcomed one of her hearty kisses, although he'd been in the habit of wiping them off his face.

'I'll get you an aspirin for it,' Seth whispered.

Although Asher swallowed it down, he knew the little white pill wouldn't fix his shoulder. It wouldn't penetrate its deep pain or the sickness of his belly. But he hadn't mentioned it again.

In the months following Mum's accident his shoulder throbbed constantly, but he'd trained himself to get used to it. By the time she returned home, he considered it a background nuisance. And by the time she was able to shuffle around with her walking frame, he'd accepted the twinges as part of his new life. Eventually he rarely gave his shoulder a thought. Not until recently, when it suddenly turned really bad again.

Kaitlyn's hair was getting a bit sticky. She would guess he'd been crying so he had to stop.

'Maybe the operation and chemotherapy will give me longer than they say.'

He pleaded with God, *Can't you give me a second chance and do a miracle?* Prayer was his last resort, but he sensed it was more hopeless than the aspirin. He'd tried it many times before but it was like speaking to thin air. Asher had never wanted to admit that before, but now that he was dying, he had to quit messing around, pretending to believe what he didn't.

'Asher, wake up.'

He wanted to groan but wasn't sure he could summon the strength. Even though they'd just operated on his shoulder, pain was raging, already cutting through the anaesthetic they'd used.

'Asher,' the nurse's voice intruded through his foggy thoughts again.

She wanted some sort of response. Who would have believed that pain or narcotics of any magnitude would ever overcome his urge to talk? Dad would have made some corny joke about it. Not only was he sore, but nausea was stirring in his depths. Every part of him that could protest was protesting, except for his mouth.

'Asher, we've finished.'

He managed to grunt but still couldn't force words. His lips were dry except for some sort of glueyness that kept them stuck to his teeth. If anyone wanted him to talk, they'd have to peel them back like a banana skin.

'We're going to wheel you to recovery.'

Recovery? He was never going to recover. Both the doctor and specialist had given him only a few years to live at the most. Nothing made sense. If he had been in the mood to talk, he knew what he'd ask. *What's the point of drawing this out? I'm feeling even worse than I did when I walked into the hospital. Why bother cutting out the primary tumour and wasting time on follow-up chemotherapy when this rotten cancer has me beaten anyway?* It was twisting its parasitic tendrils through his lymph nodes and blood. He could imagine it.

God, why don't you just take me now? Could this get any worse?

Alarming names above ward doors blended into each other as they wheeled him along the corridor. He was lying prostrate on the train from hell, watching stations whizz past. Why did they give diseases such long, convoluted, scary names? Was it to make patients feel even more intimidated by the menacing conditions in their bodies?

The bright, female voice went on, 'Your family and girlfriend have been waiting here the whole time. They'll be glad to see you.'

Oh God, it can get worse. He didn't want them to see him like this. Tears were stinging the corners of his eyes. He knew he couldn't raise his sore left arm to wipe them, but when he tried to raise his good right one, it turned out to be all connected to drips, tubes and wires.

'You must stay still for now.'

Great. So he was stuck on his back in agony while water welled from his eyes and probably his nose. *I don't get it, God. I've caused some serious harm, but you know they were accidents. I don't understand why I have to go through this.* Ranting at God in his mind didn't help. It simply made him feel more clogged up. He'd have to concentrate on something different, and the brightest thing seemed to be how soon he'd be able to face his dad and get an opportunity to say the regretful things he'd never had a chance to tell him on earth.

How does heaven work? Would his dad, who never wanted to hear those things while he was alive, want to stand around and listen now? Dragging them to light would bring down a pall of gloom, clouding the fair weather of heaven. And if Dad would be willing to listen to Asher unburden himself without spinning on his heel and striding away, he would no longer be the real Hayden Dorazio.

Perhaps there would be a ban on some conversation topics in heaven, but then it wouldn't be heaven to Asher. He'd always longed to explain his heart to his father, after the terrible night he'd burst in on Dad in the cabin—as it turned out, the last night of Hayden's life.

This isn't working. His eyes were stinging more than before.

Chapter 6

'Asher Dorazio.' The chemotherapy nurse consulted her notes. 'Chair seven.'

He and Kaitlyn followed her through a spine-chilling scene. A variety of bodies lounged on recliners, mostly elderly, and all hooked up to tubes. The fact that two-thirds appeared to be hairless added to the extra-terrestrial experiment effect he didn't want to be part of. Even the nurse's uniform looked more like a space suit from a science fiction movie.

Several pairs of heavy-lidded eyes lifted to watch him pass, then returned to books, knitting or other pastimes. Kaitlyn's hand tightened around his, communicating her uneasiness. Asher returned the pressure. In this room of washed-up, worn-out humanity, she was ravishingly out of place, almost like a slap in the face for them.

'Did Dr Jackson tell you about the medications we're going to administer?'

Asher nodded. His oncologist had rattled off some long acidic-sounding names, reminding him of either poison or the artificial gunk they put in commercial foods. He'd asked why the names of chemotherapy drugs had to be long and convoluted enough to strike fear into the hearts of patients. Without a smile, Dr Jackson replied that if he had no proper questions, he'd simply wish him all the best for the long road ahead of him.

The nurse rolled Asher's sleeve high and began flicking his inner elbow, searching for a vein. He'd been through this drill before with his blood tests, and knew it could take some time.

'Your veins want to play hide-and-seek.' The nurse paused to adjust her double-layered gloves, and then she was at it again. He watched Kaitlyn wince as the nurse finally found a vein, and slid the long needle straight into it.

'Hey, are you okay?' Asher asked. Kaitlyn had turned pasty grey.

'I will be. Just a bit faint.'

'If you need fresh air, go out to the corridor. Your boyfriend is our main concern.'

It seemed sympathy was a rare commodity for some in the medical profession. Kaitlyn's eyes shone with pooled tears and he had to do something, say something, to distract her.

'Hey, when I first came in here, I thought my best childhood dream had come true.'

The nurse's eyes, magnified behind her big squirrel goggles, looked up at him. 'And what might that have been?'

'To fly in a rocket to outer space. You're all dressed up like an astronaut.'

Her snort sounded promisingly humorous. 'Not a flattering uniform, hey? It's to protect my skin from the chemotherapy drugs.'

'Why, what would happen if some got on you?' It was probably not the wisest question to ask but he had a morbid interest in her answer.

'It would burn a hole through my flesh.'

He let out a slow breath. 'Human veins must be made like steel.' Perhaps being a chemical cocktail would have bothered him once upon a time – before he got too sick to refuse any medical protocol they decided for him. No, who was he trying to kid, it still bothered him. It bothered him a lot.

'He's going to be all right, isn't he?' Kaitlyn asked.

'As you can see, we're doing our best.'

'Hey Ash, will you be okay?'

'Of course. I'm in a hospital.'

'You're already a whole lot better, aren't you? That operation on your arm has made you much less sore, hasn't it?'

'Yeah, I'm doing fine.' Letting Kaitlyn put comforting words in his mouth was part of the routine he'd grown used to. She'd hate to hear that his shoulder was still in a lot of pain, that the unrelenting ache made him believe they hadn't managed to cut it all out after all—either that, or it was quickly growing back again, returning its roots to the terrible network it had already established in his lymph and blood systems.

He was willing to go along with anything to return the smile to the

41

pretty face he loved. Her happy, refreshing spirit had drawn him to her. It was going to be hard enough for her later on, when he got closer to death.

'You've got to say you're doing more than okay, Asher. You're doing great. Don't give up on positive thinking, because it might save your life. I want to hear you tell me you're doing well every day. Don't you dare stop fighting this. I've got to hear ten positive things each day. No, twenty.'

He imagined another, softer, snort from the nurse, but might have been mistaken.

'How long will this take?' Kaitlyn asked her.

'He won't be through for a few hours.'

'That's a lot of... stuff.' Kaitlyn's eyes focused on the needle in his arm and quickly glanced away again.

When the nurse left, she perched on the edge of the seat near his recliner. 'Hey, Ash, with that much chemotherapy pumping through, there's no way you can't get better. It's horribly depressing in here, but it'll all be worth it.'

'You don't have to stay here for the whole time,' he told her. 'Why don't you do some shopping?'

He could see she was tempted.

'I came to help you keep your spirits up. Are you sure you wouldn't mind?'

''Course not. Escape while you can. If I wasn't hooked here by my blood vessels, I'd be out of this hub of death in a flash.' He glanced with dismay at the people in the chairs on either side of him. *My big mouth has struck again.* 'No offense.'

'Stop thinking of it like that. It's the place that's going to make you well again. I'll go then. And I'll bring you back a nice treat for getting through your first chemo session.'

As soon as she left, the body in the chair adjacent to Asher's squirmed. 'Thanks for getting rid of your chick for a while, mate.' He was a shell of a man with no trace of hair. 'Pretty high-maintenance, isn't she?'

Asher forced a grin. 'She's been worried about me. My diagnosis was a big shock, and not all that long ago.'

'Just don't forget to look after yourself as well as her. My name's Ron. Non-Hodgkin's lymphoma.'

'Hi, Ron, I'm Asher.'

'And I'm Yvonne, third-stage breast cancer,' a frail voice piped up from the chair on his other side. It belonged to a tiny woman.

'Hey, it's like an Alcoholics Anonymous meeting,' Asher couldn't help observing. 'Are we supposed to introduce ourselves by disease?'

'Have you been to Al Anon meetings, Asher?' The place where Ron's eyebrows would have been formed creases as he opened his eyes wider.

'No, but my dad went once or twice. He told us all about them.'

'Was your father an alcoholic?'

That was always a tricky question to answer. 'He had a bit of a drinking problem but never officially called himself that. He was at the meetings to do some research for a role in a play.'

'So he's an actor, then?' With only a few wrinkles around her eyes, it was impossible to guess the bird-like Yvonne's age. She might have been a similar age to his mother, or merely a decade older than himself.

'Was,' Asher corrected. 'He's dead, now.'

'You're such a nosy woman.' Ron shot her a mock scowl.

'It's okay. He died five years ago. My sister is an actor too. So's my girlfriend, who was here with me. She's brilliant.'

'We could tell.' Ron's tone was dry. 'Maybe someone should recommend that she play the part of a sensible human being.'

Yvonne gave a chuckle. 'The poor girl is trying desperately to stay in the land of denial at the moment. I've been there and know where she is along the path. Listen to who's talking, anyway. Ron could give us all lessons on being sensible. That'd be the day my doctor tells me there's a cure for cancer.'

'Hey, Yvonne, what's that you're knitting?' Asher gestured to a mountain of red and white striped wool wedged beside her and spilling over the arm of her recliner.

'It's my scarf. I set myself the challenge of knitting it during every chemo session. Six metres long so far. Four more sessions to go and then I auction it off.'

'Who'd want a giant scarf taking up a whole room and getting tangled with everything?' Ron was shaking his head. 'I reckon I could teach lessons on being sensible. That thing is as useless as a chocolate teapot.'

'It's a symbol. It's not meant to be really worn. It'll raise money for breast cancer research, you mark my words. I've knitted some of my own hair into it.' She indicated a rusty-red stripe. 'Asher, what would you call the colour of the bandanna on my head?'

'Well, not red exactly. Not burgundy either. Maybe something in-between.'

'Do you like it?'

'Yeah, it's nice.' He'd had a lot of practice saying what he was supposed to say.

'It was the closest colour to my hair I could find. I had gorgeous long, auburn locks, as lovely as your girlfriend's yellow frizz, but far more rare.'

'When all this rubbish has finished, it'll grow back.' For once, Ron did sound compassionate.

'Hey, about the hair,' Asher ventured. 'How long does it take to start falling out?'

'That doesn't happen to everyone,' Yvonne said.

'Don't give him false hope. It happens to practically everyone. I started loosing mine two weeks into the chemo. You'd better warn that girl of yours that soon she won't be able to run her fingers through it.'

Asher tried to shrug as if it didn't matter. 'I probably won't grow it back, then. I don't think they expect me to live for long.'

'Ron, you didn't have to be so blunt,' Yvonne scolded.

'I'm just trying to help the lad. Bluntness is kindness in disguise. Hasn't your brush with the big C helped you figure out that life is too short to pussyfoot around, being fake and saying what people want to hear?'

Asher closed his eyes. Although he could block out the sense of sight, he could do nothing to subdue the hospital smell, that mixture of chemicals and fear that hovered, reminding him of when he used to watch Mum lying in such pain, knowing it was his fault.

Bluntness never worked for me. Just caused me to kill Dad. He had the sense not to voice that thought. Ron and Yvonne had problems enough of their own without needing to hear the story. Asher couldn't feel the chemotherapy drugs surge through his veins, but he could feel the sharp ache Ron's words caused. Emotions were more toxic than the poisonous medications that were capable of eating holes through human flesh. Toxic sadness, toxic grief and toxic guilt were buried far too deeply to deal with.

At home in America they were Goodwill stores, and here in Australia, Imogen had to get used to calling them second-hand shops or Op shops too. She wasn't sure what she was looking for on the crammed bookshelves behind the bric-a-brac. *I guess I'll know if I see it.*

Asher was having his first chemotherapy session right about now. By the time she arrived home, it would already be over. Imogen always had trouble looking him in the eye, knowing he would soon die, but didn't want him to guess that she welcomed excuses to avoid him. That would probably add more hurt to the load he was carrying. But trying to behave casually around him, as if nothing was amiss in his life, was an enormous strain.

The only person who let her emotions gush out whenever she saw him was Kaitlyn. Strangely, her unrestrained show of grief seemed to help Asher most. He seemed strongest while he was stroking Kaitlyn's hair and trying to soothe her, but his pseudo-strength would surely cave in if everyone started falling apart around him.

Poor Kaitlyn. Imogen had been envious of the bubbly, sanguine girl but now Kaitlyn's world had crumbled around her. Having a boyfriend diagnosed with terminal cancer was unthinkable.

But my envy can't have anything to do with her world collapsing. I'm so used to wondering if I should feel guilty for everything.

That was why Imogen was kneeling on the threadbare carpet of a second hand shop, browsing through musty old books. If she found one about figuring out when she ought to speak up, or even how to reverse the curse of being a jinx, she'd buy it. It didn't matter who wrote it or how old it was. Obscure, out-of-print books would be as good as any. Other stores didn't have what she was looking for. She'd checked already. Not that she knew what she was looking for, but she'd know if she found it.

There was nothing here, either. Scrambling to her feet, her elbow grazed the spine of a heavy old Bible, knocking it to the floor. Wincing at the crash, she turned to apologise to anybody within earshot, but she was alone. The Bible had fallen open to a shiny picture of Jesus with a crowd of children. The compassionate expression on his face stirred something deep inside of her. If she could have been lucky enough to meet that Jesus face to face, she would have pleaded with him not to allow her to remain a jinx, and anyone who looked that sensitive would have done something. She asked for guidance in her prayers as a matter of routine, but felt as if she was appealing to thin air. Was it because she had already made her mind not to speak up? Although it was a strange impulse, she bought the Bible anyway.

Sitting on a park bench, she began to eat her ham and salad sandwiches before returning home. The wattle trees were a crisp yellow, the gums smooth and rugged. She remembered Seth showing her the different native trees when she was a child. Imogen snapped a brittle leaf and drew the fresh intensity of eucalyptus into her lungs. It was the tonic she needed before returning to the house where she could already smell impending death.

Sure, she felt bad for avoiding Asher, but she felt anxious about so many things that an extra bit on top hardly tipped the balance. She couldn't bring herself to suggest moving out. Not now that Marian had started thanking her for the housework she did during the day. 'I don't know how I could hold everything together without your help.' That, after all, was why Imogen had flown to Australia, although had she known the circumstances that awaited her, she might have had second thoughts.

Flipping through the old Bible, she saw the former owner had underlined several passages with different coloured markers, giving the pages a patchwork effect. A fanatic, like her brother. Scotty was always 'getting stuck into the Word' as he called it, earning her parents' nods of approval.

Imogen had been given many different Bibles as Sunday school prizes. She'd read them obediently until she knew passages by heart, but never understood how people could keep poring over the same old stories as if they were discovering something fresh each time. To hear the way Scotty went on, anyone would think it was a magic book whose contents changed every time the covers were opened. Either Scotty was exaggerating his delight to impress their parents, or else he received astounding insights from God which she was too unworthy to pick up on. Possibly both.

At the front of the book was a sentence written in black ink. **This Bible is the property of Christopher Stubbins. Please return urgently!** That was followed by an address and phone number.

Imogen's first instinct was to hold the Bible by its spine and give it a shake. No loose money flapped out. From time to time, her parents used to tuck banknotes in their children's and foster children's Bibles to test whether they were actually reading them. Once, Imogen had carried around a $20 bill for two months before she found it. Mom and Dad still enjoyed telling the story.

Perhaps Christopher Stubbins simply wanted to keep his kaleidoscopic underlinings, which must have taken some time and effort. Maybe he'd accidentally left his Bible somewhere, and it had made its way to the Op shop.

Taking care not to slip on damp pine needles, she strolled to the bus stop. When she got off at the bottom of Aunt Marian's hill, she hiked up the steep path toward the house. Her shoes cracked open the small gum nuts that were underfoot everywhere. Her parents would have said they had to be smashed for new life to emerge. They used that biblical maxim as a panacea for any bad news. For something fresh and new to bloom, something else had to die. But how did the homily explain the plight of a smart and handsome man as young as Asher Dorazio? How would his death help a soul?

Somebody was kneeling in Marian's garden with his head buried deep in a lavender bush. Imogen slipped behind the drooping branches of a weeping willow. Marian had commented just that morning that she'd love to acquire a gardener for the upkeep of her property but wouldn't have time to search for several days. Seth had mentioned something about coming to clear some brush away and pluck a few weeds over the weekend, but it was only Wednesday and these legs looked too short to be Seth's.

'I'd get out and do it, but I have a fair excuse not to,' Asher had said. He was still attempting wisecracks as if he wanted things to function exactly as before, but his family found it hard to muster a smile. Only Imogen tried, because she sensed that he appreciated it when people did. That was one of the awkward parts about living with the Dorazios. Whenever she forced a chuckle at Asher's attempted humour, the others looked at her as if she was flippant and callous.

Emerging from the bush, the kneeler rubbed his shiny dome as if it had been scratched by thorns. Had she seen him before? Imogen hung back while he snooped around other plants. Should she approach him to introduce herself and ask his identity? No, he didn't look like a gardener. Gardeners surely didn't wear tailored mauve shirts and pristine white jeans. And something about the edgy way he moved, jerking his head up before resuming his search, warned her to stay concealed.

A memory stirred. When she'd driven with Asher to the doctor's surgery that terrible day, hadn't they waited for a bald fellow to cross the driveway? She ignored her accelerating heart rate. That didn't mean this man was some harbinger of death. Maybe it wasn't even him.

But the first night she'd arrived from the airport, a bald guy had

47

walked along the path outside her bedroom window. Her pulse throbbed in her wrists.

He stood up, stuffing something he'd found into the back pocket of his white jeans. With a glance up the street beyond her tree, he hurried away. Several moments later, Imogen crept out to peer in the bushes. There was nothing but scuffed dirt where he'd been pawing around.

She extracted her key from her purse, looking over her shoulder. *What did he just find?* Should she tell Marian someone was snooping around in her garden? No, Marian had all the worry she could handle. She'd tell Seth. That was the wisest idea. Seth could decide what to do about the hairless prowler.

Kaitlyn returned with three shopping bags in each hand and a wide smile on her face. 'How did you go?'

'I think I'm feeling okay… I mean, pretty good.' Telling the truth without having to choose a careful lie was a relief. He did feel strange in a spaced-out sort of way, but it was nothing he couldn't handle. One session down and only eight to go.

Her smile widened. 'Good. It's around lunch time. Are you feeling hungry?'

'I reckon I am a bit.' He hadn't expected to be.

'Then let's go to a restaurant. You deserve it.'

'You'd better stay away from public places.' The nurse came back in time to overhear their plans. 'They're hothouses for germs and it's important that he doesn't pick up any infections during his treatment. The chemotherapy will compromise his immune system.'

Now, Asher felt like some sort of weird, delicate alien that could keel over with a little puff of air.

Kaitlyn's smile vanished. 'Nobody told me that before. What if I've already picked something up when I was walking around? People were coughing all over me in the Rundle Mall.'

'You can only do what you can.' The nurse shrugged. 'Life goes on.'

'That's not going to make me feel any better if I give him some disease and kill him!' Kaitlyn's voice was rising and several patients looked up.

'Let's grab something for a picnic,' Asher made a move to take her hand but Kaitlyn stepped away and looked toward the nurse.

'Is it safe for me to hug and kiss him?'

'Physical contact is okay. Kisses, too.'

Kaitlyn took his hand.

'Just be sure not to sleep together for three nights,' the nurse continued.

'We never sleep together anyway.'

'Then you should be fine.'

'But why would there be a problem if we were sleeping together?' Kaitlyn asked.

'For the next three days and nights, there might be some toxic residue from his skin in the form of sweat.'

'You mean I might be in danger?' Kaitlyn dropped Asher's hand.

'Not if you're careful, as I said.'

Taking a step back, Kaitlyn looked at Asher with rising tears.

'Three days isn't long,' he said.

She kept her distance.

'Hey, I don't have to hug or kiss you in that time.' He'd never seen her mouth twitch in that skittish way before.

'Are you sure you wouldn't mind?'

He did mind becoming an object of distaste. Unmanly tears were not far from the surface but they would be toxic too.

'No, I can hold out, but at the end of three days, I'll expect you to make up for it.' He'd hoped to coax her beam back but Kaitlyn's smile was feeble. He supposed he couldn't blame her. He was a noxious sponge. At one time, he might have thought of using that to his advantage with his family, pretending to chase Becky and Seth with outstretched hands and threats of radioactive contamination, but they'd changed too. Nobody laughed any more. Taking care to keep a few inches of space between him and Kaitlyn, they left the hospital.

Chapter 7

'Maybe you shouldn't have knocked back that role. You would've been great and it would've given you something to fill your thoughts apart from worrying about me.' Asher's voice was growing hoarse. Even though Imogen was looking down, slicing one of Marian's chocolate cakes, she could detect fatigue in his tone.

'What happened?' Marian leaned across the table to fill Kaitlyn's cup with steaming tea from the pot.

'When we got back from Asher's chemotherapy session, my agent phoned, offering me the lead role I'd wanted. It's about a girl who finds out her fiancé has been killed in the war. But I told her it's too close to home now.' Kaitlyn's face began to crumple.

Imogen noticed Asher reach out to clasp her hand but he seemed to reconsider and withdrew it. Marian gave Kaitlyn a sympathetic squeeze instead.

'Becky, why don't you ask them if you can have that part? That'd make me feel better about missing out.'

'I did already, as soon as I heard you weren't taking it.' Becky placed her cup on its saucer with a clink. 'They said no.'

Silence followed.

'Sorry, sweetheart,' Marian said.

'They fobbed me off with the excuse that my twin brother is sick so perhaps it would be too much for me.'

'Hey, sorry this is mucking up your life, too.' Asher stared at the piece of cake he'd taken a bite from and placed the fork on his plate.

'They know that Kaity's your girlfriend, but they still asked her. And then they offered me another role which will take almost as long to learn.

They just didn't want me to play the lead.'

Kaitlyn cut in, 'Hey Asher, are you okay?'

He opened his mouth to say something and covered it with his hand instead. Then he was up, knocking his chair backward, and rushing to the bathroom. They heard him being sick before he had time to close the door.

'This is the last thing we need!' Kaitlyn raised trembling hands to her face. 'He said he felt fine before.'

'But they did warn you it could be a side effect.' Even though they all knew it, somebody ought to remind them. Imogen guessed it might as well be her. She trailed after the others to check up on him.

Asher was hunched over the toilet bowl.

'Oh no, are you okay?' Kaitlyn asked.

He gagged again. 'Not just now.'

'You poor, poor thing. What are we going to do with you?'

'Maybe you should just shoot me.' He tried to laugh.

Kaitlyn reached out to rub his clammy forehead, averting her eyes from the gruesome sight in the toilet bowl. 'Oh, I forgot something.' She groaned, wiping her hand up and down the leg of her jeans. 'He's all sweaty, and I touched him.'

'So?' Becky said.

'They said not to touch his sweat because it might be poisonous.'

Pinching her nostrils together with one hand, Becky stepped into the bathroom to draw Kaitlyn out by the arm. 'Come on, don't panic. We'll wash your hands in the kitchen.'

'But what if it's already got in?'

Kaitlyn's question was followed by the sound of Asher throwing up again. Imogen could tell by the sound of the splash in the toilet that it was a big one. The two girls turned and hurried away. Her own stomach was roiling.

'My poor son.' Marian touched his tousled hair. 'Can I do anything to help?'

Turning his head, he nodded. There were dark circles around his eyes, as if he'd given himself black eyes through the force of his heaving. 'Yeah, Mum, can you go away?'

She hesitated. 'Are you sure?'

'Yes. And please tell Kaitlyn to keep away too. Just for now. I'm sick of people seeing...' He erupted into another fit of coughing over the toilet

51

bowl. 'Mum, just go.'

Marian hobbled away, beckoning Imogen to follow. Imogen could only think to pat Marian's hunched back, holding her close.

At last, the older woman brushed the salt-and-pepper curls back from her face. 'You're a sweet girl.'

Imogen felt sick inside. *I'm not.* Marian had no idea what she'd done.

Marian squeezed Imogen's hand with her dry one. 'I'm afraid Asher is going through this nightmare because he's being punished.'

'By who?' Imogen had meant to ask 'for what?', but the other question slipped out instead. Her heart skittered, because she knew Marian meant God. 'Do you mean for your accident so long ago, when we should have been in bed? That wasn't his fault as much as mine. I was the one who started moving the…'

'No, I'm not talking about that.' Marian tugged her toward the door of the spare bedroom. It felt strange to be dragged along by someone almost as short as a child, especially because she remembered Marian as a sturdy, upright woman. It was not simply that Imogen had grown so tall herself—Marian's accident had shrunk her, causing her to cave in upon herself. Imogen almost had to stoop to keep squeezing her hand.

Marian sunk her hunched form into Imogen's cane chair in her careful way, as if her bones might collapse if she was too quick.

'I feel safe telling you this, Sweetie, because you're removed from it. You're not enmeshed in the deplorable luck of this family.'

Imogen felt her blood run cold. *If only you knew.*

'I've kept this to myself for years and it's getting too hard to hold in. Will you promise not to tell a soul?' Marian's brown eyes were heavy.

'I promise.' Imogen sat down on her bed.

'Asher did something terrible.' Marian's voice turned husky. 'He committed a serious crime, a sin, and it's caught up with him. I won't tell you what it was. I can't bear to do that, so please don't ask, but it was bad.' The wicker chair was shaking.

'But is God really like that?' Imogen's hands were clammy because she knew Marian was a very religious lady who worked as a Christian counselor. She ought to know the ways of God. 'Biding his time, with his heart bent on vengeance?'

'He's a God of justice, who can't be mocked. I can't express my fear that this cancer is a punishment meted out on both me and Asher.'

Why do Christians use weird words like meted?

'You see, I kept quiet about something I probably should have spoken up about.'

'To protect Asher?' *Is she talking about what I think she is? How can I tell her it wasn't his fault.* A sharp ache suddenly shot through Imogen's head. *How can I know what she thinks?* What if she and Marian were both keeping quiet about the same thing?

'Yes, because I was certain that what he did was an accident. But that was no excuse. I knew the moral thing to do but turned my back and did what my emotions told me to do instead.' She swallowed hard. 'And that was nothing. I think Asher and I are both reaping what we've sown. I feel as if I ought to tell him but dredging up the sin now that he has cancer seems a terribly cruel thing to do. You see, he doesn't know I know what he did... I missed my chance to speak up at the time. But would you please pray for him? Pray that he'll come clean to a pastor, if that's what God wants of him.'

Imogen mumbled some sort of agreement. Yet after watching Marian shuffle out, she flopped back on her bed and smothered her face with a pillow. *What an empty promise.* It wasn't because she wouldn't go through the motions of saying prayers. She'd been doing that for years. But she had no right to expect God to listen to any prayers of hers to make Asher own up about his thing—when she refused to own up about hers.

Is it just another sign that I should speak up myself. I just can't see how it could help, at this stage.

It was him again, snooping around in the dark. He wore a woolen stocking cap but took it off to wipe the glass of his binoculars. Beneath the street light, his head gleamed. Imogen froze. She'd told Seth about the bald guy, but Seth was no help from his own house. She had to force her limbs to move. Seth had said not to hesitate to call the police if she saw him on their property again.

Creeping out to the living room, she heard scuffling on the porch steps and halted again. He was moving things around. The metal foot scraper was being pulled along the wooden slats, and the terracotta plant pots clinked together. *Don't the Dorazios keep an extra key under one of those?* Through a gap in the drapes, she could see his stooped back as he searched for something. Her chest tightened and her heart raced.

The room filled with light. As Imogen's eyes screwed tight in the brightness, the prowler fled. Asher stood there with his mouth slightly open, his hand still on the light switch. She must have looked frightened or let out a gasp.

'Hey, what's happened? Who was that out there?' He might have heard the man's retreating footsteps too.

She tried to swallow because she knew she couldn't talk until her heart slowed down. First things first.

'Do you guys keep a spare key under the flower pots?'

'No, we're more imaginative than that.' He shook his head.

'Thank heavens.' Her stored up breath came out in a whoosh.

'But who was it?'

'I don't know. A bald guy.'

Asher's eyes narrowed. 'Hey, I've noticed him before, walking along the street. I'd started wondering whether he lives around here.'

Imogen was still trembling.

'Did he frighten you? Was that him on our veranda just then?'

If only she knew what to say. Troubling Asher with the problem was surely the wrong thing to do.

'You can tell me. Just because I've got cancer, I'm not some little kid you need to keep in the dark.' He sounded grieved but worse than that, he looked hurt. Telling him might not be the right thing to do but she went with her instinct.

'I first saw him the night I arrived here.' She told him everything and at the end, Asher sank onto an arm chair, looking pale. Her stomach churned. She knew Seth would be cross. He had specifically told her to tell nobody.

'What's the attraction for him here?' Asher wondered.

'When I told Seth, he thought it might be your BMW. It would give him the impression that rich people live here.'

Asher rolled his eyes. 'Does Seth think I'd leave the BMW sitting around, inviting crooks to come and steal it? It's always locked away in the garage, and this bloke comes and digs around in the garden.'

'And if he wants to rob the place, why doesn't he get it over and done with?' Imogen added. 'Why does he just loiter around here, week after week?'

Asher began to stretch his arms over his head but lowered the left one with a wince. 'Maybe he's the Grim Reaper.'

For an instant, her blood ran ice cold but then she shook her head. 'If he's the Grim Reaper, then he fled pretty quickly when you turned on the light. I saw him through the drapes.'

His smile flickered. 'You mean curtains? You're living in Australia, remember.'

'Curtains, then.' She felt her cheeks flushing. It had been the same when she was little. She'd tried to speak the way her hosts did but so many words were different in Australia. The twins used to correct her endlessly back then too. 'Anyway, I wouldn't have imagined the Grim Reaper looking like him, without a hair on his head.'

'Do you know I'll soon look like him?'

Looking at his wavy, damp locks, sadness swept through her. She had to force some words. 'I can't imagine you as a chrome dome.'

He chuckled. 'Hey, thanks. My family wouldn't have said that. They would've just raved on about how it's what's inside that counts, or something like that.'

'Well, that's true too.'

'I know, but I just wish someone would crack a joke from time to time.' He heaved a sigh. 'What time did Kaitlyn leave?'

'Around ten o'clock. She phoned the hospital first, to make sure everything's still okay. She told them how sick you were.'

'What did they say?'

'That it's quite normal. And they reassured her that there'll still be enough chemotherapy drugs in your blood to do its work.'

'It's going to get so much harder telling Kaitlyn I'm still okay.'

Imogen didn't know how to respond. 'Hey, why did you get up? Do you … need something?' She'd almost asked, Are you okay, but stopped herself in time. He'd been asked that question enough for one night.

'I wanted a drink. All that puking made me feel dry.'

'No wonder.' If he was trying to determine her limits, she'd show him that she could match his offhandedness. She knew he already had enough alarm and dismay to deal with from others. But as she rose, she hoped he wouldn't see her knees trembling. 'I'll leave you to it, then.'

'Are you thirsty too? Stay, if you like.'

So he wanted company? Thirst was the last thing on her mind but he was watching her carefully. She knew nodding would be the right response. 'Yeah, I'll join you.'

Soon, they sat with hot chocolates at the kitchen table. Asher took his first reflective sip, swallowed slowly and seemed to wait to see what would happen.

'Are you okay?' She let it shoot out before she had time to think.

He covered his mouth and leaped to his feet. Still clutching her cup's handle, she scrambled up, ducking for cover, but when he removed his hand, she saw that he was smiling.

'Just kidding. Serves you right, for asking me that.'

Shaking her head, she sank back onto her seat, looking at the lower level in her cup. 'You made me spill hot chocolate all over myself.'

'Sorry. I shouldn't have done that to you. It's just that I can't really do it to anyone else. They're all too close to me to appreciate it. It'd make me a real sicko.'

Sicko. Another quaint Australianism to remember. 'So you thought you'd make the most of your ammunition on me? I'll have to figure out how to get you back.' She wasn't quite sure where the words were coming from but even though they sounded flippant and wrong, they still felt right.

'You'd better be quick, then. I might not be around for much longer.'

'Oh, Asher!' The protest shot out.

'Sorry. That's taking it a bit far, even for me. You must think my humour is pretty warped. Don't worry, not all Aussies are like me. It's just a pressure valve.'

'That's okay.' She couldn't let him feel bad for long. 'You can release it on me any time.'

'You mean figuratively, I guess? I noticed you didn't want to be in the direct firing line a few moments ago.'

'You always have a quick comeback, the same as when you were a little boy.'

'Hopefully I'm not as much of a nuisance as I was then.' He took a deeper sip of hot chocolate and she watched his throat ripple as he swallowed. 'They're all driving me up the wall at the moment, but I'll really miss them.'

'Hey, maybe you shouldn't keep thinking as if you're already dead.'

He raised his right palm in a helpless gesture. 'Sorry, I can't seem to help it. To be honest, it's making me really scared. These past few weeks remind me of a time when I was small and knew Mum was coming home from hospital soon. Dad didn't want us all to be around on the first few days.' He gave a wan grin, and she smiled back, encouraging him to continue.

'That's what he said, but the truth is, he didn't want me. He said he thought I'd talk her ear off. So he arranged for me to have what he called a sleepover party with a family from his work who I didn't know very well.' Asher paused for another sip. 'I didn't know what they were going to be like, only that they had a son who loved sport, and I was nervous. But this is death I'm facing – the biggest sleepover party ever.' His forced laughter burst like bubbles in the air.

'Hey, you know, my dad is a paediatrician.' Imogen didn't know whether she'd be revealing too much but risked it anyway. 'He's seen lots of children die. It's shattered him every time, but he says they often drift to the next life peacefully with smiles on their faces. He says it's helped him handle his own fear of death.' Aware of Asher's intense scrutiny, she stared into her cup. When she looked up again, those green eyes were still fixed on her.

'Hey, Imogen,' he spoke up at last. 'Could I speak to you other times, when it all gets a bit much?'

'Of course.' Her throat was raspy. She'd better not let him see how close she was to tears. 'Maybe you'd better change your shirt. You look all damp and might catch a cold.'

Nodding, he pulled a face. 'Yeah, it's sweat. I was drenched before.' Standing, he unbuttoned his shirt and tried to ease it over his left shoulder. Clicking his tongue, he shook his head at his ineptitude. 'This is easier than a t-shirt but still a bit sore.'

'I'll help.' It felt appropriate to come behind him and slide the collar the last few inches over his broad shoulder. She felt his clamminess, although she tried not to touch him. She used to be two inches taller than he, but now he loomed over her.

'Thanks.' That voice, which used to be so vexingly high-pitched, was deep and soft near her ear. He bunched his shirt up into a ball. 'Hey, do you know my sweat is toxic? This might contaminate everything else in the wash.'

'I offered to clean the oven for your mother in the morning. I wonder how it'd work on that.'

His laugh was spontaneous and genuine. 'Thanks. You're really great to have around.'

Her heart skittered hard enough to fill her chest with the feeling of little feet. *Is this why I'm here?* She could pull off a light-hearted act for one evening, but did God expect her to do it day after day, watching Asher grow steadily weaker?

She deferred the shedding of tears to the privacy of her own room.

Asher's smile was really brave and beautiful. *Stop it, Imogen. You don't go there. Are you crazy?* She cried some more, instead.

Dear God, I don't know if you've ever answered many of my prayers before, but if you answer this one, I won't hold a grudge about all the others. You can perform miracles. Won't you please heal Asher?

He almost stumbled over in the shower and resorted to pinching himself to jerk his eyelids open for another few seconds. Swirling clouds of steam matched his exhausted brain. It seemed to be trying to drag him into another world. Asher began to hum tunelessly between his teeth to keep himself awake. Although he was edging closer to death each day, he wasn't going to be one of those invalids who needed help getting in and out of the shower.

Although still damp, he fell across his bed in his boxer shorts. His head ached and his shoulder throbbed. It was probably going to be another of those long nights when he was shattered beyond words but unable to sleep.

One chemo session down and eight to go. Pounding his pillow with his right fist, he let out an expletive he'd never let his mother hear. He would have to face that horrendous nausea again in another three weeks, but that wasn't what was making his heart ache. That was because for a few moments, he'd been able to forget about his wretched condition and have a joke with someone who treated him like a normal person instead of somebody living on borrowed time.

God, I wish you'd heal me. That was a pointless thing to pray. *Can't you please give me a sign, any sort of sign, that this isn't all for nothing? I suppose I just want to believe that you know what's going on with me. I'm sorry, but I don't feel that you are real. Maybe I've kidded myself about it all these years, just like I used to kid myself about the existence of Santa Claus when I was little. I hate to think I've been lying to myself about you too, but did I ever truly know you enough to believe in you? It's a big ask, expecting me to, isn't it? How could I ever have demanded it of myself, when praying to you always felt like talking to myself?*

Feeling thirsty again, he eased himself up on his right elbow to take a few sips of water. He longed for it to be true, because he'd hate to discover that all his mother held dear, all she'd taught her children to cling to, was a lie and an illusion.

Lord, surely you can manage a sign, can't you? If you are real, please let me know.

He paused to wait for he knew not what. Nothing.

I'll assume that silence means you're definitely not there, and I'm talking to nobody. Fine. I'm sick of playing this game anyway.

Chapter 8

Strathalbyn. I know that's here in the Adelaide Hills somewhere. I guess it'll be easy enough to find a bus route. Imogen had phoned the previous owner of the Bible she'd bought, who'd sounded delighted at the prospect of having it back. When she'd offered to bring it, he rattled off his address, so part of her day's work would be finding it. But first, she had to get home with the milk and tidy the house for Marian.

Lifting her face, she gazed into the boughs of the tall trees that lined the street and filled her lungs with their restorative scent, a blend of pine needles and eucalyptus leaves. Becky had told her that koalas visited those gum trees, but Imogen had yet to spot one. The cuddly marsupials must be elusive, appearing when least expected.

As she reached home, a flash of movement caught her eye. She glimpsed a pair of white jeans and a shiny head slipping into the garden shed. Imogen's mouth turned dry and her shopping bag slipped unheeded to the ground by the letter box. The tension in her chest was as much from anger as anxiety. His effrontery had gone on for long enough.

She'd seen a stout padlock on the shed door. It was the type she could spin around and snap into place. *Dare I?* It would simply take somebody to race to the shed and lock it within the next few seconds. The intruder would be trapped fast and she'd be able to call the police. The moment to act was now.

Careful to take silent steps, she dashed through the silky grass and swung the shed door shut.

The execution was not as smooth as she'd hoped. Instead of closing quietly, the door made a raucous squawk. Too late, she remembered Marian telling Seth that it needed a good oiling. Imogen's shaky figures snapped the lock into place.

Bang, bang, bang! Only the door stood between her and the irate prisoner, and the flimsy metal was already beginning to buckle.

Oh, no. Not going to plan at all. Her pounding heart was rattling her ribs.

Bang, bang, BANG!

'Let me out. Help!'

The cheek of the guy amazed her. Here he was shouting for assistance as if he owned the place and she was the lawbreaker for daring to lock him in.

The more he kept beating the door with his fists, the more the thin metal bowed. He'd soon punch a hole in it, perhaps one big enough to squeeze through. If she went to call the police, he'd escape. Instead of having a sneaky prowler, they'd have a raging angry prowler with a vendetta, capable of hurting people and getting really nasty. And it would be all her fault.

Imogen leaned against the door to stop it shuddering. The man's pounding richocheted through her body.

'You can't come out! The police are on their way.' She ran the backs of her hands down the door but they were slippery, as if she'd been dipping them in a water trough.

Bang, bang, BANG! 'Lady, you've got to let me out.'

'What's happening?'

Another voice came from behind her. She turned to see Asher emerging from the house in his pyjamas, blinking away traces of sleepiness.

'I've locked him in there!'

Instantly, he was by her side, raising his own arms against the door. With a wince, he lowered the left one. 'Stop pounding! You're making it worse for yourself.'

'Let me go!'

'No!' Asher raised his voice above the prowler's. 'Not if you don't shut up and listen.'

Silence. The sound of a man's commanding voice seemed to knock all courage from the crook. Asher glanced at Imogen with his eyebrows raised in a question. She shrugged back.

'We live here,' Asher went on, 'and you've been a serious nuisance.'

There was a small snuffling sound. 'Please let me go. I promise I'll

61

stay away.'

Imogen couldn't believe her ears. The dumbfounded expression on Asher's face made her want to laugh.

Keeping his hand planted against the door, Asher snapped, 'Tears won't work for you. I've seen what you look like, mate. You're not pretty enough.'

Imogen almost spluttered on the nervous laugh she couldn't hold in.

The prowler drew a shuddering breath with a sort of hiccup at the end. 'Don't call the police. If you let me out, I'll explain everything.'

Asher hesitated but curiosity seemed to get the better of him. 'It'd better be good.' He lowered his arm to undo the padlock. The bald guy shuffled out and his mouth dropped open when he took in Asher's attire.

'What are you staring at? I know I'm not dressed the part, but I promise I can still fight in my pyjamas. So who are you and why are you always hanging around?'

The guy wiped a hand across his eyes. 'I'm Jay Reynolds.'

'I won't say, "Pleased to meet you" just yet. Go on.'

'I don't know if this'll be good but it's the truth. I'm a big fan of Rebecca Dorazio, the actress. I looked her up on the internet and after a bit of detective work with the phone directory and play program from the theatre, I figured out this must be her house. She does live here, doesn't she?'

'I'm the one asking questions,' Asher said. 'You haven't explained why you keep snooping around here.'

'I wanted to find something that belonged to Rebecca Dorazio that I could keep. Then I was going to stop coming. I promise.' He swiped his nose with the back of his hand.

Imogen spoke up, 'You could have just lined up in the crowd and asked her to sign your program.'

'That's what normal people do,' Asher added.

'And she would have loved being asked,' Imogen said.

Jay was shaking his head. 'I couldn't bear to have her beautiful face looking at me. I'm so funny looking and she's an angel straight from heaven.'

Asher's lips twitched. 'Heaven needs quality control on their angels.'

'He's her twin brother.' Imogen explained.

'I think she's stunning.' Jay had a dreamy look on his face. 'I went to every performance of *Much Ado About Nothing* just to see her. She has so much class. She outshone the lead actress by far. They had some garish, frizzy-haired girl with a coarse voice that drove me nuts. You know the sort, all show with no substance? Sometimes I wonder where directors keep their brains when they make their selections.'

Drawing a hand to her mouth, Imogen stole a glance at Asher. She wouldn't have been surprised if that description of Kaitlyn was enough to make him take a swing at Jay after all, but Asher was simply squinting at him with one eyebrow cocked.

He rolled his eyes and shook his head. 'I assume you haven't found whatever you've been looking for.'

'I saw you pick something up.' Imogen said. 'Yesterday under the lavender bush.'

Jay shamefacedly dipped his hand into his hip pocket and pulled out a transparent piece of plastic. Imogen had to stare at it before it dawned on her what it was. It was a blister pack from a box of pills with all its bubbles empty.

'I'd like to think this was hers,' Jay was saying, 'but I knew there was a fair chance it'd be someone else's.'

'A very good chance,' Asher said. 'That's from my box of painkillers. Must've fallen out of the rubbish. You can keep it as a souvenir if you like, but I'm touched that you care.'

Jay Reynolds turned scarlet to the top of his head. 'You wouldn't believe what an idiot I feel like. I'm not a common stalker, I promise.' He looked down at his hands with a sigh. 'Why should you believe me? It looks as if I am. What have I turned into? Please don't call the police. I promise, if you just let me go away, I'll never be back again. Hey, do you mind if I ask…,' he glanced from the plastic to Asher's pyjamas and back to his face, 'are you sick or something?'

Asher's smile dropped off. 'Cancer.'

The colour drained from Jay's head. 'Oh wow, I'm sorry. Are you gonna be okay?'

Asher gave his lopsided shrug. 'They've given me a few years maybe.'

'Gosh.' Jay sank his face into his palm. 'I didn't know her brother was dying. Poor Rebecca.'

Asher managed a feeble grin in Imogen's direction.

'I feel like a complete heel, giving you all this hassle on top of what you already have to bear. I thought I was being low-key, only turning up when people are either at work or asleep in bed.'

'I hate to let you down then, but you were terrible.' Asher seemed to take pity on him. 'You can get going, but if we ever see you around here again, we will call the cops. That's a promise.'

The shiny dome nodded vigorously. 'I promise I'll stay away. Please don't let your sister ever know anything about this, or that I ever existed. I'm such a loser. Thank you both, and please accept my humblest apologies for the worry I caused you.'

'Why call yourself a loser? You have everything going for you because you have time to do a lot of things. I'm the one who might fall off my perch at any time. I'd swap places with you in a flash.'

'No, you wouldn't. My life is a mess. I wish I could change it.'

'Well, instead of stalking my sister, why don't you pour that energy into something more worthwhile?'

'There's nothing I'm good at. I stink at everything I try.'

'That's not strictly true. You managed to trace where your idol lives. And you keep coming all the time. That's persistence. Isn't there anything else you ever thought you'd like to do?'

Hesitating, Jay rubbed one of the dimples in his head. 'I always wanted to write a poetry book.'

'Then give it a shot.'

'Do you really think I could?'

'Well, you'd have to make a better poet than you do a prowler.'

Jay's head drooped. 'Nobody would take me seriously. I'm bald as a billiard ball and ugly as sin.'

Asher looked at Imogen and rolled his eyes. Neither of them expected he'd be called upon to speak platitudes to a prowler. 'Hey, don't say that. It makes me feel crushed because I'm going to look like you soon.'

'I just want to do something significant. I'd like my life to count for something.' Jay turned to Imogen. 'I'll ask you, because you're a female. You won't string me along. Do you think I could succeed at writing poetry?'

'I guess you'll just have to give it a try.' How could she say anything else?

Suddenly, Jay swept up her hand and brushed the back of it with his lips. Imogen drew it back swiftly.

'I'll always remember this moment and I'll never forget either of you. Thanks for being so gracious. I promise I'll do something to make you proud of having met me.' He left with a spring to his step. When he reached the road, he turned, raised his hand high above his head and waved to them.

'I hope we have seen the end of him.' Curling his lip, Asher returned the gesture with his right hand. 'Maybe we should've called the police anyway. But I have a feeling he's harmless.'

'Freaky, though.' Wiping the back of her hand on her jeans, she wondered whether she ought to apologise for waking him up and forcing him to come to her rescue. Instead, she said, 'Nice pyjamas.'

'Thanks. Do the stripes make me look tough and dangerous?'

'Well, it seemed to work with him.'

He leaned against the shed door with a grin. 'Next time you want to hold up a prowler, just warn me, will you? I might try a different outfit.'

'Thanks for coming out to help.'

He gave a mock bow. 'Don't mention it. Hey, why did you let him try that crazy chivalrous stuff and kiss your hand?'

'I had no idea he was going to do that. I would have kept my hands behind my back if I'd known.'

'Looks like you haven't learned your lesson.' Sweeping her hand into his, he seemed to be on the verge of kissing it as Jay had done. 'Don't worry, just kidding. Still too many chemo drugs in my system. Lips to skin contact is probably okay but I won't risk it. You're off the hook.' With that, he returned to the house.

Imogen followed slowly. *Is it really good for him to joke around like that all the time? Isn't that denial, or something?* Her father would soon tell her if Asher's stream of witticism was unhealthy for him, but Dad was far away in New York. *Am I really doing the right thing, encouraging him?* Sometimes she couldn't tell whether Asher was joking or not. *Was he really going to kiss my hand?* The thing she'd never admit to anybody was that being let 'off the hook', as he expressed it, made her feel strangely let down.

'Would you like me to drive you there?' Asher asked.

'You don't have to do that.' Yet Imogen's hesitation spoke volumes. He could see from her face that she would appreciate help finding the unfamiliar address.

'I don't mind. It's not on any bus route from here.' He felt better about taking her himself. After the brush with Jay Reynolds, he didn't feel comfortable about a girl like Imogen finding her own way to a strange bloke's house.

I know he was stalking Becky, but if I hadn't come out, who knows what moves the sicko might have tried on Imogen.

His first impression of Imogen had been that she was quiet and sedate—the sort of girl he assumed wouldn't offer anyone much in the way of entertainment. But he'd forgotten what she used to be like. He shouldn't have been surprised that she'd consider locking a prowler in the shed. She had the courage to leave her family to come and live in a foreign country alone, and the poise to converse with a dying guy without getting tongue-tied and weird like everyone else. She'd had that same audacious streak when they were children. He'd never expected her to follow him outside at night to keep battling him for the gold tokens, but she had. And she'd been resourceful enough to want to move that ladder.

She opened the driver's door of the BMW, groaned comically when she saw the steering wheel and hurried around to the other side. 'I still keep forgetting that the left side is for the passenger.'

'For a moment, I thought you wanted to drive.' He watched her slide into the seat beside him. Any girl as adventurous as her ought to look and act different. She should be solid and loud-mouthed, not quiet and willowy. Honestly, she was a bit of a worry.

What sort of man would write a note in his Bible that he wanted it urgently returned? It seemed almost as if this Christopher Stubbins intended all along for it to conveniently go missing. If it was some sort of perverted ploy to get naïve and kind-hearted young women alone with him, the freak would find himself outsmarted this time.

'I've really made demands on your day, haven't I?' Her voice was apologetic.

'That's okay.' He wouldn't admit that he felt the need to look out for her. He could think of several women from his office who would have been offended, and she was probably no different. 'Helps me fill time.'

That much was true. If he wasn't driving Imogen to Strathalbyn he'd be moping around, impatient, until Kaitlyn arrived later that night. He'd been aching to see Kaitlyn and show her that he was okay. He'd felt terrible when he'd been too sick to even say goodbye. Knowing how she took his condition to heart, he'd worried about her state of mind ever since, but she would be with him in a matter of hours now. They'd play a game or watch TV. It was different to the social whirl they used to engage in, but by the end of each day, he was too tired to mingle at parties anyway. By about nine-thirty each night, his eyelids began to droop.

No, that's not it at all. He was doing it again—lying to himself. Ever since he'd been sick and had more time with his thoughts, he'd been amazed how often his own mind attempted to fool him. He knew he did it with others, but never realised until now that he tried to dupe himself too. How could he have fallen for his own act so often? Now that he was dying, he might as well be honest. He felt uncomfortable socialising because the jollity ceased whenever he walked in. His friends didn't know how to deal with him. That was what was hurting him.

The house wasn't difficult to find. The new section of Strathalbyn was drier than Aldgate, reminding him of summer, a season he may never see again.

'So have you got the Bible?'

She tapped its hard cover beneath her arm. 'Right here.'

The middle-aged man who answered their knock greeted them with a wide beam. 'I'm so pleased to meet you. I'm Chris Stubbins.'

He didn't seem taken aback or disappointed to see a male friend with Imogen. When Asher extended his hand, Chris gave it a firm, friendly shake. With his dark skin, thick thatch of snowy white hair, and gleaming smile, he looked like the negative of a photograph.

He patted the cover of his Bible as if it was a beloved pet. 'I can't tell you how glad I am to see this. You won't believe how I came to have that note written inside the cover. A good mate of mine did it as a joke.' Chris' eyes sparkled with the sort of merriment that couldn't be contained within. Asher wasn't sure it made him comfortable.

'Why did he write it?' Imogen asked.

Chris turned and gestured up the short passage behind him. 'I'll tell you what, why don't you come through to the kitchen and I'll tell you over a slice of cheesecake? I made some for friends, but ended up with too many. The least I can offer the rescuers of my Bible is a slice of cake.'

Imogen looked at Asher with a questioning raise of her eyebrows. It seemed she wanted to accept the offer, so he shrugged and nodded.

The aroma inside Chris' house smelled fragrant and inviting. His small kitchen bench was crowded with fresh cheesecakes.

'Come take a seat and I'll tell you. I'm renowned for carelessly misplacing things. Keys, wallet, credit cards, anything that isn't nailed down. After prayer group one night, my mate, Joe, was ribbing me about it, and then grabbed my Bible and wrote that message. I told him what a duffer he was, but just a few weeks later, the Bible went missing. I must have put it down somewhere, because I take it everywhere with me, to coffee shops, parks and meetings. Somehow it must have made its way to that second-hand shop. I was attached to it because it used to belong to my dear old mum in England. What a blessing that a responsible young lady was the person to find it.'

'I'm glad I was able to help.' Imogen said.

'Would you like a slice of my mango and white chocolate cheesecake? Cheesecakes are my favourite hobby.'

Imogen looked across at Asher. 'Do you think you'd be able to manage?'

'Yeah, sure. They told me that's the sort of thing I should be eating.'

They ended up sitting at this stranger's table digging into the most delicious, sunshine-coloured dessert Asher had ever tasted. His spoon slid through it like a cloud and it dissolved in his mouth in a burst of tropical flavoured heaven.

'Mmm, this cheesecake is the best.' Imogen dabbed her lips with her serviette.

'I can't cook anything else. I just have a knack for cheesecakes.'

'With that sort of knack, you don't need any other,' Asher told him.

'Have another slice. So are you brother and sister? Boyfriend and girlfriend?'

'Neither. I'm staying with Asher's family and doing a bit of work for his mother.'

'I see. Now, young fellow, may I ask what ails you?'

'Pardon?' If the cheesecake wasn't so light he might have choked on it. *Is it that obvious I'm sick?* He'd lost several kilos over the last few weeks, but although his jeans were baggy and he needed to use the tightest notch of his belt, couldn't he just be a skinny guy?

'You mentioned being told that you have to eat this sort of thing. I assume that was by a doctor.'

Asher set down his spoon. 'I had my first course of chemotherapy yesterday. I had a cancerous tumour in my shoulder that spread to my lymph nodes.'

Chris Stubbins raised his great, dark eyes to his ceiling. 'Maybe you're the one I've been expecting.'

Huh? Asher wanted to be out of there. Chris could make brilliant cheesecakes but he was starting to sound like a fruitcake. Imogen was blinking, startled.

'No, I'm not a madman.' He seemed to guess what they were thinking. 'It's terrible that you have cancer. I offer my deepest sympathy. It's just that somebody gave me a word in church that by the end of this month I'd be able to help a young man. I assumed it was going to be a lad I know from work who has some serious family problems, but although I've been reaching out to him, he's been resisting. Now it's the thirty-first day of the month and maybe it's turned out to be you instead.' His wide smile was back.

'So how can you help me? If you're a doctor, you can't really help. It's already spread too far. I left it too late before I went to the doctor. They reckon I probably have only a few years to live at the most, even with the chemo.'

Chris' smile was serene. 'That's not the sort of help I meant. I was thinking more along the lines of encouragement, friendship and support. You see, I can understand to a large extent where you're coming from. I had raging leukemia and they gave me only a few weeks to live.'

Chapter 9

'So what happened?'

'I was healed. God healed me.'

Asher rolled his eyes. He hated that pat answer. It was the sort of vague but exclusive statement that did not invite dispute.

'Well, how did you put yourself in a position for God to heal you?'

Chris shrugged. 'Nothing you probably haven't already considered. Prayer…'

Asher cut in, 'I've prayed. I've got down on my knees and pleaded. All my crying out to him hasn't helped.'

Chris' eyes seemed dewy with compassion. 'Maybe you've been working on it too hard.'

Asher's heart sank. 'But you just said to pray. Now it sounds like you're telling me to ease off on prayer. I've tried both, believe me. And I can tell you, neither will get me healed.'

'Listen, son. I'm not pushing either one or the other. I'm just suggesting that you remember who the healer is. And it's not you.'

I hate it when people call me that. I'm not his son. 'Do you think I don't know that? But how do I get God to consider healing…?' He broke off. It was just a different way of asking the same question he'd asked before. They'd been around in a circle. No, they hadn't moved anywhere. He would try different words.

'How did your healing happen?'

The corners of Chris' mouth quirked. 'You really want a straight answer, don't you?'

'Yes, please.'

'Well, here's how it was for me. I took time to sit and pray, to focus on nothing but God and his promises. I'd hate to make you think it's a fool-proof method for everyone, though. God can't be worked like a formula and I don't want to say anything to make you believe he can.'

'Well, how did you think you could help me, then?' Asher made no effort to conceal his despair.

Chris remained calm. 'You've been doing all the asking, so far. Do you mind if I ask you a question?'

'Go ahead.'

'First of all, what's your occupation?'

'I'm a computer software engineer.'

'So what do you do?'

Drawing a deep breath, Asher resisted the impulse to groan. He liked talking but not about this and not now. 'I design computer software programs.' The blank expression on Chris' face told him that answer made it clear as pea soup.

'How do you actually design 'em? I don't know much about computers.'

'Well, I write coded instructions that tell a computer what to do in logical steps.' Trying to explain his job to somebody who wasn't familiar with computers was like trying to describe a fish to someone who had never seen water.

'You've lost me already. I'm only a grocer.'

'I guess it's pretty involved.'

'Forget the explanation then. It'll go over my head and won't serve any purpose. Are you the sort of person who can think with your heart or does your brain tend to hold you back?'

'What sort of question is that?' It didn't make sense.

'With a job title I can't even understand, you might be saturated in the intellectual mindset of the modern age. Wanting a quick, formulaic solution might be a sign of that.' Shaking his head, Chris cut himself another sliver of cheesecake. 'I've been told it all started with the Ancient Greeks who thought they were a cut above everyone else. Smart people aren't always our friends. They shrug off answers which can't be explained with intellect. They think everything has to be subject to science and technology. If things can't be clinically observed and proven in laboratories, they won't believe it's true. And anything that can't be measured and summed up with the five senses is given the flick.'

71

Asher wondered at the note of disdain in Chris' tone. It sounded like common sense to him.

'How do you think we should think?' Imogen asked.

'My experience has taught me that a serious diagnosis can be a wake-up call.' Chris turned back to Asher. 'If you've been looking no further than what you can see and feel about your situation, I'd encourage you to broaden your focus. I'm telling you this because I've been there.'

Asher slowly ran his spoon around the edge of his bowl. 'What am I supposed to look at, then?' He had heard his pastor talk about an invisible, spirit realm, but didn't feel in the mood to discuss airy-fairy fluff while he was so sick.

'Do you believe that God loves you dearly?' Chris' voice had turned soft.

Asher found his throat tightening. He looked down at the white knuckles on his tight fists, unsure whether he felt most sad or angry. 'It's what I've always been told.' He didn't add, *But he has a strange way of showing it.*

'Do you believe it?' Chris asked. 'Do you believe that your future, whatever it may be, is safe in his hands?'

Asher stayed silent. He wasn't sure he could give the answer Chris evidently hoped for.

Chris said, 'I can promise you, he loves you to distraction. Don't just take my word for it, though. It's all through the Bible.' He ran a reverent hand across the cover of his own Bible. 'I'm almost sorry you've brought this back to me. I'd like to think you're reading it yourselves.'

'I've read the Bible,' Imogen said. 'My parents were missionaries and elders on the church board. They tried to make sure we all knew it back to front.'

'And my mum is a Christian counsellor,' Asher added. 'She's always tried to pound the Bible into us from Revelation to Genesis. Back to front, like Imogen said. I've even taught Sunday School.' Teaching primary school kids had its fun moments. At least they thought he was cool, and he'd been able to monopolise a conversation without being told off.

'Do you think you could consider reading it with a fresh mindset, as if you've never read a word before? It's just that the people who may benefit quickest from what God might want to do are those who don't think they've already heard it all.'

Asher flinched. This was familiar territory. He hadn't said much, yet

Chris Stubbins had already summed him up as a know-it-all.

'All I'm trying to say is this. Sometimes it helps to undo any assumptions you might have made. You've got to be prepared to read over the same old stories with the expectation that you'll find something fresh and valuable each time.'

Asher and Imogen looked at each other. She raised her shoulders in a slight shrug, reflecting his confusion.

'How can doing that help heal me?'

'It might help convince you how much God loves you and wants the very best for you.' Chris' eyes were dark and luminous. 'Sometimes it's so easy for people to forget that most important thing. It will remind you that his plan for you is perfect.'

'How can I believe his plan for me is perfect when I'm dying of cancer and the chemotherapy is making me sick? And how can I believe it when I saw what happened to my mum?'

'Maybe we should go now,' Imogen spoke up.

Her nervous face was looking up at him. Asher realised he was standing but didn't recall getting up off his seat. His fists were cocked. *Oh God, no, not this.* He wasn't supposed to get so crazy mad that he didn't realise what he was doing. The last time that happened had been with Dad. With a pounding heart, he let his fingers relax and sank back onto his seat.

'Sorry,' he said. 'But if God looks after us, then why doesn't it look like it? My mum broke her spine. We prayed and prayed for her healing, and she was never completely healed. She can only shuffle around to this very day. If God wants us to believe him for something, then why doesn't he come through every time?'

Chris was watching him through a misty screen of tea steam. 'That's the saddest question ever asked. But don't assume that God was responsible for either your mother's injury or your cancer. Don't be like all those people who are so quick to suppose that whatever happens must be his will. Things happen in this fallen world that he hates, and smarter people than me have tried to figure out why. In fact, some people believe that God's faithful followers should be immune to sickness. They say that illness and disease is obviously a consequence of the sin of humankind, so now that our sins have been cleared by Jesus, why are we still dealing with the consequences?' He looked up with a smile. 'I guess I can understand their reasoning.

Before Asher could respond, Chris shot up his hand. 'Now, before you get stuck into me again, I'm in no way suggesting it's your fault that you have cancer. But some people believe scripture makes an excellent case that your body should be out of bounds.'

'So how's believing I shouldn't have cancer going to help me now that I do have it?'

'Don't bother asking how or why. You'll make yourself mad, going around in circles. Just focus on God's tremendous love for you. If he cares for you, then you're in the best of hands. Sometimes the simple things are all we have to rely on. And they turn out to be all we need. That's how it was for me. When I really started to believe the words in the Bible, I noticed promises to be grasped that I seemed always to have missed before. And I developed a strong trust that they covered me too.'

Asher glanced at Imogen's attentive face and kept quiet. He found his head whirling. It was too pat and simple. Crazy. It sounded freakishly good. He was afraid to let himself hope. Although he hadn't come to terms with the idea of dying so young, he was getting more used to it with each passing day. His approaching death was the first and last thing on his mind each morning and night. The thought of having a tenuous hope to cling to made his stomach swoop.

Better to face reality like a man than go along with something weird and have my hopes dashed.

But the thought of relinquishing what Chris was suggesting made him want to weep. He fiddled around with the handle of his teacup, careful to keep his face averted so they couldn't tell.

Chris was standing over him, clamping his shoulder—the good one, luckily. 'I know how you're feeling, believe me. I wouldn't be urging a sick man to listen to me ramble on if I thought I'd only hurt and confuse him. But I can't stop thinking that maybe you've been brought into my life… my house… because I can share my experience with you, for what it's worth. That's all. Forgive me if I've caused stress.'

Asher's shoulder gave its hateful throb. Nothing could be more real than that. Thinking about it seemed to remind the pain to happen. *There's no way this would ever work.*

'Maybe I'll think it over… pray about it.' *What a cop-out.* Asher knew he was a great phoney, mentioning prayer. He'd given nothing more than lip service to prayer for the last fifteen years, as if his faith had smashed on the patio pavers with his mother's spine.

'Hey, could I get back to you if I have any more questions I'd like to ask?'

'Of course. I'll give you my phone number. I'd be more than happy to talk any time. Thanks for asking. It shows I haven't merely bamboozled and confused you.'

But you have.

Once outside, Asher blinked in the sunshine. It was blazing with its final intensity before fading to the tired, late afternoon light. Since taking sick leave from work, Asher had been able to observe the pattern of the days. It reminded him of what was going to happen to him. Had he passed that last brave, flaming surge of life yet? Was he entering the dwindling stage?

When they were in the car, Imogen remarked, 'He was more than we bargained for.'

'Yeah. I probably won't phone him or talk to him again. But at least I have his number.'

Imogen heard Asher get up to have a shower after his nap. His mother had suggested waking him before Kaitlyn arrived to share dinner with them, but Imogen trusted that Asher would be up in time to get ready. Kaitlyn was the person he loved most in the world. When he came out in a smart green shirt, Marian joked about him looking the part for his sweetheart. Asher even blushed.

He went to answer a phone call and she could tell by the slump of his shoulders that the news wasn't good.

'That's okay, you enjoy yourself then... you deserve to have a break from all of this.' He sounded fine but whoever was at the other end couldn't see his body language. It turned out that Kaitlyn wasn't coming. She'd been invited to go nightclubbing with her fellow cast members, and decided she might as well make an effort to be sociable in her grief.

Dinner was a sober affair with each member of the Dorazio family trying to behave upbeat. Asher couldn't help showing that he was crestfallen, and Becky was gloomy because nobody had invited her to the nightclub event. As Marian tried to cheer them both up, big tears suddenly started rolling down her cheeks. The twins ended up trying to console her. Imogen had no idea how to make anybody feel better. How could she have assumed she could simply breeze into their lives and be a blessing?

Becky decided to join the party anyway, Asher and Marian said goodnight before disappearing to their own rooms, and Imogen read a book for several hours. A clatter and thump on the veranda startled her. It sounded as if somebody had tripped over the metal chair and gone sprawling.

Jay? Jay had said he wasn't coming back. There was a shuffling, breathy sound like some sort of sick animal. As she edged closer to the door, it sounded like a person crying.

Kaitlyn was sprawled across the veranda with her high-heeled shoes dangling over the steps, and her head wedged against a fallen flowerpot. Her hair was wild, covered with dirt and plastered to her face.

Imogen was down on her knees beside her. 'Are you okay?'

'My boyfriend's dying, I knocked back a first-rate role and I feel sick as a pig. Other than that I'm just ecstatic.' She finished with a loud hiccup.

'Sorry.'

Kaitlyn didn't smell good. Imogen couldn't figure out if she'd actually been sick or if the vinegary odour around her was just left over from the party.

'Come inside. I'll fix you a drink.'

'A drink? Now you're talking.' Kaitlyn tried to scramble up but the heels of her shoes got tangled together as if they were having a sword fight. She went crashing back down again. 'You'd better make it stong… slong… spong. What am I trying to say?' She let out a raucous giggle.

'Strong.' Imogen's heart was sinking. She shouldn't be putting words into her mouth. 'But I didn't mean that sort of drink. I'm talking about a hot drink.'

'A hot drink ain't gonna change my life, sister.' Kaitlyn's pencil-thin eyebrows drew together and she erupted into a stream of invective Imogen hadn't heard since the foster kid Mom and Dad had sent back because his mouth was too filthy.

'Hey, what's happening?' It was a repeat of the question Asher had asked her that same morning when Jay was in the shed. He stood holding the screen door open and even wore the same pyjamas.

Kaitlyn somehow swayed to her feet. She took a few wonky steps and pushed Asher hard in the chest. More of the sour odour hit Imogen's senses whenever Kaitlyn moved.

'I should have got to play the lead. It's all your fault. Why didn't you go sooner to the doctor? Why did you get cancer? My life is hell because of you.' Her tears combined with dirt from the pot plants to make her face muddy.

He tried to gather her into his arms. 'It's okay to feel that way. Settle down.'

Imogen heard the sharp sound of a hand striking flesh. When Asher recoiled back, touching his cheek, she knew Kaitlyn had slapped him. Imogen felt herself turn hot.

Asher had grasped both Kaitlyn's wrists and this time, held her at arm's length. 'Thanks. I've had that coming to me for awhile.'

She was threshing about, still trying to lash out at him, showing her perfectly manicured nails, wine-coloured to match her cocktail dress. 'Don't stick your chemical-laden fingers all over me.'

'I think you're emitting more noxious chemicals than him right now.' Imogen knew Kaitlyn was drunk with grief, but she said it anyhow. Kaitlyn started sobbing. Asher stared at Imogen with shock. When he smiled, she knew it would be all right.

'Take it easy,' he said. 'I've never seen her quite like this before.'

'I offered her a hot drink.' Imogen wanted him to know that she'd been trying to help.

'Good idea. Could you go and get one now? Hot, black coffee.'

'What about you?' Asher was still gripping Kaitlyn's wrists, trying to stop her lunging at him.

'No, I don't want one.'

'I mean… with her.'

'I can manage,' he grunted.

As she fixed the drink, Imogen found herself shaking. She sloshed coffee across the counter and had to wipe it up. When she brought out the steaming cup, Asher was sitting on the porch swing with Kaitlyn's head in his lap. Her mouth hung open and she was making little snoring sounds, fast asleep.

'Wow, that was quick.' Imogen set the coffee down on the glass-topped table.

'Yeah, she used up all her energy.' Asher was brushing Kaitlyn's hair back from her face in a gentle movement that made Imogen's throat tighten.

She watched the way the moonlight shone on his blond wavy hair.

'What Chris was talking about today… have you been thinking about that?'

'Yeah, but I've decided to stop thinking about it. We shouldn't have stayed listening to him all that time. It could raise my hopes too much.'

'If he was healed, don't you think healing might be possible?'

He shook his head. 'When you think about it, meeting him might make my chances of survival even slimmer. What are the odds of two people in the same room both being healed of a fatal disease? I'm talking mathematics now, probability. It's ultra-rare when one person gets healed, let alone two.'

Imogen imagined her spirits seeping all over the wooden boards of the veranda. 'Hey, I don't think Math has anything to do with the way God might choose to work.'

He shuffled as if he was trying to shrug and winced instead. 'The way I think God chooses to work is through science. If a body has cancer, it doesn't often go away. Hey, don't even mention him to…' he jerked his chin down at Kaitlyn.

'I won't.'

She's going to kick herself one of these days when he's dead, for lying there in a drunken sleep when she had the chance to explore his face with her fingers and remember it for always. The thought came unbidden, and Imogen turned and went back inside so Asher wouldn't see her tears.

Chapter 10

It's only going to get worse for her.

Asher had once joked to his happy Kaitlyn that it would take a major cataclysm to make her really upset. At the time, he couldn't imagine that she had it in her. He hated seeing somebody who had always been so cheerful dragged to the depths of despair.

She'd often given him mock slaps, pokes and punches while laughing at the jokes he'd spouted, pretending to find them outrageous, all the while encouraging him to think of more. Now that he'd found himself on the receiving end of her genuine heartfelt physical attack, it left him reeling inside.

She was really drunk, though. Mum always tried to excuse Dad's drunken tirades by insisting the dreaded drink transformed a person's personality. Asher didn't quite agree. Alcohol didn't effect a total change. Rather, he suspected it brought out all the suppressed anguish and distress a person was more or less successful at concealing when they were sober. It had happened with Kaitlyn the same way he'd so often seen it happen with Dad.

I wish he was around. He remembered the sight of Dad striding across a stage, working the crowd. His father had loved his stand-up performances even more than he'd loved acting. Sometimes they watched him on the auditorium stage at the school where he'd been a drama teacher, the same school Seth now worked at as chaplain. At other times they'd seen him play at independent venues. Asher had sat through hundreds of Dad's one-man comedy routines.

'I'm Hayden Dorazio, part Scottish and part Italian.' He'd swing around on his heels when he came to the end of the stage, with his shaggy mane tilted proudly as if that was the most impressive claim anybody could make. 'We all know the Scottish people are renowned for their fiery tempers and the Italians for their intense passion. Well, folks, that makes me a force to be reckoned with!'

Then he'd give a stealthy glance from beneath his bushy eyebrows, gauging the crowd's reaction, wordlessly demanding that they cheer. And they wouldn't let him down. Only Asher would sit with his fists wedged against his side. That 'adore me' look of Dad's used to make him fantasize about tangling his fingers in all that pretentious hair and wrenching it until there was none left. Dad wouldn't use his put-on Scottish brogue when he yelled for mercy. Dad had often called him a nuisance, show-off and big mouth, and then showed off so blatantly himself, making his family sit through it.

But that was back then. If only Dad could get a chance to make one return appearance, Asher would cheer louder than anybody. He'd probably fall to his knees and hug Dad's legs as he had when he was a small boy.

'Hey, you got it mixed up,' he'd crowed once when he was eleven or twelve. 'It's the Irish who are renowned for their fiery tempers, not the Scottish.'

Dad peered around with a finger held to his lips, then hissed, 'Don't shout these things out in public where people might overhear. Tell me in private and for heaven's sake, keep that ear-splitting voice down.' Then he'd flashed his broad smile with a hoot of laughter and shot out his hand to muss up Asher's hair. 'I'll have to think of something else.'

The stagecraft which Becky often claimed to be such hard work came easily to him. Asher had never expected that Dad-shaped cavern in his heart to remain so empty and aching.

If only Seth had believed me, Dad might never have died. Becky adored Dad, so he hadn't really expected her to accept what he had to say, but Seth should have listened. He always claimed to be open-minded and wise. The incriminating evidence Asher had chalked up against Dad was solid proof of what he'd been up to, but Seth insisted on sweeping it aside.

Asher hadn't wanted to believe it either. It made him so heartsick he could hardly keep his mind on anything else. Back then, he often left a room when Dad walked in, before he erupted into accusations which Dad would deny. He'd waited until he'd been certain, and coming to Seth with his evidence had been one of the most painful things he'd ever forced himself to do. Then Seth insinuated that Asher was a gutter-minded troublemaker who wanted to stir up a scandal.

Seth had stood there, with his heavy brows drawn over his blazing eyes. 'You're so over-dramatic. You'd better shut your sensationalist mouth because nobody's going to listen.'

'Do you think I'm enjoying telling you this?' Asher had shouted.

'Listen, I know Dad hasn't always treated you as sensitively as he should have, but there's no way he'd do that. I never want to hear you smear Dad's name again. If you do, you're not welcome here!' Seth had pointed to the door, his arm outstretched.

Asher had slammed the screen door against the brick wall, determined to catch Dad red-handed. What happened next could have been completely different if Seth had believed him. Instead of Asher tearing alone to the holiday cabin, almost blind with rage, Seth should have come with him to calm him down, a quality he was admired for.

Instead of Asher hell bent on confronting Dad with what he'd been up to, Seth could have stepped between them to talk reason. Seth could have even gone without Asher, taken Dad fishing and thrashed it out on the Southern Ocean. Seth and Dad used to enjoy their fishing trips—they'd bob around for hours as a speck on the horizon, rods dangling as they enjoyed each others' company.

Years earlier, Asher had pleaded to go with them. After they caved in and took him, Dad swore it would be the first and last time. 'I had to be a blockhead to agree to take you.' Asher had been restless, kept wobbling the boat and didn't stop talking. When they got back to shore, Dad made a big show of falling to his knees, with his hands raised in a gesture of thankfulness. For Asher's part, the experience had taught him that just because something seemed desirable didn't make was so. He'd been bored out of his mind.

If only Seth had believed Asher, Dad might still be alive. That thought bobbed up more than ever since his cancer diagnosis, but it had to be shoved back down where it belonged.

So many times, Asher could have gone out and got rip-roaring drunk to take the edge off the pain. He'd had plenty of opportunities, but his solemn fear of the power of drink held him back from having more than a glass or two. Alcohol made the rubbish and muck in a person's heart pour out, and his heart contained so much, nobody would be left standing. It was hard enough holding it in when he was sober. And he knew in some deep, dark recess that the bitterness and fury he'd felt against Dad had now been transferred to Seth. If Asher got drunk, Seth would be in the direct firing line, and Asher's reasonable side knew that his brother didn't deserve it. It would be a mistake to attack him. What happened hadn't been Seth's fault at all.

He lay on his back, blinking up at the ceiling. *Okay, I have the same combination of quick temper and passion as Dad. But I don't think anybody would take that as an excuse for the way I carried on.*

Imogen couldn't sleep. Her brain wouldn't turn off, and her legs were too twitchy. She could hear everything. Becky arrived back and offered to drive Kaitlyn home. Then Marian shuffled out of her bedroom and spoke to Asher. He mumbled something back, low and serious. Now silence filled the house, but she still couldn't rest.

She found her Bible, a token to honour her parents, pushed into the back corner of her drawer. Unlike Chris Stubbins' treasured volume, the pages were white, pristine. What if some of those hints she'd been getting were from God?

'You'll never fathom the treasures between these covers if don't read it,' Mom would say. There was still nothing but the same dry, numbered columns of words, but even though it felt like trying to crack a secret code for 'good' people, Imogen kept turning pages. She was floundering at the mouth of a cave that appeared barren, although others assured her its depths contained precious gold, silver, rubies and pearls for those who knew how to look. Even though she was in the right place, perhaps she simply wasn't wise enough to recognise the value in what lay upon her knees.

Maybe that's what the stable in Bethlehem was like. She squirmed and sighed. *There was clearly a baby in that manger, but to most people, he was just the normal son of a poor couple who'd travelled far from home. Only those who cared to look closer figured out that he was really the one sent to save the world. I guess I would've been one of the people who would have walked straight past.*

Perhaps she'd simply heard the story too often. She'd prattled 'Jesus was God's Son' from the time she was old enough to talk. Had she already transferred it to the 'Heard That One' compartment of her mind before she even grew old enough to understand its significance? She closed her eyes and tried to ponder the mystery of God's Son being born in human form. It was truly hard to grasp. Had she let history's most mind-blowing event become drab and commonplace through familiarity?

Something Chris Stubbins had said earlier that day flashed through her mind. It began to recede straight away but Imogen pounced on the heels of the fading thought, sensing its importance. She wriggled up in bed. Revelations couldn't be grasped lying down. *Got it!* Chris had said that weird thing to them—that people who are too busy thinking with their brains might miss messages from their hearts. He also suggested that they needed to approach the Bible, in all its familiarity, with fresh eyes. *Maybe he meant that seeing or hearing something a lot can make people switch off, so they might as well be blind or deaf.* She was gripping the tail of a slippery idea. *Don't get away. If looking at Scriptures with fresh eyes is what it'll take to make me get it, then that's what I want to do.*

She wanted to read one of the stories, any of them. Glancing down at the open page already in front of her, she began to read. The book was 2Kings and the story was about Naaman. She could approach this with a fresh mind. She already knew he'd been a Syrian commander, but this time she was determined to make his form take shape in her imagination. She closed her eyes until his picture came into focus.

Naaman was a high achiever who had accomplished all he'd ever set out to do. He'd secured a high position in the Aramean army and had showy chariots, money, prestige, and the respect of his peers. And although the Bible didn't mention it, she imagined him tall with wavy-blond hair, penetrating green eyes and a generous smile. His circumstances were perfect except for one terrifying fact—he had leprosy, a life-threatening disease.

Asher Dorazio, high achiever, fantastic job, great car, lovely girlfriend, only one huge problem—a life threatening disease. It was futile to hope. Miracle stories were surely rare even in those ancient times, which was why they earned their spot in the Bible. Nevertheless, when Imogen's head turned fuzzy, she realised she'd been holding her breath.

Naaman heard about a noteworthy prophet from Israel. He decided it may be worth traveling to consult him, as he'd already tried many more traditional cures for his leprosy and he was desperate. But Elisha, the Hebrew prophet, enraged him. Instead of the reception Naaman had expected, the man sent a servant to tell him to dunk himself in the Jordan River seven times. 'Then your skin will be healed and you'll be good as new.' Naaman stormed away. It was ridiculous, of course.

Asher, still trying the best twenty-first century medical science has to offer, sits and listens to an older man named Chris, a simple grocer who claims to have experienced a radically different way to be healed. 'I just believed and latched onto the promises God made in his Word. I spoke them out. It worked for me.' But Naaman-like, Asher rejects Elisha's, or rather Chris' words.

'Dipping in the Jordan River is stupid! And why seven times? Does he think I haven't washed myself hundreds of times already, with the best lotions and spices Aram has to offer? What makes him think the murky, polluted water from his backwater province is anything special? It will probably reinfect the sores and make them worse than they already are. Coming here was a waste of time.' Imogen actually heard Naaman, the Syrian army commander say all this in a manly, deep Australian accent. Who could argue with such a decisive man?

The rest of the story was Sunday school folklore. Naaman had gone down to the Jordan. On the seventh dunking, he'd emerged with flawless, glowing skin. But what had changed his mind? His servants had spoken up and said, 'Listen sir, you might as well give it a go. What have you to lose?' Perhaps the Hebrew maidservant who had first told him about the prophet was among those urging him to try the cure.

Imogen could stay in one spot no longer. She began pacing her floor. *The foreign household guest and casual employee approaches Asher.* She stopped moving. *Is that me? Is this why I'm here?*

No, she wasn't thinking straight. The analogy was severely limited anyway. Chris Stubbins wasn't some Elisha-like Old Testament prophet who spoke on God's behalf. In the New Testament, people started hearing directly from God for themselves. *Believers today are meant to do the same. I wish I could sense more.*

She sat down and rested the Bible on her lap. 'I'll try to pray again.' If God was trying to speak to her, what would he say?

She couldn't shake the impression it might be something like, *Although Chris is no Old Testament prophet, he could still be used to bring a message. He's a person set by me in the right place at the right time. I might not assign people to boom out my announcements exactly as they did then, but I still call my willing people to give timely words of encouragement. Think of all the occurrences that converged to have both of you visit the home of Chris, a stranger to you. What he said was for you and Asher to grasp.*

'Was that you or me, God? Is it wishful thinking? My thoughts have always been my own thoughts, haven't they? Am I so set on hearing what I want to hear that I'm mistaking it for you? Is it just that I so badly want Asher to recover and live?'

You can keep seeking me. You can encourage Asher to keep seeking me too. One thing you may be sure of is that I never change. I had a heart to heal people back in the Bible and I still do.

Imogen's heart started to thump. 'Tell Asher? I doubt he'll listen. I already mentioned Chris tonight. He's closed that door.'

Tell him anyway.

Dismay seeped through Imogen. 'This must be just my imagination. It can't be you, God, because what I think you're telling me to do will never work.'

Asher was far more complex than any mere Syrian commander. Even as a little boy, once he'd made up his mind about an issue he'd been infuriatingly stubborn. 'Australian Rules football is better than American sport and that's it... The raspberry flavoured drink tastes nicer than the lemon one, no matter what you say... Anybody who would want to see a movie with pretend things like fairies is a dope, and nobody can tell me different.'

Even Ginny, the placid little house guest, used to want to shake him. In fact, once she'd lost her temper and shoved him against the wall, but he still hadn't backed down on whatever they'd been arguing about.

It would be no use. Asher's opinions were always set like concrete and now he was no longer a little boy. He was a computer software engineer who knew all sorts of things nobody else had a chance of understanding. *He isn't going to listen to me after telling me not to mention this again. At least I've got his friendship right now. If I come back to him with this, he'll get impatient and tell me to butt out. It'll upset him and he'll never want to talk to me again. It's not as if I'm refusing to take up my role in the story, because it isn't really about us.*

She held her breath, waiting for her heart to settle down. The impression was still there. She hadn't reasoned it away. It was welling up stronger than ever.

Well, what am I going to say? Gazing down, she knew she had help to answer the question still in her hands. Would she stick to the script, and say something similar to what Naaman's servants had told him? 'You'd probably have listened to Chris if he'd come up with something hard to understand, the sort of thing your brain would respect. Just because this sounds too simple, why not consider the possibility that God might want you to keep hoping, that he might want to heal you too?'

He was doing a bit of work for his boss. It seemed that even though Asher had officially taken sick leave, John Thorne couldn't do without him completely. A shadow crossed his computer screen. Asher spun around and saw their house guest, with her hands clasped in front of her.

'Can I talk to you for a moment?'

'Yeah, sure.'

'Maybe you should think about what Chris Stubbins said. What he's suggesting—well, hoping and praying to be healed won't do you any harm. And God is always there, loving you.' She let out the rest of the breath she'd been holding. It seemed she'd expected it to take longer to say.

Asher shook his head. 'You don't think it'd do any harm to get everyone's hopes up, and then kick the bucket?'

'You wouldn't have to tell anyone else.'

'What if the person I'm most afraid of disappointing is me?' There, he'd said it.

'Well, even if you do kick the bucket, living the rest of your days praying and hoping for the best can't make you worse. It wouldn't do anything but make your last weeks and months more pleasant than they would have been.'

She didn't get it but he tried to keep the irritation out of his voice. 'But I don't want to start fantasising about starting a family with Kaitlyn, and traveling overseas, and cool things like that if it's all going to be ripped away from me. That'd be crazy.'

Imogen stood her ground. 'What if you don't think so far into the future as all that? What if you take each day as a separate compartment? Then you can go to bed each night thinking, *I only need to trust God to keep me alive for one more day.* Then, you might even wake up one morning with a family—little blond kids who ace whatever they do, like you and Kaitlyn.'

He tried another approach. 'Listen, Imogen. Say you were in the same position as me. Say there was a guy you thought the world of, then you talked to someone like Chris who mentioned that God gave him a miracle. What would you do?'

She didn't hesitate. 'I'd tell him to take every day as it comes and keep praying for the best. And I'd tell him not to rule out the possibility of a total miracle, because every day I'd have to spend with him would be a bonus.'

'No, I said you're in my position,' he corrected. 'Not Kaitlyn's. You're the one who's been given the death sentence, not your friend.'

'Oh, yeah.' Her face coloured. 'I honestly don't know how I'd respond in your position. I'd be scared. But I've always felt sad that I don't understand the ways of God more. If I was talking to someone like Chris, whose own experience filled me with hope, well, I wouldn't want to think I'd dismiss his words outright. Just because they might sound a bit too simplistic, maybe even silly, I might wonder if they still could be an answer to prayer. Even if I wasn't healed, but started to understand God more.'

She stood close enough for him to see that her pupils had turned huge. Asher remembered from one of his lectures that dilated pupils were a sign of sincerity. It was part of a psychology unit that went with his course. The bits about body language were some of the only interesting snippets among all the dryness and boredom he'd had to take on board.

'Do you really reckon that old man could be an answer to prayer?'

Imogen blinked. Now that he'd focused on her eyes, he noticed she had long, softly curling lashes.

'Well, what if he is? What if we don't see more answers to prayer because when they come, we reject them because we'd prefer something else?'

He swung around on his computer chair and tilted it back, with his right arm stretched behind his head. 'You know, I actually prayed the night before last, after the chemotherapy.' Somehow, she was the sort of person he could admit such things to. 'I even asked him to send me a sign. Is Chris Stubbins what He came up with?' Asher began to laugh. The idea was so far-fetched and absurd. He ignored the tiny spark of something like hope and shook his head. 'God knows the sort of person I am. If he wanted to heal me, he'd come up with something more feasible than an old country grocer who makes good cheesecakes. He'd give me something he'd know I could believe.'

'You mean like a flashing neon sign in the sky saying, "Asher, I'm going to heal you."?'

'Yeah, I might consider believing that. I wish he would.'

'Me too. But after what I read last night, it just occurred to me that maybe we don't recognise prayer answers because we're too busy looking out for God to give us the answers we'd prefer in our own heads. Maybe we try to box him in. What if God's answers are more inventive and unexpected?'

'Hey, what were you reading last night?'

She hesitated, with a bit of a grin. 'Okay, I'll tell you.'

He could stretch both arms over the arms of his chair without too much discomfort, or maybe her story just drew him in. When she finished, he said, 'So you see me as Naaman, hey?'

It was good to see Imogen could still laugh at his jokes, even though nobody else would. 'Don't kid yourself. It's just an analogy. Do you get the point I'm trying to make? Maybe our visit to Chris was part of the answer to both our prayers. Maybe God wants to encourage you that complete healings are always possible.'

'You prayed for me?'

She nodded sheepishly. 'I prayed for you that same night, that God would heal you.' She swiped a hand across the back of her eyes.

He could ignore her tears but that might be awkward, since her plight was so evident. She'd know he was pretending not to notice. 'This has been tough on you too, hasn't it?'

Her small, responsive noise sounded like an affirmative.

'Hey, buck up. Isn't that what you Americans say?'

She pulled a face and shook her head. 'We never say anything as corny as 'buck up.' That sounds more like the language in old Nancy Drew stories.'

'It does a bit, but I guessed you wouldn't want to hear what we say in Australia.'

'And what might that be?'

'Okay, you asked for it. Don't be such a wuss. See, you'd prefer buck up, wouldn't you?'

'Something like, "Keep your spirits up," might do the trick.'

'Keep your spirits up, then.' He waited until she looked at him. 'Imogen, it's really important that you do. I'm probably being a bit selfish, but it's been a relief to have you to talk to, somebody who doesn't care too much for me, a simple friend. You're a great outlet for me, so please don't get all weepy on me now, like the others.'

Her smile looked forced, but showed she was trying.

'And in return, I'll think over what you said. I promise.' *What am I saying? What does it matter what she thinks of me when I'll probably be dead soon?*

'Just remember, if you do, Kaitlyn might thank you some day.' She turned and fled, as if she couldn't escape from him fast enough.

'Yeah, goodbye,' he spoke into thin air. Her departure left him realising that he wasn't ready to be alone with his boring report again yet.

There was no way he could make such a huge jump of belief as Chris Stubbins had. Their cases were completely different. And just because the Bible was said to be God's own word, he'd been reading it all his life. It'd never made a difference to him. It was just a book.

Chapter 11

'Why are you pulling out of the table tennis finals?'

Imogen watched Seth's shoulders stiffen at Asher's question, or maybe it was the slightly belligerent tone with which he asked it. Seth calmly carried a shovel and set of hedge clippers from the shed to add to the pile of tools on the lawn. He had organised a gardening blitz for his mother, but with all the raking, pruning, clearing and mowing to be done, it would take them all more than the few hours until Marian arrived home from her friend's house.

'We just don't have the heart for it any more,' Seth told Asher.

'But you were looking forward to it, we had a good team and you put everything into it. Just because I'm not well enough to play… everyone else is still fit.'

'It's okay, Asher, we really don't even want to.' Jodie was on her haunches, untangling an old clothesline from the tongs of a pitchfork.

He wheeled on her. 'Do you really not want to, or is it because he doesn't want to?'

Seth dropped a spade with a clang and straightened. 'Will you leave Jodie out of this? Do you want us to play in the finals? If that's what'll make you happy, we'll do it.'

Asher shook his head as he stared at Seth. 'Forget it. What's the point of playing table tennis with that attitude? You'd just lose.'

'No matter what I decide, I can't please you then, can I?' Seth's words were slow and tight with the control of a person holding something back. 'Asher, I can't help being upset that you have cancer. What's your gripe?'

'My gripe is that pulling the team out of the finals won't make me better. Then you'll always be able to say that you might have won if it weren't for your poor, sick brother.'

'So it's all about you?' Seth pushed his hand through his tight, brown curls. 'Other people have feelings as well as you, Ash.'

Hey, what's going on? The tension had escalated so quickly, Imogen felt her heart quicken.

Jodie was up off the grass in a flash, an impressive move for a pregnant woman. She clasped Seth's hand. 'Guys, don't do this. You'll both feel bad later.'

Squeezing her hand, Seth kept glistening eyes on his brother. 'Sorry, I know I stuffed up. I should just keep quiet, and let him treat me however he likes.'

'Treat you how I like! C'mon, I'll tell you how I'll treat you. I'll leave you the BMW in my will and you'll have to cope with all the repayments.'

'There you go again! Even while you're so sick, you can't help rubbing it in that you're so much more successful than I've been.'

Even though she knew his shoulder was sore, Asher threw both hands up in an exaggerated gesture of defeat. 'Of course that's what I'm doing. According to you, that's what I always do.'

Seth swung a pick into the ground, leaving a brown gash in the lawn. 'I don't want to listen to any more of this.'

'What's new? You never want to listen to anything I have to say.' Asher swung around and began striding down the road away from them, his right hand wedged into his jeans pocket and his left one dangling beside him.

Seth groaned. 'I'm an idiot. Why did I have to argue with him in his condition? Somebody better go after him.' Raising his voice, he called, 'Kaitlyn!'

She and Becky stepped outside the house.

'Would you go after Asher?' Seth hung his head. 'He and I had a few words.'

'Nice start to the day.' Kaitlyn hurried after his fast retreating form.

'I reckon she's pleased,' Jodie assured her husband. 'Now she won't have to break a fingernail helping out here.'

'Hey, you've got to be nice about people.' Seth tugged Jodie's short, springy ponytail.

'Sorry.'

Becky was squinting at her sister-in-law. 'You don't like Kaitlyn

91

much, do you?'

Jodie sighed. 'I know she's your best friend… I don't dislike her.'

'But…?' Becky prompted.

'I think you might be better off not getting all those big breaks and great roles that she gets.'

'So you think she has tickets on herself?'

'I think Asher could've done better. That's all.'

'Jodie, stop it, before you go too far,' Seth warned.

'Well, you won't have to worry about her being around for too much longer.' Becky's eyes began filling with tears. 'First my dad dies, and now my twin brother is going to. Does God hate me or something?'

Seth was over in a few strides, wrapping his arms around her. 'All we can do is trust that God has his reasons in all this, Beck.'

She pulled away. 'Seth, I can't bring myself to say this to Mum but I'll tell you. Listening to you raving on about God and his reasons sickens me. I'd rather think there's nobody than believe that someone's watching me and doing nothing to help.'

'You think God isn't real?' Seth's hands dropped to his side.

Becky cocked her head. 'What if I do?'

His handsome face blanched. 'Then you're effectively saying that you reject everything Mum and I stand for.'

'Oh, get that horrified expression off your face. I'm not putting up with any more spiritual guilt trips. You might be my older brother but I'm a free agent with a right to believe what I like. I'm going along with this clean-up plan of yours and washing windows, but I'm not letting you try to force me what to think.' She raised her soapy water bucket with a slosh, and stalked around the corner of the house.

Seth gaped after her. 'How can I help the kids at the school believe in God when I can't even convince my own sister to keep her faith?'

'It's my fault,' Jodie told him. 'I shouldn't have wound her up about Kaitlyn. I'm sorry, babe.'

Imogen watched a muscle twitch in Seth's cheek.

'I don't know why this horrible thing had to happen to Asher, but we'll just trust that God will help him through it.' He planted a grim kiss on his wife's head. 'Come on, let's do what we can control and get to work.'

Asher waited for Kaitlyn to catch up to him.

'Seth's such a bossy git,' she said. 'When he says, "Jump," everyone's supposed to ask, "How high?"'

'Yeah, nothing new to me.'

'Slow down a bit. I'm puffing.'

He paused and motioned her to his right side. 'Come around here. This arm's easier to put around you.' When she hesitated, he added, 'It'll be safe now. No traces of chemotherapy chemicals.'

With a sigh, she moved against him in the old way with her head nuzzling his shoulder, but didn't wrap her arm around his waist as she used to.

'Why is he doing this working bee for your mum? To earn brownie points in heaven?'

Asher could hardly force a laugh. He used to feel exhilarated around Kaitlyn, in a slightly guilty way. Listening to her say the things he kept bottled up was a bit like living on the edge. Now he just felt sad. 'He likes doing hands-on things so you can see the difference afterwards. It makes him feel as if he's achieved something, even if the elephant he's avoiding is standing there as huge and grey as ever.' He closed his mouth. He was rambling.

'He's so busy wanting to surprise your mum, but I'm your girlfriend and nobody thinks to give me a break.'

He tried to tease her into a lighter mood. 'You had a break the other night, remember. No, maybe you wouldn't.'

She raised her pert nose. 'It doesn't count because I was miserable that night. I can't remember trying to bash you up, like you said. I'd like to go out tonight, to Darius' poetry reading gig.'

'Who's this Darius?'

'The guy who plays the hero in the new play.' Kaitlyn lowered her voice, even though nobody was around. 'Becky has a serious crush on him. I might take her along. She's been suffering over your diagnosis too. We all need a break from it.'

'Yeah, I'd love a break from it. I hate being the main man in this drama.'

The friendly smile of Chris Stubbins returned to his mind. Chris' escape route from the tragedy surely couldn't be possible, even though Imogen's way of reasoning kept playing through his head. *What if we keep God in a box? What if we reject his answers because they're more inventive than we expect?*

Asher knew he must be dreaming, because heaven wasn't quite the way he would have imagined it. Surely there must be more to see than this thick forest? Yes, he was vaguely aware of his bed and the pillow beneath his head. He was having a nap and seemed to be suspended in a hazy place between sleep and wakefulness. Although he knew this at the back of his mind, it didn't stop him racing around dodging trees and looking out for his dad. *I just want to talk to him.*

A voice broke into his consciousness. 'Asher Dorazio, welcome to heaven, but you didn't need to arrive just yet.'

He looked around for the person who had spoken in his dream. 'Well, I didn't have much choice, did I?'

'You don't have to give up hoping. You prayed for a sign, and then shrugged off the words of the people who have come into your life. Why not consider what they say instead of rejecting it without a thought? You've probably heard that humans are my hands and feet. Well, have you considered they may also be my voice? You were always such a talented talker but maybe you're not so good at listening.'

Hold on. Asher had to protest. *I did think about what they said.* His mind felt hazy. Had he? *Of course I did. Chris and Imogen said I should keep my hopes up because I never know what might happen. I know all that, but I've been given a prognosis. It isn't reasonable to hope that I might be able to live. It's crazy.*

'For somebody who likes being presented with facts, how's this one? An infinite number of so-called crazy people like Chris Stubbins have pushed in and lived. Those who you say weren't healed are part of God's mystery. There's no way you can measure their faith, or decide they didn't have enough. But those are their stories, not yours. Just because your human reasoning can't understand or explain everything, that's no reason to give up praying and hoping for your own healing. Here's a definite fact you can grasp. If you throw in the towel and blindly believe the dire words of the doctor, based on limited human facts, then you're more likely to die just when they predict.'

Hey, leave me alone.

Asher jerked out of his slumber. His brow was damp with perspiration.

This is ridiculous. Whenever he tried to sleep, restless impressions from his jumbled thoughts played through his head. Chris and Imogen were getting to him even in his sleep. It was just Chris and Imogen, wasn't it?

It had been a bad day from the time he woke up. He shouldn't have let himself get irritated with Seth. Being mad at people exhausted him. Perhaps all the crashing fatigue was the sum total of times in his life when he'd lose his cool without even registering it. Thumping his Bible onto his desk, he didn't know why he was bothering. If a peaceful sleep wasn't possible, he might as well do something.

The book fell open, and he read where his eyes happened to land. Eleven blokes in a boat, panicking. Those storms on the Sea of Galilee could obviously get pretty wild. *Is this it? I've heard it all before.* He could understand the disciples' fear. His boat was shaking too.

Thanks a lot, God, for reinforcing what I already know. Yes, I'm terrified. They weren't actually going to die at all but I really am.

Jesus came walking to them on the water. *As if that's going to happen to me.* Asher remembered Chris' lifeline again. *Give me a break. That wouldn't work.*

Peter cried out, 'Lord, if it's really you, tell me to get out of the boat and come to you.'

Jesus stretched out his hand. 'Come.'

Peter climbed over the side and went walking on the water. He did fine until he remembered that he was doing something impossible. Humans couldn't walk on water. If those waves crashed over his head, he would surely drown. With that thought, he immediately began to sink. But Jesus steadied him.

Asher snapped the book shut. That was enough. It hadn't worked for him as the Naaman passage had for Imogen. It was just a story. Nothing would happen even if he did look toward Jesus and cry out for help.

Or would it? Chris Stubbins had been sinking in a storm of leukemia. *How do I know that for sure? That's what he says, but what if it really wasn't leukemia at all?* He supposed he should take Chris' word for it. What did he say he'd done? Something about reading and agreeing with God's words in the Bible as if they were written just for him. Chris ought to know if his doctors had given him just a few weeks to live. Was his response to the terrible prognosis his way of climbing out of the boat?

But I'm different. I could agree with the Bible until the cows came home and nothing would change. I'm sick. I'm going to die. How can I agree with anything that seems weaker than the facts I can see and feel? God, if this is your way of telling me to get out of the boat as Peter did, I'm sorry but it's not strong enough. It sounds like my own imagination and wishful thinking. Now I don't know what to think. Why did I even bother to pick up this Bible? Just as I expected, it hasn't helped. I'm a total mess now.

'Hello, it's Asher Dorazio here. Remember, I came to visit you the other day.'

'Asher Dorazio!' Chris' voice on the other end of the phone sounded jubilant. 'How are you?'

Something in the sheer joy of Chris' tone worried Asher. It was sort of familiar – yes, the pressure of having to live up to expectations. 'Not the best, but I want to hear more about… well, when you were healed. I want to find out which parts of the Bible you focused on. But hey, when… if I die, you won't blame me, will you?'

Chris laughed a rich, mellow sound like bells. 'I wouldn't stomp around saying, "That accursed young man died on me and made me look like a fool!"'

'Well, good. Just so long as that's clear.'

'Got it, but can I ask you a question?'

'Yeah, I suppose so.'

'If you're dead, will it even matter? Why are you so anxious about letting people down posthumously?'

Asher was surprised Chris Stubbins even knew a word like posthumously. He hadn't seemed the type to have a large vocabulary. 'It's just because I've let people down in a big way… I mean a huge way, more than once in my life. I'm always on guard.' He was saying something factual so why were his eyes brimming? He cleared his throat before it crept into his voice.

'How old are you?' Chris asked.

'Twenty-four.'

He heard the man click his tongue with pity.

'You've worn your health and spirits down to stumps at such a young age.'

I shouldn't have phoned. Asher wasn't asking for any of this. 'Are you saying I've given myself cancer?'

'On the defensive again, are you?' Chris sounded playful. 'Of course I'm not saying that.'

'Well, you're not expecting me to do anything weird, are you?' If Chris told him to dunk himself seven times in the Murray River, Asher suspected he would be more resistant than Naaman.

'Such as?'

'I dunno. Like stopping chemotherapy and drinking squashed beetle juice.'

The deep-throated laugh rang over the line again. 'If I had you here in front of me, I'd say yes, just to see the look on your face. I can imagine some people agreeing to squish insects but not you.' Chris seemed to find everything Asher said witty and delightful. How could he trust someone who cackled at his lamest jokes, when his family had always simply rolled their eyes at his funny ones?

'I'm not recommending that you stop your chemotherapy either. That depends entirely on what God leads you to do. But instead of catching beetles, catch your thoughts and attitudes. You must train yourself to believe beyond a doubt that God loves you and wants the very best for you. He can heal you and he can also help you find strength in what you're going through every step of the way.'

There it was again. Was the old guy going on about positive thinking? Asher knew that alone, was useless. A mere change of thoughts would be far too simple to cure such entrenched cancer. His own thoughts were too deeply embedded to change anyway. The thing Chris suggested was ridiculously easy and impossibly difficult at the same time. But the part about God's possible willingness and ability to heal him, that was the part he couldn't simply argue away so easily.

Chris' soothing voice spoke on. 'Don't make your days harder for yourself. When fear of dying comes, you just take it to God and talk to him about it. He doesn't expect you to bear it all alone. It's natural that you feel fear, but it doesn't need to overwhelm you when you remember who is on your side. His love is the biggest peace you can ever find, but I hope that you find that out for yourself'

'Okay, thanks.'

'I'm glad to help. I'll do as you ask and send you some scriptures to focus on. You can find more of your own too. Make sure you get them planted deep in your spirit and believe them in your heart, because they're true. Remember, they aren't just ordinary words. You can't take the Bible as just any old book. That's where I believe many people become unstuck.'

Asher's head spun. Now, Chris sounded like a teacher, and he still wasn't sure he could buy what he was touting. 'So is that my homework?'

'Call it that if you like. Do you think it funny, me setting you homework when I'm only a grocer and you're a computer software engineer?'

'Hey, you remembered what I am.'

'You thought I wouldn't, didn't you?'

If he said yes, would that suggest that he felt superior to Chris in his inner heart? *Oh God, I'm not conceited and full of myself like Dad, am I?*

'You can admit it. Part of you would trust what I say more if I was a certified doctor and had some head honcho doctor who writes all the medical protocol telling me what to do. You'd be more impressed if I'd taken the hypocritic oath, wouldn't you?'

It was Asher's turn to chortle. 'I think you mean Hippocratic.'

'Ah, do I?'

Asher fell silent. Had Chris just made him the butt of a joke?

'Hey, don't just take my word for it. You can ask for God's guidance for yourself. You have more time to seek him now, and get quiet before him. That might have been more difficult when you were at work full time. Make the most of it, my friend. And here's another thing I did which probably wouldn't hurt you to try. I reckon you should find at least one thing each day to be thankful for.'

'Thankful?' He was careful not to blurt out the first scathing rejoinder in his mind.

'There'll be plenty if you search. For example, if it was me, I'd say I'm thankful you're giving me the opportunity to help you. Write 'em down somewhere. It's a wonderful way to start renewing your mind.'

Asher let out a carefully measured sigh. 'Okay, here goes. I guess I'm thankful you dropped this on me now, because if you'd said it straight away, I probably would've made excuses and hung up. It sounds pointless, but I'm interested enough to go along with it for the sake of whatever wisdom you think might be behind it.'

He remembered the days when Mum had made him and Becky sit at the table and write thank you notes to friends and relatives for things they hadn't wanted. He'd thanked Auntie Sheila for the soap on a rope. What ten-year-old boy would want soap on a rope? And Imogen's parents, Uncle Tom and Aunt Patti, had sent him a preachy old story book.

'That's the spirit. You can always call.'

Asher had to get it all sorted out in his head. He used to look for somebody to talk to, until his family told him that listening to him ramble bored the socks off people. But one person might be interested because she had put him up to it. He found her on the veranda, sitting on the swing and reading in the last dim light.

'Hey, Imogen, have you got a moment?'

She placed her book face down. 'Yeah, sure.'

'Well, it might be a long moment.' He had to be honest and fairly warn her. 'Remember how I can talk?'

She smiled. 'I sure do. Go ahead, then.'

It was the following afternoon and he returned to the swing where he and Imogen had sat talking. *I guess if I'm really going along with this, even a little bit, I'll have to change my attitude.* Asher smiled as he remembered her enthusiastic opinion that answers to their prayers might be rolling in already, such as coming across Chris and the possibilities he'd given them to ponder.

The other night, well, maybe I was a bit unfair to expect you to answer my prayer that instant. I mean, I can understand that if your answers involve input from other people, then there are going to be time and space considerations. Maybe I shouldn't have demanded instant feedback. I'm sorry but I'm sure you know about my control-freak tendencies. At least, Chris Stubbins seemed to insinuate that I'm a control-freak and he might have a point.

Asher leaned back against the warm vinyl of the swing. *Pretty dumb of me to have that attitude, especially when nothing I've tried hard to control ever worked out. Whatever the reason I've got cancer, it might have been unfair of me to demand that you respond like a human being, when you're God. Of course you're bound to be totally different in the way you relate to me.*

He stretched out on his back so that his feet were hanging over one arm of the long swing seat while his head rested on a cushion. *I'm willing for you to do your own thing. I suppose that's what I feel the need to say. I've chosen to believe that you do exist, and that it's true that you want the best for me. I'm tired out. I just want to let go and let you take charge. It doesn't matter any more whether I'm healed or not. It doesn't matter if you don't reveal yourself to me the way I wanted you to. When have you ever caved in to my demands? I'm just willing for you to do whatever you have to do.*

He found that lifting his arm slowly and incrementally made it possible to rest it behind his head without too much discomfort. A wave of sleep rolled over him, and sudden tears welled up with it, warming the backs of his eyelids. *Why on earth am I crying?* The sun's rays felt good, soaking through his shirt and jeans, gave him the impression that someone was hugging him, and maybe even congratulating him for not giving up.

He didn't want to open his eyes or do anything else to make it end. He didn't even want to do his usual thing and form his experience into words, but simply basked in it.

Chapter 12

Dear Triple-Strength Paracetamol,
    Thanks for taking the edge off the pain in my shoulder. And pain, thanks for being slightly weaker than the paracetamol.
    Cheers, Ash

Smiling and shaking her head, Imogen handed the paper back. 'I'm not sure this is what Chris meant.'

'If he expects something soppy about birds and flowers, he's not getting it from me.'

'At least he already knows you're a tricky case.'

So she thought him cynical and difficult. Sighing, he ran his fingernail down the metal slats of his Venetian blind. 'I don't have anything against gratitude. It's just that I find it... I don't know, scary or threatening, being thankful for things I'm going to lose soon.'

'Hey, you're not on board with your agreement,' she reminded him. 'You said you were going to start trusting that God is handling your case, instead of simply getting ready to die.'

He scrutinised her earnest expression. 'Imogen, could I ask you a favour?'

'Sure.'

'Will you help me believe? I want to rest in God's love and trust him, but they've given me such a poor prognosis, and they ought to know. They're the doctors. I want to live, but whenever I decide to let go and trust that God is working in my life, I feel as if I'm pretending because I can't force myself to believe something I don't. All my life I've spoken this stuff, but do I really believe he loves me personally and wants the best for me? I have to be honest and say I wouldn't have a clue. I can't physically see or hear him, so how would I know? Maybe it's all been an act on my part. Becky's the one who signed up to be an actor, not me. I'm sorry for dumping all this on you. It's just that the time you spoke to me about Naaman was the first time I felt a faint flicker that I might have a chance to recover.'

'Do you know what? I don't know if this will boost your faith but it's helping me. I've been looking things up in books and the internet. And it's not only Chris. I've found plenty of true stories about other people who have been diagnosed with incurable diseases and beaten the odds.'

'Will you show me some?'

'You mean now?'

Nodding, he booted up his computer. 'Oh, well, only if you have time.'

'Sure I do.' She sat in his computer chair and free-wheeled over beside him.

Imogen dared to let her muscles relax. Her fingers ached from being squeezed together but it was all right now. He'd left the bathroom sooner than she'd expected.

Although his complexion was pale and his hair damp again, he managed a weak smile at her as he passed along the passage. 'A bit better this time.'

It was the evening of Asher's second chemotherapy course. His prediction that he'd be hanging over the porcelain bowl again proved to be true, but it wasn't for as long. Breathing a sigh of relief, she fell across her bed. If only she knew for certain that listening to Chris was wise. Perhaps she wouldn't be so determined to cling to his encouragement if there was any other hope for Asher, but there wasn't. *I've got to believe it. Meeting Chris was an answer to prayer, and then the story of Naaman came just when I needed to read it.* A person in Asher's position needed others to encourage him to believe.

She'd studied more of her Bible in the last few days than she'd read in as many years. With a pen and notepad beside her, she copied down anything to do with healing and used it to form her prayers. Praying still felt like talking to herself, but Imogen shrugged off the feeling of futility. If she expected Asher to take Chris' advice to strengthen his faith seriously, she had to do the same. God surely heard them because he'd promised.

She and Asher had sat together at his computer, reading about people who'd recovered from seemingly impossible odds and lived to tell their stories thirty, forty, even fifty years later. Asher hunched his shoulders, leaning his chin on his right fist, reading each article over and over, looking for some common ground. She'd been afraid his hopes would be dashed by all the repetition that these cases were rare aberrations, but Asher didn't seem to mind.

'That fact that it's happened at all gives me hope. If only one or two people, like Chris, lived to defy the odds, I'd want to hang onto that as enough proof that it could happen for me too. But when you really start to research all this, there are hundreds of documented cases.'

'And we've probably only scraped the surface,' she added.

Thoughtfully, he nodded. 'Yeah, the fact that we've found plenty is convincing enough proof that there'll always be more. Maybe I could be one?'

'That's right, why shouldn't you? Hey, maybe you can use these stories for one of your exercises.'

'Hey?'

'Chris' thank you exercises. Seeing that there are hundreds of survival stories from people who have walked a similar path before you, and beaten the odds, is something to be thankful for. Because it encourages us that miracle healings have happened and that, for all we know, your story could end up being one of them.'

'Yeah, I'll do it.'

'And you can thank me for thinking of it.'

'Hey, hang on.' Although his competitive streak used to irk her when they were small, the familiar old flash in his eyes pleased her now. 'You're taking the credit but if you think back over our conversation, I'm the one who thought of it.'

'But I brought these stories to your attention in the first place. Then I reminded you of the thank you notes.' She dared to add, 'Face it, you're not as good as I am at finding things to be thankful for.'

'Okay, game on.'

Since then it had become a joke between them. He'd write thank you notes to show her which never failed to make her smile.

Dear Becky's Alternative Albums,
Thanks for being deplorable enough to make me run for cover

103

where my ears can bleed in peace. Sometimes I feel so tired and crook, I fear nothing will motivate me to move, so it's good to know that something still works.

Dear Daytime Soap Operas,
Thanks for being so lame and predictable that I'd rather sleep than watch you. I can have a doze without the regret of missing anything. Thanks for being a handy scapegoat when I want to vent some frustration, but don't want to keep directing it at my condition. If I do, I always find it hard to stop. You're a fairly satisfactory substitute.
Cheers, Ash

'Don't show this to Jodie. She loves those soapies.' Imogen was proud of herself for picking up some Australian jargon. 'She tapes them while she's at work to watch when she gets home.'

'I hope that's just a bad side-effect from being pregnant. I feel sorry for Seth if it isn't.'

'Don't you think these are just veiled grumbles?'

He threw back his chin in a flamboyant gesture of feigned offence, reminiscent of Uncle Hayden. 'How can you say that about my genuine attempts at gratitude? Here's what my next one's going to say. I'll be thankful that I'm not as skeptical as Imogen.'

Becky's voice from the lounge room, loud and protesting, broke into her reverie. 'Kaitlyn, don't do it now. He only just had his chemotherapy today.'

'Waiting longer just makes it harder.'

At once, Imogen's muscles were taut again. The insides of her fingers felt bruised as they curled together.

She heard Kaitlyn rap on Asher's door. 'I have to talk to you.'

Imogen sat at the kitchen table, nursing her coffee, as she listened to Becky tell Jodie about the scene the previous evening.

'I pleaded with her not to but her mind was set. What makes me maddest of all is that she's using his religious mumbo-jumbo against him.' Becky squinted across the table at Jodie and Imogen in the early morning light. 'Sorry, I know it's your mumbo-jumbo too. But the way

Kaitlyn's using it is really awful.'

'What are you talking about?' Jodie rested her hands on her small podge.

'She reckons God prompted her to break up with Asher.'

'You're kidding!'

'I'm completely serious. I told her she should have the backbone to own her decision rather than passing the buck on God.'

'That's so hard on Asher.' Jodie's eyes were wide with the surprise Imogen had felt the previous night.

He still hadn't emerged from his room since Kaitlyn had left. When they knocked earlier, he'd called out that he wanted to be alone. *Nothing I could say would help him, anyway.*

'Who goes and dumps a guy with cancer?' Jodie spread her fingers across her bump as if she was trying to cover her baby's ears. 'Sorry, Seth would say I shouldn't speak this way, but I can't help it.'

Becky was drumming her fingers on the table edge. 'It seems God's been telling her that she needs to put herself first. Staying attached to Asher was starting to crush her spirit. She told me she can't even bear being close to him any more. On the day we did the working bee, he wanted to put his arm around her as if everything was still the same, but she felt creepy, as if she was walking with a dead guy.'

'So she decides to rip him out of her life as if he already …' Jodie's eyes fixed on something up the passage. Imogen turned and there stood Asher. His eyes were hollow and smudged.

'Hey, you shouldn't have been eavesdropping on us!' Becky's face was blotched.

'I wasn't.' He cleared his throat. 'I just walked out here, like I normally do.'

'How much did you hear?' Jodie seemed to sink lower in her chair.

'Just the last bit. Listen, I appreciate that you all feel bad for me but I'd rather you didn't pick on Kaitlyn. She really did feel terrible.'

'Sure she did,' Becky muttered. 'I'll bet I can predict where she'd be right now. Lying in Darius' arms, telling him how much it tore her apart to break up with you.' A tear slid down her cheek.

Asher stared at her. 'What?'

'She didn't tell you that part of the story, hey?' Becky was snuffling.

'Not about him. I thought he was the guy you were interested in.'

'Yeah, but I've been watching him trying to chat her up for days now.'

Asher pulled out another kitchen chair with his foot and sank into it. 'Well, don't you think he's someone you'd be better off without?' He began raking his fingers through his hair. 'What sort of bloke tries to steal someone else's …' He stopped to look down at something he held between his fingers. It was a lock of his ash-blond hair. Imogen watched him try to smile. 'Hey, Jodie, it looks like you'll be out of a hairdressing job soon, as far as I'm concerned.'

'Oh, Asher, you'll still be the same person without your hair.'

'I know.' He spoke quietly. 'That's the problem. Kaitlyn knows it too.'

Asher had driven off in his BMW without telling anybody when he'd be back. Imogen slipped inside his room to put his folded laundry on his bed. With a lurch of the heart, she stopped short, wondering if he'd even noticed more thick hair over his pillowcase and sheets. She brushed some off but didn't want to drop it in his rubbish bin.

On his computer desk was another of his funny thank you notes. He must have been working on it just before Kaitlyn knocked. He probably wouldn't mind if she read it.

Dear Kaitlyn,

Thank you for ever looking my way, and for the great times we had. Your blue eyes were like the clear sky that beamed down on me. I'll never forget the way your gorgeous hair tumbled around your shoulders. I suppose I loved that because it's free and unfettered, happy to be itself, just like you.

I'm sorry for hurting you, even though it's unintentional. I don't know if my body turned traitor on me or if I somehow caused this cancer. Either way, I couldn't stand seeing you cry tonight. I've set myself the challenge of trying to recover, just as hundreds of other people have done.

Thanks for giving me a great incentive to prove all those doctors wrong and get better again. Thanks in advance for the way your face will light up on the day I tell you I'm all clear. I won't give you this letter yet, in case it doesn't happen. I hope that doesn't

*mean that in my heart, I still think I won't recover. Right now, I have
to concentrate on the strong possibility that it may happen.*

*I can't think of a better goal than being able to tell you again,
so maybe you leaving me for a time will prove to be a good thing.
As soon as I'm well, I'll get you back again.*

All my love,

Ash

Imogen tried to leave it on the exact angle she'd found it. She
shouldn't have read it. She shouldn't have. Her eye sockets burned but
letting tears out would do nobody any good. He'd written it after Kaitlyn
had been. *Poor Asher. And poor me.* No, it served her right for reading
through a letter that was never intended for her.

Opening her fingers, she left Asher's hair back by his pillow. She was
supposed to be helping him, not falling for him.

Chapter 13

Asher focused his mind on the rhythmic squeaking of the porch swing. It was supposed to be hypnotic. He wanted to stop thinking about how sick he still felt, and what he'd just seen.

He'd gone to the café near Kaitlyn's drama studio because it was a good place to get a frothy latte, and he supposed he should put something in his belly. It had been a big mistake. The greasy, fried breakfast smells had stirred up his chemotherapy-induced nausea, and then he saw Kaitlyn walk past along the footpath with a guy.

She'd worn a flowing gipsy style skirt, probably a costume from her current play. Kaitlyn liked to wear clothes from her different roles out on the town. It was one of the quirky eccentricities all their friends admired, making her unique and interesting. Asher watched her burly companion lean down to speak to her. Kaitlyn responded with one of her spontaneous laughs, like a peal of bells. She squeezed the fellow's arm and leaned her head on his shoulder. Then she'd raised her face for a kiss. She hadn't seen Asher sitting all alone at one of the outdoor café tables. That was the only bright spot. He'd left without buying a latte.

He couldn't blame her for not wanting a shell of a man whose scalp no longer had enough energy to hold in his hair. Maybe he should even be relieved for her. If he died, she'd be okay. He'd be leaving her with somebody who could keep her happiness level cranked as high as Kaitlyn's was supposed to be.

But I'm not even dead yet. Perhaps that laugh was what disturbed him most. She'd been sobbing when she told him it was over. How could she change so quickly? He could understand her reasons for wanting to pull back from him. Well, he could understand some of them. He'd assumed she wouldn't laugh in quite the same way for any other man so soon, let alone kiss him. *Get over yourself.* Should he be hurt that he proved to be replaceable so quickly? *She's a woman. What would I expect?*

The cynical thought shot through his defenses from nowhere. No, he was fooling himself again. Why did he keep trying to lie to himself? He knew exactly where it came from. Whenever he read allusions to the seductive temptress in the book of Proverbs, he knew instantly who she reminded him of, although he'd never set eyes on the woman.

She, must have been in the holiday cabin just before he got there on that horrible evening five years ago. If it wasn't for that stranger, Dad might not have died. He'd do far better not to think about her.

Was something intrinsically wrong with the female nature? Perhaps women were generally more shallow and promiscuous than men expected.

He thought of Jay Reynolds, the poet with his heart set on idolising Becky, and found himself shaking his head. Becky was nothing like the angel Jay had devoted so much time trying to track down. She could be self-focused, demanding, shallow, teasing and downright annoying.

That train of thought was no good either. Wonderful women like his mother were everywhere. Marian always behaved like a loyal, loving hero, no matter what was happening in her life. There was Jodie, too, who would never dream of looking at any man but Seth.

As the front door opened, he flinched, not wanting to talk to Becky about Kaitlyn and the other man. It was probably the Darius guy, who Becky had mentioned. When Imogen stepped out instead of Becky, relief filled him.

'Hey, are you feeling any better?'

'Like death warmed up, actually.' At least he could be honest with somebody. Imogen was nice enough to sympathise with him but she wasn't family. He didn't have to worry so much about depressing her. There was a distance there he appreciated. 'Your dad's a doctor, right? He probably pumps chemotherapy into people too.'

She nodded. 'Some of his kids are cancer patients.'

Asher quickly shied his thoughts away from the image of little boys and girls having to undergo his ordeal. That was more than he could bear. His mind was like a pinball machine. There were so many obstacles to dodge to get the ball safely home. Wanton women, suffering children…

'It's supposed to help people heal but makes us feel sicker and weaker than we did at the start,' he said. 'Common sense would tell me that my body is meant to be stronger to fight back, hey? Well, when I go for a treatment, I feel as if I've been run over by a road train.'

'A what?'

'A road train. You know, like a big truck with carriages. You haven't heard of them, have you? Maybe I should've said I feel like I've been run over by a lorry or truck.'

Grinning, Imogen sat on one of the metal chairs. 'You know the purpose of chemotherapy is to destroy the bad cells. Killing good ones along with it is just an unfortunate side effect.'

'Yeah, I know all that. But while I was heaving over the toilet bowl last night, I couldn't help wondering if it's like leeches.'

Her eyebrows raised. 'How do you mean?'

'We say how dumb people were in the Middle Ages, yet I can see how their standard treatment would have sounded reasonable to them. Drain out the bad blood and the sickness runs out with it, right?'

She drew up her legs beneath her. 'You would've been a convincing medieval quack. Go on.'

'Thanks. Now zoom your imagination forward in time, maybe a couple hundred years from now. Two people are sitting around talking about our generation. One says to the other, "What barbaric drugs they used to pump into cancer patients. Instead of giving their immune system cells every chance to build themselves up and help the body recover, they massacred them!"'

'And then they drive off in their super hover-cars to get their routine all-round cancer vaccines,' she added sadly. 'I wish chemotherapy didn't take such a harsh toll on people's bodies. It has been shown to work, though. My father would often say it's dramatically improved survival rates over the last couple of decades. He hates the side-effects in his patients but says it's been well worth administering so many times.' Her eyes were wide with sympathy.

'Hey, I'm sorry. I'm not trying to knock your dad's profession, or anything like that. I know chemo is not the equivalent of snake oil. I'll try to imagine it as healing liquid gold running through my cells. That's how some of the other patients I saw yesterday tell me they deal with it. I just wish I had access to the possible medicine of the future. They reckon some day there might be ways of targeting cancer through the immune system. I've been reading about the research. Maybe I was born too early.'

'But don't forget there's something that's far older and more powerful than any of that stuff.' She seemed to be almost trembling.

'What?'

She tilted her head. 'Have you forgotten so soon? It's God's miraculous healing power.'

'Oh, yeah. Sorry, I let my thoughts drift again.'

'Well, I know it's only been a few days, but the more I've been reading about it, the more sense it's beginning to make. It's clear now that I've actually started reading the Bible instead of just owning one. What if God always has a perfect plan for every person, but sometimes his plans don't necessarily materialise unless we learn to listen.'

She'd managed to intrigue him. 'But wouldn't that be relying on our works instead of his grace?' The usual stale old words were right there, ready to spout.

'I wondered about that too. But I guess, in this case, they're the same thing because relying on his grace is our work.' Her eyes were glowing. 'Since that night I read about Naaman, I've been reading and studying the Bible more. There's still so much I don't understand but I'm beginning to get why it's so important. I never prayed much before because I didn't get why it's so important, but now that I've seen this, I'm not going to stop praying for you, Asher.'

Her quiet enthusiasm was like nothing he was used to from other girls. When Kaitlyn got excited, she squealed and squeezed his arm tight, or punched him. Kaitlyn wouldn't have got interested in anything like this, though. She was into freedom and living for each moment, not getting tied up in philosophical or theological thinking. When it came to coping with a cancer diagnosis, she was just into crying.

'Now, your mother told me you haven't eaten anything yet. I came out to see if I could tempt you.'

While he'd been talking to her, the quality of his bellyache had changed. Instead of being nauseated to the core, it was now more of a hollow, gnawing emptiness. His body was still reminding him to eat. That had to be a good sign.

'A vanilla or caramel milkshake from the corner shop might go down okay.' Something soft and colourless would probably be wise.

'Let's get you one, and then we'll go to the library.'

As they walked along a path half an hour later, he drew deep breaths of fresh air. Even though he'd felt empty enough to order a medium shake, he couldn't quite get through it. That was okay. He'd be able to finish it later.

'What does that flavour taste like?' Imogen had finished her small cherry shake.

'Really nice. Try some if you like.' Only when she accepted his paper cup and drew a mouthful did he remember. 'Hey, stop!' His heart was thumping.

She stared, with her lips still around the straw.

'You shouldn't have had any. I shouldn't have offered it to you. The chemotherapy was only yesterday.'

'Is that all. Don't worry, I'll survive.'

'Are you sure?' His pulse was still racing with fear for her.

'Of course. Even though we believe you'll get over this cancer, that doesn't mean you have super powers.' She gave a teasing grin. 'They call him Mutant Man. Keep away from his food and drinks.'

Asher let out a spontaneous laugh, surprising himself. He hadn't done that for weeks. In fact, he couldn't remember the last time he hadn't had to force a jovial response.

The library table had looked large when they arrived, but seemed to shrink when they filled it with books. All those science magazines looked spine-chilling, but perhaps that was just because Imogen recalled her father often poring over similar-looking volumes. They signified shedding of tears and Dad having to tell more grieving parents that their children were not going to make it.

She'd wanted Asher to join her at the spiritual section of the library instead of perusing the medical and scientific. When she'd said so, he grinned and replied that he wanted a few observable and provable facts to balance the airy-fairy stuff he was getting in spades from her and Chris. Imogen found it hard to muster a smile.

He doesn't realise those books might reaffirm that his cancer will win. Imogen didn't want to open her mouth to suggest such a thing but watched him over the top of the Bible commentary she was pretending to read. It was hard to concentrate.

'This book is interesting. Sorry, I'm off on a tangent here. It's all about the brain structure and neural pathways. I like this sort of stuff. Scoot over here. It'll help if you can see the diagrams.'

Although she doubted any illustrations would impress her, she didn't need to be asked twice to move closer to Asher. While he rambled on, she watched him from the corner of her eye instead of looking at the page.

The spark in his eyes triggered a memory. Years ago, when she used to visit their local library with Aunt Marian and the twins, Asher would always want to borrow stacks of books. Later at home, he'd annoy everybody by trailing after them, trying to interest them in stories and facts from his library books.

He'd been given a chemistry set for his birthday. She and Becky would run away, giggling and squealing, whenever they saw him with it. 'It's Chemistry Boy!' Seth used to cry out. 'Duck for cover, girls.' Ginny and Becky would slam Becky's bedroom door behind them, laughing and panting. At the time, Imogen enjoyed her shared joke with the Dorazio family. When she remembered Asher's slumped shoulders and crestfallen expression, she realised she'd been very mean.

Sometimes he'd kick the door and yell, 'Stay dumb then, for all I care!' Other times he'd try to entice them out by chattering on about whatever was in the library books or chemistry set from behind the closed door. One day, Uncle Hayden had scolded, 'We bought you that chemistry set so you'd stop beleaguering other people.'

She drew her mind back to the present. Dwelling on sad old memories served no purpose.

'Sorry, I'm probably boring you to tears,' he suddenly said.

'What? That's okay. I mean, no, you're not boring me at all.'

Grinning, he asked, 'Have you found anything interesting?'

'I have, but it's just from the Bible. Whenever Jesus was documented as healing anyone, he often encouraged them and acknowledged their faith. Have a look. I've been writing them all down.' She showed him a piece of paper. 'The woman with the issue of blood, the centurion, the Canaanite woman with the sick daughter. The list goes on and on and I haven't finished yet. His usual line is, "Go in peace, your faith has made you well," or something like that.'

'Yeah, I didn't realise how often he commended their faith.' He was already pulling over her Bible.

Imogen kept her eyes on Asher's expression as he quickly turned up

Bible verses.

It must be evident to passers-by that he wasn't well. His face was gaunt, eyes hollow and skin slightly sallow. But he was one of the people who could be ravaged by illness and still look good. Perhaps his sickness even revealed how handsome he basically was with his chiselled cheekbones, forehead and chin, and his bright green eyes. Her foster sisters would have definitely called him a real 'hottie.'

Interest in what he read radiated from him. She imagined touching him, wondering if she'd feel a tangible buzz of excitement passing from him to her. The thought of touching Asher made her blush, and she glanced away.

You're absolutely right,' he pronounced after flicking through a number of Bible stories. 'Although I know these stories so well, the implications of what he said can't have registered with me. I must've assumed it was just his nice way of saying, "Good on you and thanks for coming."'

Imogen felt a smile spread across her face. It wasn't often she'd ever managed to impress Asher.

Dear Caramel Milkshake,

Thanks for tasting good. I thought I might be able to handle a few sips of you, even though I still felt crook. You were delicious enough for me to eventually finish you off. The slurping sound at the end reminds me of the times I used to race Seth, Becky and Imogen to finish our last few inches. Those were fun memories, and the same sense of achievement was back when I finished you.

Cheers, Ash

He peered into his mirror, squinting more deeply into his own eyes than he felt comfortable doing. Resisting the urge to glance away, Asher said what he'd planned to tell himself. 'Okay, I'm going to try a different style of praying, along with my usual way of just winging it and expecting God to go along with everything I say. I'm about to pray your own words back to you. Don't know why I hadn't thought of it before.'

He turned his Bible to one of the healing scriptures Chris had given him, Psalm 103. 'Here we go, Lord, I bless your holy name with all that is within me. I don't forget your benefits because they are listed here in front of me. You forgive all my sins, you heal all my diseases, you redeem my life from destruction and crown me with loving kindness and tender mercies. And I don't have to worry about these feelings which are telling me that you didn't mean it. It's here in writing. You said it. However it works out in my life, I believe you keep your promises.'

Chapter 14

Dear Sincerity,

Thanks for giving me a mystery to ponder. I received a 'Get Well' card from some of the people at work. Did they really mean a fraction of the nice things they said or did they just come up with drivel for the sake of having something to say? As it's not the sort of question I can come straight out and ask, I guess I'll never find out. Still, unsolved mysteries keep the world interesting. Thanks that even if they didn't mean it, they made it sound believable when they wrote that they miss me. In fact, now that I'm reading over this, I feel like a cynical prat for writing it. Perhaps I should trash this thank you note and start over again.

Cheers, Ash

'This one is chocolate almond fudge,' Chris Stubbins said.

The delicious aroma made Asher's stomach begin to rumble as he raised his spoon and knocked a cloud of chocolate shavings off the top. At least if nothing else helped him, a visit to Chris' house was good for the cheesecakes.

'What have you been up to?' Chris asked.

'Not much, but being away from work has been nice.'

'Don't you enjoy being a computer software engineer?' Chris seemed to enjoy bringing the name of Asher's occupation into every conversation.

He shook his head. 'It's as tedious as watching paint dry.'

Chris' big, dark eyes widened. 'Even though you were so good at it?'

'Being good at something doesn't mean you like it.' Asher had often come across the notion that they were one and the same.

'If you hated the work, how did you end up working there?'

'It's a long story. I was offered a scholarship. It was a high profile company with an excellent salary. None of my friends had opportunities like it. I would've been crazy to have knocked it back.'

'Maybe you were crazy for taking it. Did it ever occur to you that you were doing two people a disservice? You, and another young person you were keeping out by accepting it, who might've loved working there.'

This was hardly worth the cheesecake. He'd sacrificed years of anything more fun for the biggest success of his life. Now he was being criticised for it. 'Dad would have killed me if I'd knocked back that scholarship.' Asher caught himself short. He was talking in ridiculous hyperboles; one thing that had always annoyed his father. 'I mean, he never would've stopped rubbing it in—that I had a chance to work for Lewis and Thorne, and told them no.'

'So let me get this straight. Until the cancer, you were still working hard at a job that bored you to please your father? And he's been dead for how long?'

'Five years.' Dad would have made him feel like an idiot for not taking the job and now Chris was trying to make him feel like an idiot for taking it.

'You really shared your father's beliefs, didn't you?'

'What? No, I didn't.' Asher almost laughed out loud except Chris' total misconception wasn't funny. 'He was completely different to me. He was more like my sister. She's happiest on a stage lapping up applause, just like he was. Hey, talking about my dad is a waste of time because he has nothing to do with helping me deal with this cancer. Can we please talk about something else?'

Chris was squinting at him as if he was a bug under a probe. 'If you want to suppress any thought or memory of him, it's beginning to look like he's very important.'

'I'm not trying to suppress him. It's just that I've had enough to make me sad without having to think about Dad too.' Asher drew a hand to his face when he realised what he'd said. 'Forget I said that, will you? I didn't mean it. Can we just leave him out of this? I've got a big mouth.'

'No, not at all.' Chris leaned forward to pat Asher's shoulder as if he was a schoolboy. 'Here's one thing I learned when I was sick. Sometimes it's a relief to talk about the things we haven't wanted to face.'

Asher felt his lungs fill with a deep, sharp breath, poised for rebuke. 'Not in my case. Trust me, it'll be much better if we don't talk about him.'

A serene smile flickered over Chris' lips. 'Here's something I've noticed about you. You often refer to your big mouth. You always seem to want to keep an iron guard on the things you might say.'

'Yeah, of course.' Asher slowly let out the remainder of his breath. 'I've been practicing for years. Are you still raving on about how repression might have made me sick? I'm telling you, I'm over that. I don't want to hear another word.' It was Chris who was making him sick.

The big man simply asked, 'Why?'

'Because keeping quiet about things is better than lashing out and blasting everyone with what I really think.' He'd tried that. A scathing diatribe from him had ended up killing his father. Now there was a lump in his throat of something harder than cheesecake. 'And better than driving people up the wall the way I always used to.'

'So you've been giving them the Asher you thought they'd prefer, instead of the real one?'

That was enough. 'Will you get off your high horse? You're just a grocer, not a psychiatrist!' The backs of his eyelids were burning. 'There, that's what you get when you ask me not to repress things.'

Chris was softly clapping his hands together. 'Bravo. That's the real you.'

Asher kept his eyes fixed on Chris' big, dark hands. 'That might be the real me, but you don't get it. You're weird. I can't go around talking to normal people like that. I needed to shut up. I was a pain in the neck. I had to learn social skills.'

A mellow laugh seemed to well up from Chris' belly. 'There's nothing wrong with toning down a response for social decorum. But condemning yourself for the way you were made is where you let yourself down.'

'When did I ever say I condemned myself?'

'There are more ways of talking than with words. As you were a chatterbox, maybe that's a hard concept for you to swallow.' Chris' eyes twinkled. 'Your dad might've thought you were a nuisance, but that doesn't make it true.'

'Hey, hang on. When did I ever tell you he thought that?'

Chris folded his arms in front of himself, grinning. 'You don't have to be a mind reader with a person like you.'

The skin at the back of Asher's neck prickled, although he could hardly fathom why. What else was he revealing without knowing it? Perhaps he wouldn't go back to Chris again. If Chris tried to wheedle out of him what had happened on Dad's last day, he couldn't stand it. He just couldn't go there.

Dear Guys at Work,

Thanks for the card. I appreciated the thought.

Tom, I know you took a risk talking the others into choosing a funny one, but I did laugh at the caption on the front. You made the right choice, although I appreciate the girls for wanting to choose a mushy one. But just because I have cancer, it doesn't mean I've lost my sense of humour. I've found they can both fit in the one body.

I guess you might've noticed there are a few more Tim Tams in the morning tea room for the rest of you since I've been away. Kelly, you asked whether I think I might return. To be honest, I really hope not.

Thanks for the nice things you all said. I think maybe I've been trying to smother my own cynical thoughts for so long, I have trouble taking others at face value. But the more I think about it, the more I know that some of you would never have stepped out and said all that if you didn't mean it; it just wouldn't be worth the embarrassment, so thanks. The card did help make my day. Maybe not the day I got it, but today, as I started reading it over again. If you wonder whether I'm being sincere, yes, I really am.

Cheers, Ash

PS I might even send you all a real thank you message. Not this one, though.

As he put down his pen, he heard the sound of Seth's car grinding to a halt in the driveway. It sounded like an old grandpa who couldn't stop wheezing after he'd sat down. As he walked out to greet him, Asher noticed Seth's sober expression.

'I'm glad you're home. I need to talk to you.'

'What about?'

Sinking into a lounge chair, Seth raised his eyes to the ceiling as if praying for guidance. 'I'm not sure where to start. I'm saying this as a trained Christian counselor as well as your brother.'

Uh-oh. A cold, snaky feeling coiled around Asher's stomach, although he had no idea why. He glanced across at Becky, who was sitting on the carpet, highlighting lines from her play. She shrugged.

'Just come straight out with it.'

'Well first, how have you been going?'

'Pretty good, I think.'

Seth pursed his lips and shook his head. 'You see, that's why I'm worried about you.'

'Huh? You're worried about me because I'm coping okay? What sort of logic is that?'

Seth let out a groan. 'I'm really concerned about you. It seems wrong that I've displayed more visible grief over your cancer diagnosis than you have. All the counselling courses I've done tell me you shouldn't be like this. You must be holding something back.'

A wave of annoyance swept through Asher. 'I'm dealing with the grief in my own way. Just because I'm not showing the behaviour of some text book prototype, you're coming here to nag me?'

'Don't get defensive. It's just that you've been on my mind a lot. Mum's told me that you've latched onto some old guy who has been giving you Bible verses and advice.'

'Yeah, Chris Stubbins. Imogen and I met him not long ago when we went to return his Bible. He's okay. Just giving me some moral support because he's been through something similar.'

Seth's brows furrowed. 'I wish I could talk to him myself and find out what he's been telling you.'

Irritation prickled Asher's skin. 'So my word that he's okay is worth nothing?'

'Keep your shirt on,' Seth said quickly.

'But it's always the same with you. You won't simply take my word for anything, will you?' Asher's thoughts were getting dangerously close to the occasion of Dad's last night alive. It had been welling up in his mind more than ever.

Seth held up his hands in a placating gesture that made Asher want to rip them off his wrists.

'Please stay calm. You're in no condition to think rationally. Nobody would expect you to.'

'Now you're telling me to stay calm, but when I was calm, you said you were worried that I wasn't showing enough grief. I can't win with you. This has nothing to do with my condition. There's always been some reason why you won't listen to me. I'm too young, too reactive, too naïve, too talkative.'

Seth sank his face into his hands. 'Just listen to yourself carry on, and you'll see why it's hard to reason with you.'

'That's another thing you often say. It never occurs to you that you might be the problem as much as me. It feels like a waste of time whenever I try to make you understand anything.'

'What are you talking about?' Seth's expression of aggrieved innocence added fuel to Asher's fire.

'What's the point of trying to explain, when I know you won't listen? You always have to be right. You're the guy with all the pat answers. You think you can organise other people's lives because you have a direct line to heaven. There are hundreds of possible ways a person might respond to his own unique situation, but everyone has to agree with your theory before you'll stop bothering them.' Asher was up, striding across the floor.

Seth rose to his feet too. 'That's ridiculous.'

'Of course it is. Anything I say is ridiculous to you. Do you want to hear something else?'

'What?' Seth's voice held a note of challenge.

'You have so many great solutions, even though your mind is too rigid to consider anything it doesn't want to hear. You'll never consider the possibility that you might be wrong, or limited in your view. Can't you see there might be more to life than what you've memorised from your neat little text books? If someone behaves out of your comfort zone, you always try to prod them back into line, because things won't be right until they see the world according to Seth.'

Seth's tense jaw was working in and out. 'How can you say that, when I'm just thinking about you?'

'Well, stop thinking about me!' Although Seth's face had the 'shut up, Asher' expression he'd seen so often over the years, he was going to keep talking. *He's the one who came here to have a go at me, after all.* 'Can't you think beyond your narrow limits, for a change? From things I've heard you say, you're the same with the students at your school. If they don't agree with how you think they should behave, you won't stop until you've done your best to convince them to see things your way. Maybe you can't help it. Maybe you can't show any real empathy or imagination because you haven't got any.' Asher's pulse was racing. Perhaps it really was time to shut up now.

Becky pretended to clap her hands in a silent 'hooray', but looked across at Seth's broken, pale expression and stopped.

Seth cleared his throat. 'I never knew you felt that way. Thanks for making your feelings about me completely clear. I won't bother you again.' With a sniff, Seth lurched out, slamming the screen door behind him. He had to turn his Toyota's engine a few times to start it. Through the window, Asher could see his face behind the wheel. He was dashing tears off his cheeks. At last, he left with a screech of tires—totally unlike Seth.

'Whoa, you really let him cop it.' Becky let a page of her script fall to the floor. 'I wouldn't have been quite so hard on Big Brother, knowing all he's poured into that stupid job. He thinks he can drag every student in that school to heaven by the force of his will, one by one.'

'I know.' Asher's heart was still thumping. 'I should have kept quiet.' He'd often imagined delivering a comeback to Seth for the times he'd been left feeling alienated and deserted. Now, he just felt churned up inside, like a complete creep.

'Well, I don't completely blame you. Maybe it's time he was told a few home truths. He's been judgmental and holier-than-thou for far too long.'

Imogen stepped inside with some shopping. 'Hey, I just passed Seth speeding down the street. He cut off the corner as if a wolf pack was behind him. Is everything all right?'

'Yes, apart from Asher tearing strips off him with his tongue and revealing his whole life as a useless farce. You should ask Seth about it, if he ventures to poke his nose out of his little hole again any time soon.' It seemed Becky was beginning to enjoy herself.

Imogen turned to stare at Asher. He nodded back.

'I shouldn't have listened to Chris Stubbins.' Loosening his guard on the things he'd been holding inside was a cruel thing to do. What if Seth reacted the same way Dad had when Asher confronted him? He felt himself break into a clammy sweat. *I've got to find him and apologise.* But he knew Seth wouldn't listen.

Chapter 15

When Imogen saw Jodie's small Barina turn into the driveway, she rushed outside to meet her. 'How's Seth? Asher's been trying to call him.' She'd managed to elicit the basics of the conversation from him, little by little. After pacing the floor with the phone, Asher had sunk onto a couch with his head between his hands.

'Seth's been home and gone again.' Jodie stepped inside after Imogen. 'He kicked the kitchen bin across the floor, then stormed through the house slamming every door. All I could get out of him was that he'd had an argument with Asher. I've never seen him so upset.'

Asher lifted his face. 'Jodie, I'm really sorry. Didn't he say anything else?'

She hesitated.

'You can tell me. It's okay.'

'You asked for it. Earlier this morning, just before I went to work, he said he was going to visit you because he was very worried about you.'

'So what did he plan to do?'

'He wanted to help, and to make sure you're thinking straight.'

Drawing a ragged breath, Asher balled his hands into fists. 'Because Seth knows how everyone ought to think, doesn't he?'

'Asher, don't be bitter. Seth means well. We hate it that you have cancer, but we want to see you get through the ordeal as best you can, now that God's given you this challenge.'

No! Imogen had been bombarded with words like Jodie's all her life. Her father would say similar things to the families of his dying patients. Back then, her stomach would twist with the agony of believing it was true. Now it was lurching for the opposite reason. Accepting terminal diagnoses as always true was the kind of thinking that put people in early graves. She wouldn't let Jodie do that to Asher, however kind her intentions were.

'Jodie, no. I know that sounds good and spiritual, but I've been studying, too. We always say the sort of thing you just said with no idea what we're talking about. Healing is one of the things that Jesus died to give us. It's part of the agreement. If he died so our sins could be forgiven, then why should we still have to put up with the consequences of our sins? I don't know why I never got it before. I'm the daughter of a couple of missionaries, including a paediatrician, and none of us understood this. It should be elementary. How can a smart young guy dying of cancer glorify God?'

She'd almost blurted the word *gorgeous* instead of smart. Peeping at Asher through the corner of her eyes, she went on, 'It's not the way God meant it at all. For centuries, people have been accepting sickness, when we should've been pushing in and not letting go of the truth. But it's so easy to miss that truth. Why do so many churches let us think we need to put up with illnesses and diseases?' As she saw Jodie's eyes well with tears, her own voice began to quake. 'It's like signing for a parcel delivered straight from hell, when we should be saying, "No, you have the wrong address!" Maybe we get sick because we don't see ourselves the way God does.'

All the grief she'd seen through her dad's work over the years pressed down on her shoulders. The times she'd answered the telephone to the sound of tearful voices pleading for Doctor Browne. Often she'd overheard her father's wracking sobs from behind his bedroom door. She'd met some of Dad's cancer patients at picnics organised for sick kids and their medical staff. Those children often had no hair and frail, spindly limbs. Sometimes they'd smile at Imogen and ask her to play with them. She would hang back because she shrank from the idea of making friends who were doomed to die, and now she couldn't prevent a tear from sliding down her cheek.

A hand came down to rest on her shoulder where she sat, and without looking, she knew who it was. She could smell his spicy cologne, and hear him breathing. That was touch, smell and sound filling her senses. She couldn't bring herself to look up. One more sense added to the mix would push her over the edge. She knew he was gorgeous, anyway. Not only would it be humiliating, but wrong to let him read her heart. It wasn't only because he loved Kaitlyn. She couldn't allow herself to entertain feelings for him, after what she'd done.

Jodie was close to tears too. 'Then if this isn't in God's perfect will, why doesn't he stop it happening? Why doesn't he heal Asher here where he stands? I really want to believe what you say. Why did he even let Asher get cancer?'

As his hand tightened on her shoulder, Imogen heard him clear his throat.

'I don't know, Jodie. I don't think this world is anything close to how God originally intended it. But I've accepted that he's still in control and that he loves me intensely enough to want to help me through this. When you think about it, isn't that the best answer? It's better than speaking out all the negative, depressing thoughts that occurred to me as soon as they came into my head. That's what I used to do. At least this cancer's shown me that. And for all we know, I might still recover.'

Jodie's chest heaved and fell. 'Asher, I really don't want to get my hopes raised to have you die on us. Neither does Seth. We want you to live. We want our baby to have an uncle.' She flicked a tear off her cheek.

'Hey, you know I love you guys too. Don't talk me out of what I'm saying, because I need the support.'

She wiped her face to look at him. 'But I don't know if the way you're talking is making me hopeful or terrified.'

'Be hopeful,' he told her, 'because I want to beat this thing, and if you guys are always looking at me as if I'm already past tense, it'll make it so much harder. Hey, where is Seth now, anyway?'

Jodie ran her hands down the front of her maternity smock. 'I'm not sure he would want me to tell you.'

Asher seemed to catch his breath. 'No need to. He's gone to the holiday cabin, hasn't he?'

That place. Imogen sat still while anxiety roiled inside of her. She might have guessed.

'Even if he has, I don't think you'd better go after him,' Jodie told Asher. 'I know you guys. You're not ready to speak to each other yet without getting uptight. If you turn up there, he'll feel as if I've sold him out by telling you.'

'Well, you didn't tell me. I guessed.' Asher looked as if he was about to argue further, but sighed and shrugged instead. 'I suppose you're right.'

'I've got to be with him, though,' Jodie said. 'Imogen, would you like to drive to Port Elliot with me? I don't feel like driving all that way by myself.'

Her mouth turned dry. She couldn't swallow, let alone answer.

'You used to like it there,' Asher reminded her. 'Remember how it was built on a rise, so we had an ocean view?'

'Come on, please,' Jodie wheedled. 'Seth might be more likely to come around if I bring somebody with me who's trustworthy, but not family. And he likes you. He thinks you're a nice girl with a good work ethic.'

Doom wrapped itself around Imogen's windpipe. After five years, it seemed the time had come to revisit that place. If she hung out and kept refusing, it would just appear weird.

Squeak... squeak ... squeak.

The frequency of the creaks from the veranda swing indicated to Asher that he was rocking faster than he'd thought. As he slowed down, he realised that the pattern had been in sync with his skittering heartbeat.

I'm a raving idiot with an incurable big mouth. All the years he'd spent trying to keep a guard on his mouth had been nullified in five minutes. Perhaps it was Chris' fault. He'd listened to the clueless old geezer and let his guard slip just a little. Chris said expressing his feelings would be good for Asher. But what had happened? The sheer force of the steam inside of him had swept Seth right off to Port Elliot, where Dad had been when he died. He should see Chris one last time, to blast him with his share. The old know-it-all was a danger and a menace.

Lord, I've tried hard to keep quiet all these years. You know I was sorry. Please don't let Seth consider doing anything like what Dad did. The squeaking of the swing springs accelerated. Prayer didn't help at all. It raised images of Jodie and Imogen turning up at the cabin to find Seth ... *No! It's not going to happen.*

A car turned into the driveway. It was Mum, home from work, and now he'd have to tell her. She must've noticed something amiss by his expression.

'What's happened?' Marian's face was ashen.

'Calm down. I just argued with Seth.' He gave her the briefest summary. At least Mum wouldn't grasp the similarities, because she didn't know about the day he'd sped off to tell Dad a thing or two.

'Don't worry. The girls will help Seth to understand.' She sounded more as if she was trying to convince herself. Sinking into a metal patio chair, she studied his face. 'He shouldn't have gone storming off like that, with you in your condition. You look terrible. When did you last eat anything?'

He shrugged.

Marian rose from her patio chair. 'I'm going to fix you up a banana split with ice cream and chocolate topping.'

Although she surely wouldn't understand, he tried. 'Mum, I don't think you should wait on me like that. If I feel I have an excuse to sit around getting things done for me, I'll just sink lower. I'm sick of being in the victim's role.'

Her face fell. 'Now you know how I've felt all these years.'

Something in her tone made him glance up.

'Do you know what I've missed most since my accident? The chance to do favours for my family without others jumping up, telling me to relax. Please let me make you a banana split.'

The springs had stopped squeaking altogether. Asher started the swing moving again. 'Okay. I'd like lots of coloured sprinkles too. Thanks.'

Beaming, she patted his arm. 'You got 'em.'

He watched her limp to the door and heard her grunt as she heaved her stiffest leg over the threshold. Way back in his memory, she used to be trim and active. Since her accident, she'd had no chance to jog and hike as she used to. Marian had grown broader and heavier. The flesh on her upper arm wobbled as she turned the door knob. Asher's fingers twitched in his lap; his feet were shuffling with the instinct to get up and assist her. He forced himself to keep rocking the swing, although his senses were shouting that he was discrediting his father's memory. He almost heard Dad's reproachful, 'Pssst. Get off your lazy behind and help your mother.'

All this time, I've been reading her wrong. More to the point, he'd never been listening.

Soon after Mum had been discharged from hospital, Dad beckoned the twins into Becky's bedroom. Seth hadn't been included, because being thoughtful and perfect came naturally to Seth. Dad mumbled, 'You'll both have to pull your weight far more often from now on. Don't expect Mum to run around after you any more. She'll get tired much quicker. You both have perfectly good arms and legs. Anybody I see slacking off and letting Mum wear herself out will have their buttocks warmed by me faster than you can say, "I was just about to."' Asher knew Dad was mimicking him; putting on the high-pitched treble he'd always used for Asher's voice.

I've been reading her wrong. He'd heard Mum say that she wished she could take on more housework more often than he could count. 'I wish I could do nice thing for my family... I'd love to be able to carry out a huge load of washing... I'd be down on my hands and knees scrubbing those tiles in a flash, if only I could.' For fifteen years, he and the others had taken her words as a cue to spring to action. Never had it occurred to him that she meant it.

He'd heard her but hadn't listened. Or had he listened without hearing? Whichever way around it was, he'd done the very same thing he hated people doing to him.

How incensed he'd always been when he had some interesting yarn and people told him to keep quiet. It was far more frustrating when they fobbed him off with the right grunts and noises, as if they genuinely got it, while he could see from their facial expressions that they couldn't care less. He'd hated them for letting his words drift in one ear and out the other, but all that time, he'd been doing the same thing to Mum. Whoa.

Had he done it to anybody else? He'd certainly done his share of mindless reciting at church. *Hey, someone said that not long ago!* Was it Chris? No, he thought not. It was someone gentler and far more phlegmatic, with a cute smattering of freckles across her nose. Imogen. She'd been saying it quite a lot. She'd been going on about how the words of the Bible had been passing through her senses year after year, but she'd never taken them on until now. And even though he'd nodded and thought he was listening, he hadn't really heard.

He'd echoed maxims like, 'I'm redeemed from the curse of the law,' without giving the meaning of the words a bit of thought. He and Imogen had only just begun to plumb the depths of what that really meant.

When Marian placed the banana split in front of him, he began chewing slowly, thoughtfully. The softness of the banana, wetness of the topping and crunch of the sprinkles made a good blend in his mouth. He could write it a thank you note. Maybe he'd write one to Mum too. *Hold on. Forget it.* If he was going to stop his visits to Chris, he didn't have to bother with thank you notes any more.

Asher sighed before shovelling in another spoonful. Perhaps he'd still write them. They were harmless fun. He could write a thank you note to the thank you notes, for being enjoyable. *I'm twisted.*

Imogen had almost forgotten how bright and pretty the South Australian coastal towns were. She remembered how the shimmering expanse of blue ocean would appear around bends in the road just when she'd started thinking about something else, forgetting to look out for it.

Set way back off the main road, the Dorazios' holiday cabin hadn't changed much. Built as an A-frame cottage on stilts, with a triangular window for an upstairs loft, it had always reminded her of a one-eyed wombat peeping down at people. Off to the side was Uncle Hayden's lookout platform up a huge gum tree. The trunk was so thick, she, Becky and Asher could never manage to link their hands all the way around it.

Uncle Hayden had built the platform to give his family a glimpse over the sea from their backyard. Since she'd last been there, the platform had tilted over in the leafy boughs. Some of the wooden rungs nailed into the trunk were cracked and crooked. She doubted if anyone had climbed up there in years.

When Jodie opened the cabin's front door, a forgotten odour filled Imogen's senses. The air inside was musty from being contained within doors and windows that were only occasionally opened. It was a relaxing mustiness, redolent of her holiday swimming and rock climbing with Seth and the twins. Her heart began hammering fast. It also rushed back another memory of the more recent, terrible thing she hadn't told anybody.

Seth was seated near the window on a low cane armchair with a sagging cushion. 'Hey, what are you two doing here?'

'Coming for you, of course.' Jodie was on her knees beside him, reaching for his hand. 'I'm not going to let you pine away here alone during your first week of school break.'

Seth raised his other hand to rest in her golden hair. 'I really needed to think. I had a decision to make and I've almost made it.'

'What decision, babe?'

'To give up.'

'Give up what? School chaplaincy?'

Instead of answering, he said, 'I've figured out what my problem is, and why I've always been so miserable.'

Falling back on her haunches, Jodie turned pale. 'I never knew you were miserable.'

'Not with you. You're the brightest spot in my life. My problem is I have no imagination.'

'Hey? That's not true.'

'Asher didn't mean it,' Imogen said.

'It is true. And Asher did mean it. I've been doing life all wrong.' Seth's voice cracked slightly on the last word.

'What do you mean?' Jodie appeared close to tears.

Seth cleared his throat once, twice. 'I've been living straight out of textbooks, blindly following other peoples' instructions. When have I ever tried to figure out anything for myself? I can't even read my Bible without having five different commentaries open on the table at my elbow.' He removed his hand from Jodie's, but Imogen saw a tear drip before he had time to wipe his face. 'I might as well face the truth. I have nothing of any value to teach my child.'

'How can you say that?' Jodie's eyes widened with horror. 'You'll be a fantastic father. Don't just take my word for it. Imogen, you tell him.'

She had to respond but Seth's profile was stony. He surely needed more than an obliging agreement.

'At least now that you've recognised a problem, you can start to change it.' That probably wasn't the right thing to say. Imogen wanted to take the words back. She couldn't bring herself to glance at Jodie but least Seth was smiling now. It turned into a grim laugh.

'I can't just change, Imogen. A person with no imagination can't suddenly get it because they decide they want it. It's something you're either born with or you aren't.' He hunched over to fiddle with his shoelace. 'I guess the twins always had it in shovel-loads and I missed my share completely.'

'You're as good as they are!' Jodie told him.

'Not in the imagination stakes. Look at Ash, writing thank you notes to his navel, for heaven's sake.'

'I don't think he's done his navel yet,' Imogen said. 'He's written to his shoulder and feet.'

Grinning, Seth leaned back. 'You see, if I tried writing those letters, it'd be a total flop. But somehow he can pull them off. Book learning's not the same. I never realised what I lack, but at least now I know. And look where I work. The education department.' He was up off his chair, striding an already well-worn track across the carpet to the kitchenette. 'The least imaginative place you can think of. And I'm making things worse. I'm trying to put kids in touch with God when I'm not even in touch with him myself. All I spout is second-hand drivel. I'm a hypocrite.'

Jodie scrambled to her feet. 'But you're so clever. I'm always boasting to everyone about my clever husband.'

'Intelligence without imagination is a cold, hard combination.'

'I don't have imagination.' Jodie said. 'My teachers always told me that and I don't mind. I get along well enough without it.'

Seth caught her along his path back to the window and kissed her head. 'You probably have more than you think. You create hairstyles which make customers happy. I'm in a sterile pit that I can't wriggle out of.'

'And you just used imagination,' Imogen observed.

Seth spun around to look at her. 'Hey?'

'It's imagery. The sterile pit.'

'That's just a cold, hard fact. I've trapped myself into a thankless job where I'm the butt of jokes. Do you know what most of the students call me? Mr God-Botherer. At last I get where they're coming from. We stifle them. Heaven forbid that I keep going on, making them clones of me.'

'Do you really want to give up chaplaincy?' Jodie's voice was soft.

'Yes, but what else am I good for? I'll have to tell Asher he's completely messed with my head, so I don't know what to think. He's screwed up my thoughts, and I can't make any sense of the tangle they're in.'

'You just sounded like Becky,' Imogen put in. 'I can imagine her delivering a dramatic line like that.'

His eyes narrowed. 'You're telling me I'm like a neurotic, insecure prima-donna Becky but I don't even have her acting talent to back it up. That's just great.'

'And now you sound like Asher, with the quick comeback.'

Seth groaned. 'Like his annoying, smart-alecky part. Why do I have to share the worst parts of my siblings without getting any of their talent?'

'Well, you're the one I married, not them. You're the one whose baby

I'm carrying. You're the one I want. And for all their imagination, neither of them have anybody who loves them with all their heart.' Jodie turned to glare at Imogen. 'Hey, stop saying mean things to him now.'

'How was I being mean? By comparing him to the twins, or proving that he does have imagination?'

Seth let out a reluctant laugh, and even Jodie's smile flickered.

Imogen had said enough. 'I might take a look around outside.'

It was a good time to leave them to themselves and scramble down to the beachfront. As she walked along the scrubby path, golden sand edged between the toes of her flip-flops, even though she was still way back from the water. The longer she stayed in that cabin, the more her palms perspired with the horror of what had happened there.

Chapter 16

'Asher, I just want to say I don't hold what you said against you.' Seth stood with his hands jammed inside his pockets. 'Maybe I was out of line but I was worried about you. I couldn't help wondering if you were in denial, or pretending you're not even sick. You're my brother. It hurt me to see you burying your head in the sand and pretending like cancer wasn't even there.'

They'd all returned from the beach. Now Jodie and Imogen were talking quietly in the kitchen as they washed dishes, to give the brothers some privacy. At least, that was what they said, but Asher noticed how plates and cups stopped clinking and the girls' voices turned silent once Seth started talking. He didn't mind if they were listening. What he had to say to Seth would do for everybody.

'Hey, I know it's there. I've been having chemotherapy, haven't I? I'd be an idiot not to acknowledge the cancer, but I'm not accepting that it's going to kill me. Hey Seth, did you realise that the Bible is full of awesome promises for healing? I never did until I started reading it properly. If the Bible's true, they're the words I'm speaking and believing about myself. God said that he'll honour his words when we speak them. His words won't return to him void, so I'm not going to stop saying them.'

Seth ran a shaky hand through his dark brown curls. 'Do you really believe all that?'

Asher nodded. 'I didn't before, but now it's my only lifeline. Don't you believe it? You're a chaplain. You've studied the Bible more than anyone I know. Things that are impossible with man are possible with God. Others have been healed of fatal diseases. So might I be. I've got to believe I'll die at the perfect time he's planned for me, whether it's soon or years down the track.'

'I want to believe it.' Seth sank down into a couch. 'I can't bear the thought of you dying. It's in my mind all the time, and it sucks.'

Asher closed his eyes briefly, amazed that the words of people who were supposed to be on his side still had the potential to fill his heart with fear if he took them on board. This was Seth, his big brother who had offered to donate blood or bone marrow to him, who he knew really did love him dearly.

Seth laced his fingers together behind his head. 'I had time to think at the cabin. Perhaps I should make time to get away on my own more often. I figured out I owe you an apology for another reason. It's because of the way I've been thinking about you.'

'How have you been thinking about me?' This was getting weird. Seth never apologised to him or Becky for anything.

Heaving another enormous sigh, Seth bowed his head. 'This won't be easy to say. I've been feeling it's not fair that, in the eyes of the world, I've been outclassed by my younger brother in every way.' He spoke down to the shoes at the end of his outstretched legs rather than to Asher. 'I've been resenting that you've been earning a far higher salary than me without as much work. And you don't even have a family to support.' Glancing up, Seth made a hand motion, as if he anticipated that he'd have to stop Asher from butting in. When he saw that Asher was making no attempt to talk, he let his hand drop to his side.

'Dad even said as much to me, not long before he died. I know he was just having a joke, but he said, "Chaplains are a waste of space. If you'd played it smart, like your brother, you wouldn't have to slave your guts out for nothing." And even though I knew he was joking, those words stuck with me.'

So their father's words hadn't affected only him, and they were further reaching than anyone had realised. Even though his impressions clamoured to be spoken, Asher made no attempt to interrupt Seth's train of thought.

'I think Dad was right, because deep down, I've been wondering if I'm even making any impact on those kids at the school. Only the serious ones brought up in Christian homes ever bother to listen, and they'd surely be on the right path without my influence anyway. The others think I'm a total wally. I'm wasting my time earning chicken feed and not even helping save those kids' souls. Ash, I didn't realise how far I'd taken my jealous thoughts, but here's how I looked at you. You get paid big bickies, and people admire you into the bargain. It's been eating away at me like acid ever since you got that job. Then when I found out you had cancer, I felt really guilty, as if my bitter thoughts somehow caused it.'

Asher would have spoken up about now, but Seth's hand motions indicated that he still hadn't finished.

'I'd love to be paid for doing what I love all day. I like playing around with computers, doing a bit of sport and putting model transport together. I can't afford to do any of that though. It sucks that I don't have enough time and money, because I'm too busy being a chaplain to these rebel kids who don't even want to listen.'

Asher waited until Seth's pause was long enough to indicate that he'd finished. He cleared his throat first, just to be sure. 'Do you want to know how I see you?'

Seth raised his weary brown eyes. 'Go ahead.'

'You've always been "the good one." You're the one who grew up wanting to impact the world. Mum and Dad thought the sun shone out of you. And, as far as I could see, you were doing what you always wanted to, giving people hope for their future. I was jealous of you. I'd prefer a job where I get to talk to people rather than being holed up in an office trying to be a magician. I get these boring, high-pressure projects that need weeks, but I'm supposed to finish them in a few days. The next one gets dumped on my desk before I finish the one before, so there's never a break. And the boss is always poking his head into my office, looking harried and asking me to work overtime. I always thought you had the things that mattered most. I hate that job and I'd swap you for school chaplaincy any day.'

Seth forehead was furrowed. 'Would you still swap even now?'

'Yeah. I'll tell you the best scenario. I could keep the BMW and be a chaplain, and you could be a computer software engineer and keep your old bomb.'

Seth grinned, shaking his head. 'I want you to stay alive. If you die, I'll be a mess. I'm afraid of taking those words in the Bible as a definite promise of what God's going to do for you, though. He doesn't heal all that many people. If a body has cancer, it doesn't often go away. That's a law of nature.'

Asher had so recently spoken the same words himself. Why did hearing them from Seth no longer fill him with the same sick terror? Was it to do with the prayers and reading he'd been doing? Or maybe the warm, cherished feeling he'd experienced while lying on the porch swing, having given his life over to God?

'It is a law,' he said slowly, 'but higher laws can override it.'

'What are you talking about now?' Seth rubbed his eyes.

Asher wondered where his own observation was taking him. 'Well, gravity is a law, but an aeroplane overrides it by using a stronger law of aerodynamics. That's the sort of thing I mean. The law of sickness and disease is valid, as you say. And so is the law of positive thinking.'

Seth's eyes were fixed on Asher's face. 'Go on.'

'But neither of those laws is as great as the law of God's sovereign power.' The declaration made his heart rate suddenly speed up. 'I believe he loves me.' He peered at his brother. 'You would agree, wouldn't you?'

Seth's throat twitched as he nodded.

'Then all I need to do is trust that he wants the best for me, and that he can bring it to pass. If that means overriding those other laws and healing me completely, then he'll do it. If he doesn't, then for whatever reason, it wasn't the best. He knows more than we do. I don't know why we had such a shouting match about it earlier today, when it's that simple.'

Seth was up off his seat, pulling Asher toward him and patting his back. 'It really is as basic as that, isn't it? I can't believe I needed to be reminded. I'm sorry for upsetting you, too. And Ash, thanks for showing me a few things I needed to see today. I reckon you really might be onto something great. Keep the faith.'

'Don't worry, I will.' Asher realised he'd longed for such praise from Seth all his life, but now that it had come, what a high cost he'd had to pay.

Dear Seth's New Drivers' License,

Thanks for looking so funny. I couldn't help laughing when he pulled you out of his wallet today. Those bits of hair sticking up and that squinting expression make him look like a sloth on sleeping pills, and he's stuck with you for the next ten years. Not only did you make me think I'm not looking so bad for a guy with cancer, but you proved that reasons to laugh may come any time. I may add that I'm not the only one who thought you were hilarious. Becky and

136

Imogen cracked up too, and Jodie tried her hardest not to.
Cheers, Ash

Dear Imogen's Terrible Poker Face,
   Thanks for always amusing me. You are so easy to recognise whenever we play cards. I can always tell when she has something good in her hands, as hard as she tries to conceal it, because her lips keep twitching and there's something really mischievous about her eyes. You crack me up but she has no idea how to stop. And I'm not complaining because I don't mind winning.
   Cheers, Ash

Dear Pen and Paper,
   Thanks for the chance to help me save face and not be a pain in the neck. When I read through some of the other stupid baloney I've been churning out, it gave me chills to think that's the sort of waffle that would have once poured out of my mouth. Maybe I should have been writing thank you notes years ago. Everyone would've been more thankful. I suppose I should say thanks to Chris for giving me the idea.
   Cheers, Ash

Dear Gift of the Gab,
   Imogen saw the last letter I wrote, to my pen and paper, and warned me that I might be getting a bit negative on myself again. So here's my attempt to fix it up, focusing on the positive side of what I've always thought to be an annoying problem.
   I never thought I'd say this, but thanks for being reliable. We were talking about you this morning. Imogen says she sometimes gets 'brain freeze' and panics for things to say, which makes her anxious and upset. It surprised me to hear that because I always have a plethora of things to say any time. My problem has been learning to shut up and not say everything I could. So thanks for being so closely connected to my brain that I never need to fear being lost for words. I think I've done a pretty good of being thankful for something I've deplored for such a long time.
   Cheers, Ash

Chapter 17

Imogen froze when she answered the door. There stood Seth with a person who made the bottom of her stomach dip. He was a teenage boy with a bony frame, no hair and the type of glassy expression in his eyes she'd come to recognise over the years. There were layers of pain, glazed over by medication, more pain and more medication until there was no way of knowing how deep the layers were.

'Hi, Imogen. This is Robbie. He's a Year 9 student from the school I work in, and I'm taking him for a day out. Is Asher around?'

'Sure, I'll get him.' She turned and tried not to flee.

When they returned, Seth introduced Robbie to Asher. 'He likes reading science fiction novels, and I told him about your collection. Could he borrow some?'

'Of course. I don't have as many I used to, but you're welcome to borrow the ones I do have.'

'Don't worry, I won't be alive for long enough to read many.'

Imogen flinched at Robbie's matter-of-fact manner and watched him follow Asher in the same careful, almost surreal, way she'd seen some of her dad's patients move. It appeared partly as if he was afraid to tread heavily for fear of pain, and partly as if he already belonged in some transition phase between one world and the next.

Seth put a hand around her shoulders to guide her to the kitchen, where he plopped down on a chair and looked up at her.

'I wanted Robbie to see Asher and be inspired that others are facing cancer too, and are determined to beat it. I hope I'm not doing the opposite, and making Asher feel as if he's facing a losing battle. I know Robbie looks pretty sick. He was such a healthy, sporty kid at the start of last year when I met him.'

Imogen found her throat swelling hard. 'What does he have?'

'A malignant brain tumour, which he's had chemotherapy for. It seemed to go into remission but the treatments caused leukemia. And while he was being treated for that, the tumour came back again.' Seth sank lower in his chair. 'He doesn't have long left.'

Colour was receding from the room, so even Seth's complexion seemed grey.

'His parents are gutted. I think they're grateful I'm taking him to a movie. Today's one of his better days. The pain is manageable, he says. It'll give them a chance to fix his bedroom and have a bit of down time before he gets back.'

When Dad used to talk about his patients, Imogen had got into the habit of trying to steel her spirit deep inside, so the words would trickle through instead of lodging in some crevice where they'd hurt. The problem was the initial words always sliced a clean gash before she had time to put her guard up, so some of the grief couldn't help penetrating.

Asher and Robbie joined them, with a handful of dog-eared novels. Robbie was even smiling. He had the endearing, gappy grin of a boy who should have had his whole life ahead of him.

'You can keep them, if you like,' Asher told him.

'No, that's okay. I'll be gone soon and you might want them back for your kids.'

'So, which movie shall we go to see?' It seemed Seth pretended not to hear Robbie's pragmatic words. 'Do you fancy basketball or fantasy?'

'Fantasy. I tried watching a movie with Dad last night, but fell asleep. I might be able to stay awake today.'

'Okay, then that's the one it'll be.'

On his way out, Robbie turned to Asher and Imogen and raised a hand. 'See you, and thanks for the books.'

Imogen and Asher stood by the window, watching them leave. 'He's going to die.' It was a simple, husky statement.

Asher nodded. 'I was talking to him. He's been through some horrific pain, and I think God's given him a glimpse of what heaven will be like. He seems to be at the stage where he just wants to bail out and get there. He's tired of fighting. I can understand that.'

'Are we saying that Robbie doesn't have enough faith to live and overcome?' The unspoken question hung between them—it might as well be put to words.

Asher shook his head. 'No way. I'm not having a go at him. Earth isn't our eternal home and heaven is. Robbie's been in such a lot of pain, it seems reasonable for him to want to get there.' He looked at Imogen's face. 'But I'm not saying I think my story is going to be the same as his'

'I was nervous for a moment. You might think that Robbie was a believer who died. It didn't work for him, so why should it work for you?'

'Hey, stop talking that way. You sounded just like the others—Seth, Jodie, Becky and Mum. I don't want to have you imagining me in a casket too.'

'Sorry.' So he saw her as a vital support person. Wasn't that even better than what she longed for him to see her as? *He never will, because that's what he sees Kaitlyn as.* If only he would see her as both, but there was no point in dreaming. She had to take up what was probably her God-given role in his life. 'You're right, we can't let other people's experiences shake our faith. We've got to stay focused on God's Word.'

'Yeah, now you're talking. I don't know why it didn't work for Robbie and other people. It's not my job to figure out why others don't get healed, but that doesn't change his plan for me.' He flashed her a sudden smile. 'Hey, do you want to go and have lunch somewhere?'

'Pardon?' Was he asking her on a date?

'You look the way I feel. Let's not stay stuck here. We'll go where there are people and life.'

'Sure.' Her heart stopped fluttering. It wouldn't be a date, of course, but it'd still be good to be out with Asher.

An ambulance siren blared so loudly near their alfresco table, she could hardly hear anything else. It was stuck in the traffic for a few moments, screeching in vain. She saw Asher open his mouth to speak.

Imogen cupped her ear with her hand and shook her head.

Smiling, he raised both hands in a *don't worry* gesture.

At last a row of cars managed to part and she watched its flaring red lights disappear. Imogen realised her shoulders were slumped.

Asher blew his breath out in a whoosh. 'Hey, how do you feel whenever you see an ambulance come zooming past?'

She found it hard to focus on her potato wedges, and closed her eyes to clear her sight. She'd been rushed back to the past as if that ambulance was a time machine. Its image signified not only dread, but weeks of heartache for her father. After being on hand at an emergency site, it often took him days before he'd emerge from his den of pain, pale and baggy-eyed. She remembered poking her head into his office to ask him if he'd like anything to eat or drink. Even the air used to smell stuffy and thick, as if her father was exhaling pain. She managed to find the words to describe it to Asher.

'So, for me, it means people getting sick, dreadful emergencies and dying. I guess terror floods my body before I even realise.'

Asher chewed his last morsel of toasted sandwich, looking thoughtful. 'I'm the same. Whether or not it started with my mum's accident, I'm not sure. You were there to hear those blaring sirens stop in front of our house.' He rested his face in his hands. 'When they carried her off in the stretcher, I was so scared.'

She couldn't catch his eye. Instead, she watched the two middle-aged men at the next table. One was twirling the pole of the sunshade in the centre while the other leaned forward, talking.

Asher went on, 'While that ambulance was just screaming in our faces, I started thinking I'd still like to change more of my thoughts.'

The middle-aged men had turned and seemed to be looking straight at them. Flushing, Imogen turned back, in case they thought she'd been staring. 'Then how do you think we should react whenever we hear an ambulance siren?'

'Well, instead of getting tense and imagining people dying, we could turn it upside down and think, "There's an ambulance off to someone's rescue".'

She slowly nodded. 'Hey, just when we think we're coming along, some other way of thinking gets challenged, doesn't it?'

He grinned sheepishly. 'Yeah, I've been realising how much time I've wasted trying to be like Seth.'

'Why did you want to be like Seth?'

'Who wouldn't want to be like him? He was always right, always a good mate to everyone, and always getting pats on the back. And when he wasn't right, people agreed with him anyway, because he was Seth.'

'So how did you try to be like Seth?'

He heaved a sigh. 'I tried to shut up more. And for years, whenever

I wanted to say anything, I'd stop to consider whether Seth would say it.'

Imogen had worn a rubber WWJD bracelet her parents had given her for several months, until it started to irritate her skin. It had stood for *What Would Jesus Do,* and now she found herself chuckling. 'So forget wearing a WWJD bracelet. For you, it would have been WWSD.'

'Yeah, but I didn't need any jewellery. It was branded into my brain.'

'What a total waste of time. You're completely different people.'

'I can see that now. You heard what he said a few nights ago, didn't you?' Asher rolled his eyes and shook his head. 'Even Seth can't live up to being Seth.'

The sound of scraping metal made her turn. The middle-aged men had pushed back their patio chairs and were approaching their table. The stockier one, with a grey pony-tail and loose, white cotton trousers looked past her to Asher.

'Hey, aren't you one of Hayden Dorazio's kids?'

'Yeah.'

The man's smile widened, revealing a checkerboard of white teeth and silver caps. 'I told you, Gus, he is a Dorazio. Hey, young fellow, I almost didn't recognise you because of your headgear.' He glanced at the green bandanna covering Asher's head, and bringing out the colour of his eyes. 'Have you joined a band, or turned gypsy? Never mind, I'm Ross Fletcher. At one time, your dad was one of my closest friends. Gus, you remember Hayden, don't you? The drama teacher and talent scout.'

Anxiety prickled beneath Imogen's hairline. She ducked her head in case these men were people she'd come across, although she didn't think so.

'Yeah, I remember that guy. He was so talented.'

'I'll say he was. He could have an audience weeping like a baby one moment, and roaring with laughter the next. He'd brighten anyone's day just being around him. Hayden always seemed to glow with energy. A real original.'

'Yeah, that was my dad.' Asher sounded sad. If Imogen had been Kaitlyn, she could have reached for his hand.

'Hey, what happened to him again?' Gus asked. 'Died tragically, didn't he?' He glanced apologetically at Asher. 'I hope you don't mind me asking.'

Asher shrugged. 'That's okay. It was five years ago now.'

Ross had the grace to flush. 'Maybe I'll tell you later,' he mumbled to his friend.

Asher drew a deep breath. 'I don't mind you telling him in front of me. Dad was down at our holiday cabin at Port Elliot.'

'Neat little set-up, he had,' Ross interjected. 'You should've seen it, Gus.' He glanced at Asher again. 'Are you sure you don't mind us talking about this?'

Asher shrugged again. 'If you're going to tell him anyway, it might as well be here.'

Ross paused for a second longer, and seemed to decide it would be more awkward to stay silent at that point. 'Well, okay. Hayden went down to do some fishing on the rocks. He ignored the beware signs and climbed right down to the most slippery rocks by the ocean. That was Hayden for you. He'd stamp where angels would fear to tread.'

'Thought he was immune to trouble and accidents,' Asher added quietly. 'Typical Dad.'

'And a freak wave washed him off. That's about all there is to it.' Ross stretched back in his chair.

If only it was all. The alarm bells ringing inside Imogen's head were louder than the ambulance siren had been. She had to get out of there.

'Yeah, Dad was a good swimmer, but that sort of current on such a rough day was too much for anyone.' Asher managed to sound matter-of-fact.

'Wasn't there something strange about his death?' Gus asked.

Imogen almost gasped. If it wouldn't have looked suspicious, she would have bolted.

Ross sank his face into his hands. 'Gus, won't you drop it now?'

'Sorry, mate. It's just that I remembered hearing something long ago, and I forget what it was.'

'He had a set of iPod earphones wrapped around his neck,' Asher said. 'The surf hadn't managed to wash them off.'

'You mean there might've been foul play? Someone did the dirty on him? Strangled him and pushed him?' Gus' little grey eyes were like marbles.

'No,' Asher said firmly. 'He'd been listening to music, that's all. Nothing suspicious.'

'Gus watches too many crime shows, the silly old geezer,' Ross excused his friend. 'Sorry, young fellow. We shouldn't have been rehashing it all like this.'

'So which one are you?' Gus asked. 'The elder son or one of the twins?'

'I'm one of the twins.'

'He's the boy one,' Ross chimed in.

'I'm glad you figured that out.' Asher grinned.

'I reckon you were the one who used to chatter like a wind-up toy,' Ross told him.

'Yeah, that was me.'

Ross settled on a chair. 'I wouldn't mind catching up with your mother while I'm in this neck of the woods. Marian was a good friend too, and she's been through a lot.'

Suddenly, Imogen's cell phone rang. She had a legitimate reason to leave the table. Excusing herself, she stepped inside the café where it was quieter.

The person at the other end was trying to hold back sobs. 'Imogen, it's Jodie.'

'Jodie, what's happened?' Imogen's body was poised in panic mode—motionless, as if her heart had suspended its beating.

'It's the baby. I started to bleed.' Jodie's teeth were clearly chattering.

'Oh, Jodie! Is it bad?' Now Imogen's heart was thumping like a lead ball, hurting her rib cage.

'Enough to soak through a cloth.' Jodie made a hiccup noise. 'I tripped over at work, and my stomach hit the side of the table. I winded myself, but I would have thought I'd be well padded enough to protect the baby.' Her breathing was heavy. 'I called an ambulance. I'm on my way to hospital.'

An ambulance? Could it have been the one they'd seen? 'You try to stay calm and the bleeding might stop. Asher and I will be right there.'

Jodie drew a shuddering breath. 'I'm sorry to upset Asher, but I couldn't reach Seth. I know he was taking Robbie to the movies.'

Imogen's head spun. Poor Seth. She imagined him sitting in a dim theatre with his phone switched off, oblivious to what was happening to his little family. *God, you have to make it all right for them. Please.*

'Mum and Becky are always hard to get hold of during the day, and my family live in Melbourne. I didn't know who else to phone.'

'You've done the right thing. We'll jump straight into the car and be with you. I'll keep talking to you on the phone all the way. Sit tight and don't cry too hard.' If only she could remember some tips from her dad but he was a paediatrician, not an ob/gyn. He didn't deal with babies until they were on the outside, where this one wasn't supposed to be for several more weeks. Random phrases whirled through Imogen's head. Ripped placenta... early delivery... still birth. She snapped her mind shut. She was doing what Asher had warned against and jumping to the most horrible conclusions. She didn't have a clue. 'The ambulance crew know what they're doing.'

Imogen swung around to where Asher was still talking to his father's old friends. He stopped mid-sentence when he saw her face.

'We have to get to Jodie. Right now. I'll explain in the car.'

'Right.' He didn't stop to inquire further.

Chapter 18

'Asher, do you think the baby will be okay?' Jodie's teeth were chattering even though the hospital air conditioning was warm. He was sitting in a chair on one side of her bed while Imogen held her hand on the other side. They were waiting for an ultrasound technician.

'Jodie, come on. You know what you believe. God is looking after you and Seth and the baby. He isn't going to stop.' Yet Asher's insides were quaking, convincing him that he was speaking platitudes. At any moment he'd drop his guard and say something that revealed his state of mind.

'Tell me more of those things you were saying the day Imogen and I went to Port Elliot to find Seth.'

'Hey, what things?'

'You know, about God's great love for every human being, including those who haven't been born yet.' Jodie squirmed on her sheets. Her blue eyes bored into him so bright her tears appeared azure. 'I love this baby and the way it wriggles. It doesn't deserve to be hurt because I was the careless one who tripped over. I was trying to remember the things you said that day.' Her face crumpled.

So he found himself talking. He told Jodie some of the insights he'd had along his cancer journey, starting from the time they'd first met Chris Stubbins, and Imogen had read the story of Naaman. Jodie even managed a wan smile at the comparison Imogen had made.

He heard reassuring words pour out of his mouth, about God's promise to stay close to his children. They couldn't have been from him because he, Asher Dorazio, was petrified at the thought of anything happening to his niece or nephew. He began listening to his own words instead of just saying them.

She squeezed his hand tighter. 'Thanks, Ash. You're awesome, do you know that?'

He blinked down at her coral-pink nail polish, not sure how to take her words. But the ultrasound technician was there, saying, 'Let's see what's happening here.'

The following half hour turned out to be one of Asher's most fascinating ever. While Jodie's belly poked up like a dome, the screen revealed what was happening beneath it. He craned forward in his seat to watch the tiny person twitching, swallowing and wriggling. Jodie's stomach looked too still for all that busy activity.

'Everything looks fine,' the technician said. 'Your placenta is in a good position, and the baby is active and healthy. I'm sure there's no need for that bleeding to alarm you.'

Jodie covered her face with her hands and let out a huge sigh. And Asher turned limp inside while relief spread through him. He found words bubbling up, just as they used to when he was much younger.

'That baby has Seth's profile. I'm sure that's the Dorazio nose.'

'Do you think so?' Jodie wore an ear-to-ear beam. 'I do too.'

'Stay still, Uncle, so I can check.' Imogen pretended to cock her head and study Asher's face. 'Yes, the Dorazio nose.'

The door opened and Seth rushed in, dripping puddles from his clothes onto the floor. 'I came as soon I saw your text message. What's happening?'

Jodie stretched a hand toward him. 'Everything's okay. Come and see our baby.'

'Thank God.' Seth ran a shaky hand through his damp, brown hair.

'Babe, you're soaking.'

He nodded. 'The storm they predicted has come early, but who cares about that? All the way here, I was praying as hard as I could.'

Asher was master of himself again. 'Well, they were answered.'

Sinking into the chair Imogen had just vacated, Seth craned his head to look at his brother. 'You're one of the people I owe the biggest apology to.'

'Hey? What are you talking about?' Two apologies in as many weeks?

'I've spent years indulging in a pity party like a spoilt brat.' Seth ran his thumb across the back of Jodie's hand. 'I didn't even realise it until today. I was sure I was working so hard doing God's work for him, but inside, I've been having a hissy fit. God's given me everything that matters to a man, and it took the threat of losing it to show me how precious it is.' He pressed the back of Jodie's hand to his cheek. 'You'd think the idea of losing my brother would be enough to help me come to my senses. I'm glad God stays so patient with me.'

'Come closer. I don't care how wet you are.' Jodie's eyes were streaming as she tried to wriggle higher up her pillow to rub his damp face.

Imogen was swiping her eyes and heading toward the door. Asher had the same idea. Seth and Jodie needed to be alone.

In the corridor, she drew a deep breath. 'I was so nervous.'

Asher nodded, with the sudden urge to sweep Imogen into his arms and hold her tight.

'I'm glad we were there for her.' The opportunity to hug Imogen had slipped past, yet all the way home he cast sideways glances at her, wondering what would have happened if he had done it. She probably would've taken it the right way, as a friendly gesture of relief after an anxious day.

But was that your motive? He felt his heart speed up. Cancer had taught him not to ignore internal questions. Once again, he'd caught himself trying to lie to himself, and almost succeeding.

He stole another peep at the curve of her creamy smooth cheek and the soft canopy of her nut-brown hair. He hadn't hugged her because he knew he'd wanted to do it.

'Are you okay?' Imogen asked.

He fixed his eyes on the road beyond his windscreen wipers. 'Yeah.' His heart wasn't settling down. Imogen was a perceptive girl who might read his mind. 'Why?'

'Because you haven't spoken for such a long time.'

'Yeah, five minutes must be a record for me.'

He had to think about something else. He tried to remember when he first hugged Kaitlyn. She had actually made the first move. He'd been helping her and Becky with lines from the play they were working on. Asher had cracked jokes and delivered the leading man's speeches with comical accents. Becky ended up on the verge of frustrated tears, but he kept clowning around because he relished the way Kaitlyn grinned at him behind Becky's back. And the next day, she'd phoned.

As soon as he heard her bubbly voice, he offered to fetch Becky, but Kaitlyn said she was calling to speak to him. He wished he could remember exactly how she'd encouraged him to ask her out. Her smooth finesse was one of the many things he'd loved about Kaitlyn. *Hold on, why am I thinking in the past tense?* It was one of the things he still loved about her.

It was time to summon a mental picture of Kaitlyn's tanned, heart-shaped face with its cute snub nose and long, blonde eyelashes. She was the reason he was trying so hard to get well again.

Why had another face suddenly made his pulse race? A delicate face with a blanket of freckles so fine many people might miss them.

But Imogen will go home to America, and she knows I'm just a friend. Kaitlyn is my reason to stay alive. I've got it all written down.

A sheet of water from a cloudburst hit the window. He really did have to concentrate on the road.

They arrived home to find the house empty. Asher flicked on the heater, shivering. 'I thought Mum would be home by now.'

'She left a note.' Imogen stood by the kitchen table gazing down at a page of Marian's jerky handwriting. She cast her eyes over the black, spidery scrawl. Although it was written to Asher, he was standing beside her and didn't tell her to stop reading.

Dear Asher,

I need to talk to you. It's been overdue for five years and I can't ignore the issue any longer. I guessed what you did. I'm sure it must have been accidental, but that doesn't change the fact that I shouldn't have ignored it.

I've often wondered if bad news has hounded us because of what you did. Well, today I had a phone call from an old friend of your father's, moments before a text message telling me there might be something wrong with the baby. If poor Jodie and Seth must suffer too, because of this, I can't bear any more. I've decided to drive down to the holiday cabin. I have to think about what I should say to you.

I still love you, my son, make no mistake about that. It's

149

because I love you that I kept quiet but we need to talk about this, at long last.

Love, Mum

Imogen's stomach churned into a hard coil before she finished reading. The puzzled angle of Asher's eyebrows told her that at least part of Marian's letter confused him.

'You must be wondering what I did,' he said.

'You don't have to say.'

'Well, I don't know what Mum thinks she knows. It was bad, but more to do with me wanting to stop another person doing something worse.' He was shaking his head and pacing the floor. 'I'd better call her before I do anything else.' He pressed buttons on his phone and waited. 'I wonder who she was talking to.'

'Those guys we saw earlier at the café.' Imogen sensed that with certainty. Her heart was pounding.

'But what could they know about anything?'

She shrugged. Whatever it was didn't bode well for her.

Every second seemed to fall like a heavy weight while she waited. Even though Asher held the phone against his ear, she heard the buzzing. He finally placed it down.

'She's not answering.'

'Try again in a few minutes.' *I'll bet Marian knows what happened.* Imogen didn't know how long she'd have to plan what she needed to say.

After several more attempts, Asher shook his head. 'She's not picking up. I wonder if she accidentally has the phone on silent mode. She might be getting herself worked into a flap waiting for me to call, and it's not going to happen.'

'Should we drive to the cabin to find her?' Imogen asked the question she guessed was at the back of his mind too, judging from his immediate nod. She scooped up her damp coat. Uncle Hayden's holiday cabin was the last place she wanted to go but it may be far worse if she let Marian tell Asher whatever she had to say without her.

The storm was furious by the time they arrived at the cabin. Trees flung debris in front of Asher's wheels and tossed their limbs. A palm tree Uncle Hayden had planted while Imogen had been there, to help give the place a holiday atmosphere, whipped its leaves like a whirling dervish. She remembered his beam of satisfaction as he asked Becky to pat down the last trowel full of earth.

Marian's car was parked beneath the rickety carport, and a dim light was on inside the cabin. They both knew there was no point waiting for a break in the teeming rain.

'Let's make a run for it,' Asher said.

Slamming the doors, they dashed up the veranda steps. Even those few seconds were enough to soak Imogen to her skin.

Inside, the cabin was as empty as home had been. They checked every room.

'Mum!' By now, Asher's voice held an edge of panic.

Imogen's stomach churned so badly, she might have doubled over and gone to bed if she'd been home. Looking into Asher's bright green eyes, she wondered what he could read from hers. If Marian had gone for a walk and not returned, that alone signified that something bad must have befallen her in such a storm. A sharp crash of thunder made her jump.

What if she's drowned, like Uncle Hayden? Imogen tasted bile at the back of her throat.

Asher was rushing back out the door into the pitch black storm. 'Mum!'

When Imogen followed, her ears picked up a doleful sound. She stood still while rain streamed down her face and clothes. Sure enough, it was a cry for help.

'Where are you?'

'Up here!'

'Asher, come back.' Imogen shouted so hard her throat ached, although her voice seemed to be sucked away in the wind. 'I hear her calling.'

He returned and stood panting beside her, directing the sluggish beam of his flashlight up into the elements. Strong and laser-like in the dark back home, it wasn't up for such weather. Lightning struck, and she glimpsed a brown blur at the top of the old viewing platform.

'Up there!' She snatched Asher's hand to direct the beam. Imogen gasped when she saw that it was Marian's head. Soaking hair fell around her face and into her eyes, but her hands gripped the sides of the sloping platform as she squinted into the light.

'I can't see you.' Marian's voice was frantic.

'Down here. It's Asher and Imogen.' He sounded incredulous. 'Mum, how'd you climb up there?'

Different questions whirled through Imogen's head. How long had Marian been there? Why had she done such a reckless thing? She'd never get to ask, because Marian would surely have enough questions of her own. The blocks of wood Uncle Hayden had nailed up the trunk to use as steps were lit by another jagged flash. Only one question had a clear answer, and that was why Marian had not dared to try and venture down.

Marian drew a shuddering breath and shouted, 'It took a long time... really hurt my back. I knew I shouldn't, but I wanted to see the view one last time.' Her breath was coming in gasps. 'Then the storm started... the platform slipped. All I can do is hold on. I can't get down. I'll die if I try.'

'Mum, you're not going to fall. I'm coming up to help you!'

Chapter 19

As he raised his arm to test the strength of an upper rung, Asher's shoulder gave a familiar grinding ache. He couldn't climb up that far without causing it trauma, even without the added problem of a raging storm.

'You can't.' His mother's terror-stricken cry echoed his thoughts.

Suddenly, he had enough. 'I will!' The sick shoulder wasn't going to prevent him helping his mother down from the sloping platform. *Lord, please help me get her safely down. If ever there was a time I needed a quick answer, it's now. I'm a man of faith and my body is a temple of the Holy Spirit. It has to be whole for this. No weapon formed against it can prosper. You know I've had enough of cancer and pain! I'm going up this ladder to help Mum.'*

Once he made it up, he'd have to come down behind his mother, shielding her with his arms to prevent her slipping and falling. Dad had never been a careful handyman. The gaps he'd left between the rungs weren't even, so they wouldn't be able to judge the distance between the hand and footholds.

'I'll tie the torch around my neck,' he said aloud. He tugged off his shoes and began fumbling to pull out one of the laces. In the darkness, he'd be more confident with his bare feet anyway.

'Torch?' Imogen was standing beside him and he heard the question in her word.

'Flashlight or whatever you call 'em.' There would be time to tease her about semantics later.

For now, he had to climb. He used to know every lump and hole in those rungs by memory, but hadn't been up there for years. Gritting his teeth, he felt along the surface of each crude step to determine whether they were skewed, crooked, weak, or broken. His fingers were so icy they seemed to creak with cold whenever he let go of one rung and stretched them to seize the next. He was leaving the ground further behind while the deluge drenched him.

'Mum, I'm nearly up,' he called at last. 'I'll grab one of your feet and set it on a rung.' Water filled his mouth, making him splutter. 'Then I'll help with your hands.'

'But I can't see!' Marian's voice was frantic.

'I have the torch. Just keep your hands and feet where I put them.'

Her thick ankles loomed above him, reminding him of the time she'd been hanging off the roof over the patio. 'I won't let you fall.'

Puffing and sobbing, she began to move, following his directions. He felt her legs tremble.

'We'll take it slowly. Take a deep breath.' Every muscle in his body was taut with the effort required to support her weight. 'You need to calm down.'

'My feet are numb. I'll die!'

'Mum, STOP!' Wasn't cold water meant calm hysterics? She was getting a flood but it made no difference. 'Just listen. Forget the numbness. Trust me. Wherever I put your feet, it's firm. I'm right behind you, surrounding you. Get your head right!'

She let out a whimpering groan.

After their first few steps, an ear-splitting crash of thunder seemed to knock her backwards as if it was made of force instead of sound. He'd just moved high behind her to guide her hands. Marian slumped back and screamed but Asher's arms tightened around her. He couldn't tell whether his left shoulder was giving its normal protest or if it would have hurt anyway, with his muscles stretched to their full capacity. He kept his fingers wrapped around the rungs with all his might, holding them both in place.

'I've got you.'

'I won't make it!'

'You will. Trust me.'

As he prised her hand loose to lower it to the next step, her elbow jolted the torch. Although he'd tied it tight, the shoelace broke. The light plummeted, leaving them in total darkness.

Mum gasped and he flinched, waiting for the thump on the ground but the storm noises must have covered it up. *Stupid!* Without any light, she would refuse to move.

'I caught it.' It was Imogen's voice from far below. A feeble beam played over them.

'I'm coming up,' she called.

It was the obvious solution. 'Be careful!' Instant regret filled him. They were not words to instil confidence. Mum's sagging weight was bearing back on him, and his arms were quivering. His frozen fingers grew steadily stiffer. Keeping his eyes fixed on the ascending beam of light, he was careful not to do to Imogen what Mum had accidentally done to him. *I won't kick the torch.*

'Mum, we'll just move down a few more steps.'

The higher Imogen's upturned face moved toward them, the more his heart raced for her. She'd been safe waiting on the ground, but now she was putting herself in danger too. He squinted down through the rain, willing her to stay up. Her face was not oval, as he'd first thought all those weeks ago, but the most delicate isosceles triangle, with her knob of a chin in perfect alignment with her cheek bones. Her eyes were bright, mouth set in a line of concentration.

Imogen jerked downward and cried out. She must have stepped on a rung that gave way.

'Imogen!' Light flashed before Asher's eyes.

'I'm okay,' her assurance floated up.

All the warmth in his body converged to the relief of his quaking stomach. He couldn't feel his numb hands and feet, let alone the rungs they were standing on and clinging to. How he treasured all the contours of that strong, sweet face.

They continued their painstaking way down. Mum was making a rasping, groaning sound with each step she took. He guessed it must match the grinding of her sore bones and didn't even bother asking. Having it confirmed would help them down no quicker.

It could have taken fifteen minutes or an hour. His concept of time had stopped working.

'I'm back on the ground!' Imogen called. 'You two have only a few more yards.'

Although he could have told her Aussies didn't normally measure things in yards, he knew she meant a very short distance, and continued to work his way down. Finally, he felt solid ground rather than a slippery block of wood with the potential to suddenly twist or give way. Even though his brain was trying to tell him that the ground was lurching and pitching like ocean waves, he knew that was just an illusion. It was hard and reliable, like God who had helped them all up and then back down.

Marian hugged the massive trunk, panting and crying. Asher took that moment to wrap his arms around Imogen. He lifted her right off her feet to hold her close to him and spun her around. He'd raised her high enough to rest his forehead in the crook of her neck.

'Thanks for your help,' he mumbled into her wet hair.

Even when he let her feet touch the ground, she kept gripping him tight and burrowed her head beneath his chin as if to shield her face from the rain, although she was already soaked through.

'Asher, this time we did it!'

'Yeah, we did it.'

'Asher, I know you killed your father.' They'd all showered and climbed into musty clothes that had been folded away in the cabin. Mum's soft words crashed into him like a torpedo.

'What? No, I didn't.'

'Don't lie about it. You've never been a liar. Are you afraid I'll tell the police at this stage? Keeping quiet about this for five years is my proof that I won't, but please don't bluff or cover up any more.' She stretched a hand towards him, but he wasn't going to admit to something he didn't do.

'I didn't kill Dad. Why on earth do you believe I did?'

'Can't you just accept that I know? I put two and two together.'

'You came up with some crazy number, then.' He was hardly able to believe she was earnest.

'I'll tell you how I figured it out. We know that your father had the cords of your music player wrapped around his throat when he was found.'

Asher closed his eyes. This was turning into some nightmare inquisition.

'Do you reckon I strangled him? The tide did it. Even the doctors and police thought that. He went on the rocks listening to music, and he was swept off.'

'But why did he have it with him?'

'He borrowed it from me. Didn't that occur to you?' He was giving his mother a mouthful of backchat, something his father would have disapproved of.

'But I know for a fact that you had it with you at home the morning before he died. And he was already away at the cabin.' Her voice was quiet again, almost chilling in its intensity. 'I went to wake you up for work, and you were lying on your pillow with your hands behind your head, listening to music with those plugs in your ears.'

Blood gushed through his eardrums. 'He borrowed it.' Would repeating that convince her?

'Asher, please stop trying to fool me. Hayden was found drowned the very next morning before the crack of dawn. And when you were asked, like the rest of us, you declared you hadn't been anywhere near here that day. So, how did those earphones travel from your ears to his?'

His stomach turned to lead.

'I kept quiet about it for all these years,' Marian went on. 'I knew that if you were on those rocks with your dad and shoved him off, it wouldn't have been intentional.'

'But why do think I would have done that?'

'I don't know. You two were always arguing. Work, money, it could have been anything. And Hayden was dead. We couldn't bring him back.' Her chin began to quiver. 'But I could protect you from going to jail. If I told the police what I suspected, they might have done something. You were nineteen, an adult in the eyes of the law. I felt I had to save you, but it's been playing on my mind all these years.'

'Mum, I did come here. That's the only lie I told. I just wanted to talk to Dad.' *Please don't let her ask what we talked about.* He almost groaned with scorn at himself. What sort of foolish prayer was that, with no hope of being answered? 'I drove here after work. I'd been to see Seth and had words with him too. Then I turned up here about nine thirty, had an argument with Dad and drove straight back home again. I was probably here at the cabin for ten minutes, tops. I'd been listening to the iPod in the car on the way down.' He'd been thrashing it at top volume to match his anger level. 'Later on, I couldn't find it. I can only guess what must've happened. It probably fell off inside, and Dad picked it up to take with him when he went out on the rocks.

His mother's deep brown eyes were filled with sorrow. The question he dreaded came next. 'What was so important that you had to drive all the way from home to Port Elliot to argue with him about?'

Answering the question was a no-win situation. She might refuse to believe him, as Seth had done—and then think him a deluded murderer, instead of just a plain murderer. Or she'd believe him and feel wretched and terrible, which was what he'd tried so hard to prevent five years ago.

'I had a really good reason for not wanting to tell you.' That wasn't going to cut it. They could talk round and round in circles.

Imogen spoke. 'The reason Asher went to have it out with his father was that he found out Uncle Hayden was with another woman.'

His heart jolted as he swung around to look at her. He was used to Imogen being right beside him, offering her support, but this was just plain weird. She couldn't read his mind any more than Seth or Chris could. 'How did you know?'

She drew a ragged breath and cast her eyes down.

'Are you going to tell him or will I?' Mum said.

Imogen looked up at him. There was some sort of desperate, pleading quality in her eyes.

'What is it?' Asher wanted to hug her again but had to find out what was going on first.

'The person Uncle Hayden was with was me.'

Imogen felt sick to the stomach. Marian seemed to think she had to fill in the slack. Her hands twitched as she talked, explaining what had happened during the day. Ross Fletcher, an old friend of Hayden's, had phoned her out of the blue. He'd come across Asher and a young woman having a bite to eat at a café. Asher was the one who had passed on her phone number. Ross had always been a pleasant fellow, and had phoned to ask how she was bearing up five years after Hayden's death.

'He said, "I've never spoken to you much since the accident. I guess you knew Hayden was seeing someone." And I said, "Yes."'

'How did you know?' Imogen's stomach lurched.

Marian paused to stare at her. 'You can tell when your husband is having an affair, Imogen. All the signs were there.'

'It wasn't an affair. I didn't know what was in his head until he…,' Imogen stopped and pursed her lips together. This was Hayden's wife and son. She had to be careful what she said. They might not even believe her. She had to find out what Marian thought had happened. 'What signs?'

Marian rolled her eyes. 'Where do I start? Hayden had been getting hard to reach on his phone during the day. It was often switched off. For those few weeks, he wasn't where I thought he would be, where I'd known I could find him in the past. And he suddenly seemed to be needed at far more student dress rehearsals than usual. Whenever I mentioned this, he'd snap defensive comments at me, then apologise. Just the fact that he wanted to spend a few nights alone here at the cabin was suspicious.'

Imogen should have guessed that would be the case for a woman who had loved one man for so long. She looked at Asher, who appeared white and sick. Would he even listen to her explanation? Would Marian?

'And other times he'd be far more loving and solicitous than normal,' Marian went on. 'He'd smother me with attention. I never came straight out and accused him of having an affair, but I had a gut instinct. I was trying to figure out the best way of letting him know that I suspected, and trying to win him back again. I wasn't blaming him.'

Asher's head snapped up. 'What do you mean, you weren't blaming him?'

Imogen froze at the iciness in his tone.

Marian heaved a deep sigh. 'I wish I didn't have to explain this to you. I hadn't been able to be a proper wife, in every sense of the word, since I had my accident. I knew he still loved me, but things had changed. A virile, red-blooded man like your father....'

'Stop!' Asher flushed bright red and turned his face away. 'I don't want to be hearing this and I still say no, he shouldn't have done it.'

'I'm sorry. It's the last thing I ever wanted to tell you, but I need you to understand him.' She was watching his slumped form, with his face sunk into one hand. 'I'm guessing you worked him out too, didn't you?'

Without moving, Asher nodded.

'That's why you came here to the cabin, isn't it? To tear strips off him.'

'I did tear strips off him ... but I didn't kill him.'

'You shouldn't have done that on my behalf. If only you'd spoken to me, I would've pleaded with you not to confront him.'

For a moment, Marian's bleak words hung in the air.

'I'll tell you what Ross said over the phone today. This is the one thing I didn't know before.'

Perching on the edge of her seat, Imogen waited. Her heart was thumping and Asher wouldn't catch her eye.

'Hayden had confided in Ross.' Marian's voice was hoarse. 'He admitted that he was seeing a much younger woman, a mere girl. But he asked Ross to say nothing about it to any of us because it would all be finished soon. The girl was going to fly home to America. She was only in Australia for a few weeks. Hayden just longed to feel like a young man again for a short time.'

Imogen's eyes were burning hot with pain. Rain streamed down the grubby, unwashed cabin windows.

'Hayden told Ross that it was the same little girl who'd been staying with his family when I had my accident. All grown up now, and stunning. Imogen, how could you not tell me? Why did you even come back?' At last, Marian brought her hands up to mop her wet cheeks. 'Then straight after talking with Ross, I read Jodie's text message. She was bleeding and afraid she might be losing the baby. I'd had enough bad news. Asher a murderer and Imogen an adulteress? I had to get away to think and pray, and the only place I could think to come was here.'

It was Imogen's turn to speak but what she had to say would blight Uncle Hayden even more. 'He might have called it a fling, but I had no idea what was in his mind. He was affectionate, but I thought that was still just because I was the daughter of his old pen pal.' She might have been foolish and naïve but she was not an adulteress.

Chapter 20

Imogen had been nineteen years old. This time she was staying with Aunt Ally, her mother's sister, who had married an Australian. Her parents were on another missionary trip. No thought of visiting the Dorazio family had entered their heads this time. Although she was no longer a little girl who'd be creeping outside after curfew, it was still out of the question. Her parents had kept in touch with Uncle Hayden's family sporadically, but the old camaraderie between the boyhood pen pals was gone. Imogen had felt the sting, as she knew it was her fault.

The rest of her childhood had been fraught with guilt. Even when she was supposed to be thinking about school work, her spirit would well with sadness at the thought that she'd ruined several lives. Her family was back to its familiar old lifestyle in New York, but the Dorazio family was still suffering and it was all because of her.

In Australia, Imogen's mind kept returning to the Dorazios. She was back in their city and longed to hear about them, but hesitated to pick up the telephone or even more daring, knock on their door.

Uncle Hayden might still work at the same school he was teaching at before. The thought struck her one morning while she was buying groceries. After thinking about going there all day, the afternoon found her leaning against the school gate near the office, toying with the idea of enquiring after him on the remote chance that he was still working there ten years later. Uncle Hayden had been her hero. She didn't necessarily have to talk to him, and if she did, she could tell him how horrible she felt.

Saying the words wouldn't change things back or make poor Aunt Marian's life easier, but hearing the beloved voice from the past telling her she'd been forgiven might help her go home feeling a whole lot better.

It would be better still if she could see that he'd recovered some of his old bounce and pizzazz. She'd never forgotten how her nine-year-old heart would fizz with anticipation when she heard him return from work. She couldn't bear to think of the broken man he'd been when she left, a man who couldn't muster the energy to raise his head and say goodbye to her when her parents and brother came to take her away.

'He's doing a drama rehearsal with the Year 11s and 12s in the auditorium,' the school secretary told her.

Imogen felt her heart ignite inside her. After so many years, Uncle Hayden was in the same establishment she stood in.

'You can sit in there and wait for him, if you like. Lots of students' friends and families are there too.'

She couldn't back out of an invitation like that. She'd sat at the very back corner, trusting that he might not recognise her if he looked in her direction. If he was still harbouring a grudge about her part in Aunt Marian's accident, she hoped he'd think she was one of the student's friends. He was directing students with all his usual flair, and his enthusiastic voice filled the auditorium. *I wish I was one of those students.*

Suddenly, he saw her and stopped talking. He excused himself to the students, hurried into the aisle and beckoned her to follow him outside to the corridor. With a thumping heart, Imogen stood up to oblige him.

'Little Ginny Browne?' A smile spread across his face.

'I didn't think you'd know me.' Her voice caught in her throat.

'Of course I'd recognise you. Your mom and dad email me photos sometimes, but never as often as I'd like.' He grasped her hands between his large, warm ones. 'I hope you were waiting to come and say hello to me.'

'I was thinking about it. I wasn't sure you'd want to speak to me,' she admitted.

His eyes widened to green saucers. 'I wouldn't have missed catching up with you for the world. How could you think of not speaking to me?'

'Well, after what happened before …' she was horrified to feel tears rising.

Uncle Hayden gently raised her chin to see her face. He pulled a clean handkerchief from his pocket to mop her cheeks. His soft breath smelled like the peppermints he must have been sucking.

'You didn't think I'd reject you, did you? That makes me so sad. It wasn't your fault. Did you think we blamed you all these years? It was that naughty Asher who crept outside first. We know the whole story.'

Relief was trickling through her veins, although she knew it wasn't entirely Asher's fault either. She didn't speak up to defend him. She was so happy to find Uncle Hayden held no grudge she didn't want to take the chance of talking him into one.

'How are they all going ... your family?'

'Listen, I could answer that in a flash or we could have a good catch-up later over a drink, when work finishes.'

Nodding, she felt a smile replace her tears.

'It won't be long now. Would you like keep enjoying the show while you wait for me? There are a few rough edges in the performance but you can be one of our guinea pigs.'

She nodded again. Suddenly, the school auditorium felt like the most fascinating entertainment venue. He wrapped her tight in an impulsive hug that almost took her breath away, leaving her with a warm, cushioned feeling of safety, protection and acceptance she'd never experienced before. Then, with another smile and a wink, he hurried back into the auditorium.

'Are you a friend of Mr Dorazio's?' The question came from a curious girl with dark dreadlocks who hung back nearby.

Imogen had never found it more of a pleasure to nod.

The student let out her breath in an expressive sigh whose admiration was plainer than words. 'You're lucky. He's everyone's favourite teacher.' Lowering her voice, she added, 'Most of the girls are crazy in love with him.'

Imogen returned to her seat on shoes of air. By the end of her wait, she didn't have a clue what the play was about, but she could have written a book on Uncle Hayden's dynamism, the way he tossed his attractive, blond hair and his warm, easy way with people. Whenever he caught her eye he shot her another of his sunshine burst smiles. He was every bit as wonderful as she remembered and more.

She hated to speak of what happened next. Hayden had taken her out for a pub meal. Although Imogen completely forgot what she'd ordered, she remembered what he had. It was lemon chicken on a bed of noodles like Styrofoam, and he made up some funny magic tricks, winding them around on his fork. It was the same sort of thing she used to love watching him do when she was a little girl. This time she was aware of his green eyes flickering frequently to her face to gauge her reactions. Her nerves tingled every time because she wasn't used to people seeking her admiration.

Uncle Hayden described how well Becky was going with her studies. Although she'd longed to find out all about her old friend, Imogen was ashamed to realise by the end that she'd not taken in many words. She'd been too flustered by Hayden's smile and waving, expressive hands.

'How are the boys?' She had to prove to herself that she could pay attention this time.

'They're well. Seth got married a few months ago to the sweetest and loveliest girl you could ever hope to meet.'

'That's great.' Imogen felt a pang of envy for any girl lucky enough to become part of the close-knit Dorazio family.

'And Asher's just landed himself a plum job with a posh firm as a computer software engineer. He won a scholarship. Blitzed all his school mates and most of the state. He'll be one of the youngest workers at his new firm with one of the most responsible jobs.' Uncle Hayden crossed his arms in front of him and tilted his chin. 'My young chatterbox has made good.'

'Well, good for him.' It seemed Asher was as clever as he'd always claimed to be. 'And how's Aunt Marian?'

She couldn't help noticing the length of Hayden's pause. She could hardly swallow her mouthful of whatever she'd ordered. A ripple of dread passed through her and she pressed her toes against the soles of her shoes. Was he going to tell her that she'd passed away?

'She's been recovering well over the last several years.' Uncle Hayden let out a sigh and took a deep swig of beer. 'She's not flat on her back like she was for the first several months. She can shuffle around and do practically anything she needs to do for herself.'

Imogen hardly knew whether to offer congratulations or condolences. His words seemed intended to be happy but didn't match his doleful tone.

'I'm glad she's more independent.'

'Me too.' Arching his back, Hayden ran a hand through his bushy waves of hair. 'Because we've split up.'

'Oh.' Imogen's heart was thumping as she tried to figure out what to say because, once again, she couldn't tell whether the news was supposed to be bad or good. 'I'm sorry.' That, at least, must be safe.

164

'These things happen.' He smiled across the table at her. 'Now Ginny, how long did you say you're back in Australia for?'

'Another three weeks.' She hadn't mentioned that nobody ever shortened her name any more. It sounded so bewitching from Uncle Hayden's lips.

'Let me make it a good three weeks for you.' He leaned forward with his forearms on the table. 'I'll take you sightseeing to some of the best places in Adelaide. Places that the general public don't even know about. Would you like that?'

'Are you sure it wouldn't be too much trouble?'

'It'd be a very special privilege for a solitary chap like me.'

And her spirits had soared because she'd forgotten how lilting his light Scottish brogue was. She shouldn't make him sad by showing how the news about his break up with Aunt Marian shocked her. She had to remember that although it was fresh for her, they'd made the decision and grown used to it.

'It'd be great for me too.'

'He actually told you that we'd split up?' Marian's gaping mouth showed this was news to her.

Imogen nodded, miserable. Although it had been Hayden's lie and not hers, she still felt responsible. Was telling the truth even the right thing to do? Marian had stated that it was high time she knew the truth about everything, but perhaps it was far too cruel. She stole a peep at Asher's green gaze, so bleak and truculent all at once. *Of course it is.*

'That was a total lie,' Marian rocked herself back and forth on her chair as if her belly hurt.

'I found that out,' Imogen said softly.

But not until it was too late.

Hayden had taken her for hikes up hills with sweeping views, and to magnificent beaches with tremendous, pounding waves. As she spoke of her studies and family, he would lean his chin on his hands and listen to her every word. She knew he'd actually been listening when he'd probe her with further questions. She realised nobody had ever really listened before, and felt like a dry sponge expanding.

Then came that last terrible night—the night Hayden had told her he was going to fix her a special dinner at his cabin. 'Do you remember that little place from when you were small?' When she saw how he'd lit it up with candles, alarm bells should have rung for Imogen, but she'd still assumed Hayden's gesture was simply the fatherly action of a man who wanted to cheer up the daughter of an old friend. She recognised them as some of the same chunky, homemade candles she'd made with Becky and Asher years earlier, although Hayden had forgotten.

Should she reveal that much, without saying what Uncle Hayden expected to happen afterwards? The thing that had started to unfold in that hour before Asher would be able to take up the story?

Surely her turn to speak was over. If she was going to go on, she'd have to know if he'd even listen. Her voice came out as a croak.

'Asher, aren't you going to say anything?'

I can't think of anything to say.' Asher knew he could think of a thousand things if he just opened his mouth but had just enough self control not to do it.

'Are you okay?' She was watching him with her teeth biting down on her bottom lip, as if she cared.

He nodded without thinking, because he knew people were supposed to nod at rhetorical questions. He wasn't okay. He felt sick in a horribly empty way as if all happiness was draining from him.

'I'm sorry.' Imogen was clearly trembling.

'I think we all have a lot to talk about,' Marian added.

Talk! That was one thing he couldn't agree to yet. Talk was what had landed him in messes all his life. Any talk coming from him right now would be damaging. He could say plenty which proved that he wasn't empty after all. But he knew from the quality of his turmoil that any talk coming from him would be full of scathing, blistering, harsh words that would make everything worse. He would say only one thing.

'I don't want to talk yet. I'm going for a walk.'

'But it's still pouring,' Imogen said.

'A drive, then.' He grabbed his keys. He'd already said two things when he'd intended to say just one, and every word brought the volcano closer to the surface. He had to get out of there fast.

'Where are you going?'

Why did she keep asking him questions? He pretended not to hear. *What would you care?* was all that sprang to mind and he knew that she really did care. That made it even worse. He stepped out into a barrage of hailstones that stung his face and took his breath away.

Slamming his car door behind him, he drove as far the sheep gate near the edge of their property, then turned off his engine and sat watching slush bank up his windows. Judging from the queasy adrenaline that pulsed through his twitching limbs, his heart was pumping poison. It had probably surged through him every day for years, but he thought he'd purged it from his system with his visits to Chris Stubbins and the thank you notes he was writing. Yet now it was back, stronger than ever. He could taste the sour toxicity in his mouth, making him want to spit.

It was Imogen *with Dad.*

A shaft of pain stabbed through his head. For years he'd assumed that Dad had been beguiled by a shameless seductress like those in the Bible. Now what was he supposed to think? If it had been any other woman, Dad might have stayed forgiven. But Imogen?

Even if she hadn't realised what the old fox was up to, she should have said something earlier. *She must have guessed how terrible I've felt about the whole thing all this time.*

He couldn't stretch behind the wheel but his ribs ached with something like an intense stitch. He could barely breathe without a feeling of knives slicing through him.

It was like an impossibly implausible play script from Dad's or Becky's archives. How did Dad do it? How did he attract her? How did he make her agree to everything he suggested? How could she agree to go there? It was that which rubbed his rawest nerve. How could she?

He rested his head on his steering wheel. He and Imogen had never been together. He hadn't even seen her during that visit to Australia. She'd never cheated on him but he felt as if she had. Well, hadn't she, in a way? She'd cheated him by not being as forthcoming as she must have guessed he would want her to be. Her smile would light up the mind of a middle-aged smooth-talker like Dad. It was sick and wrong. Imogen had been nineteen years old and Hayden had been forty-eight. To think that his lips could've touched her. Asher scrunched his eyes tight and groaned but it didn't extinguish the image.

Disgusting. Sickening. Horrible. Words shot like bullets through his head and his shield wasn't a fraction thick enough to deflect them.

It left him clueless. What should he do? He had no way of fighting back. Any reaction would be ineffective for an unarmed man. Talking, his native weapon, would be counterproductive. Throwing words at Imogen wouldn't help.

Yet what if Chris was right, and suppressing hurt had contributed to his sickness in the first place? Maybe it had filled his cells, trapped deep inside, twisting and mutilating them until the hurt spilled out into his blood. Well, Chris hadn't said all that, but Asher found it easy to fill in the details.

But apart from releasing the pain in words or suppressing the deep hurt, there seemed no other option. In fact, words never helped him release pain anyway. God knew he'd tried.

He rested his cheek against the fogged-up window. He couldn't ignore the pain. It was like a second skin. Chris had said nothing was worth getting so upset about. A grim laugh filled Asher's consciousness. He wasn't sure whether he laughed out loud or just heard it in his head. Chris had never had anything like this thrown at him.

Chapter 21

It was five years ago but still felt like yesterday. When they'd finished the dinner Hayden had cooked for her, he gave Imogen a small package. It contained a beautiful cascade necklace, dripping with Australian icons moulded in silver.

'That's something to remember me by when you go home.' He had beamed at her.

Imogen ran her finger over a delicate silver kangaroo with all the gratitude she felt. 'There's no way I'd ever forget you, but this is beautiful. Thank you. I'll always wear it.'

Hayden enfolded her hand in his. 'You are the most wonderful young woman I know.' He kissed the back of it.

She had never heard anything like the words he was speaking, but something about the pressure of his hand made her skin begin to prickle. It was uncomfortably intimate. Hayden's hand felt clammy, and looked sort of old, with its looser skin and the fine lines across the back of it.

She gently tried to pull hers away but his grip tightened.

'Come on, Ginny, why don't we go and sit on the couch?' He came around the table and began kneading her shoulders with those large, warm hands. 'You feel tense. I tell my drama students that it's okay to use your bodies in self-expression and I'll tell you the same thing.' He leaned down and planted a kiss on her neck.

Imogen gasped, 'Uncle Hayden, no, I…'

'I won't hurt you. I promise.' His green eyes were gleaming. 'Please, Ginny, just let yourself go for one night. I want to send you home to America with a night to remember.'

She was up off her seat with no idea what to say or do next. If they hadn't been interrupted, would he have forced himself on her? That was the question she had often wondered.

They heard a car screeching along the driveway and Hayden sprang off the couch to peer out the window. She'd never forget the pallid dismay that spread across his face.

'It's Asher. We need to hide you somewhere, keep you out of his way.'

Imogen had no time to ask questions. Hayden sounded too urgent. She crouched behind the couch but he seized her wrist and pulled her hard. 'Not there!' His rebuke sounded harsh. 'It has to be somewhere he won't think to look.'

As a car door slammed, she spotted the long storage cupboard that ran two feet above the floor. It would be a tight squeeze, but she could manage. She was flat on her stomach, squirming in like a snake moving backwards. Sharp, pointy objects grazed her arms. The door didn't slide shut all the way, leaving a slit for her to peep through. She saw the front door bounce off its rubber stopper.

'What are you doing here?' She heard a faint tremor in Uncle Hayden's voice.

'Don't play innocent.'

Young guys intimidated Imogen. She'd been taught to be wary of possible gang members home in New York, and this voice belonged to one of the most irate-sounding young men she'd ever heard.

'Where is she?'

'What are you talking about?'

Imogen felt a tiny clink as her elbow nudged some sort of cold tool. Her breath stopped and her heart almost burst. She was living one of those smutty comedies in which a man had to stow away his illicit lover. But she wasn't Hayden's lover at all. It was anything but funny. *Why has he made me hide? I've done nothing wrong.* If Uncle Hayden had simply told Asher she was a friend, that was the simple truth, wasn't it? But it was too late to wriggle out now.

'You know what I'm talking about.' Asher shouted. 'How can you cheat on Mum after all you've been through together?'

'You're out of your mind! I'd never cheat on Mum.'

He said he'd left her. The truth flooded through Imogen in sick, heavy waves. Where did Uncle Hayden's role of actor leave off and his real life begin?

Asher seemed to be striding through the cabin looking for the woman his father had tucked away. She heard swift, angry footsteps and doors slamming as cupboards were opened and shut. If his voice hadn't been so loud and furious she wouldn't have heard his words over all the banging and thumping.

'I'm not that stupid! You might be able to fool Seth but you can't fool me.'

Imogen didn't have to see to know that goose bumps were prickling her flesh. Some pointy thing was digging into her leg. It was the corner of one of the square candles she and the twins had made long ago out of milk carton moulds. Back when Asher was still little and skinny with a high-pitched voice that never stopped talking. She'd die if this irate man found her. Even if he wasn't a gang member, he sounded enraged enough that he would be if he discovered her.

'How could you treat Mum this way?'

'I'm not doing anything to her. If you tell her any of this nonsense, you'll be the one hurting her, and all over nothing.'

'Who is she?' Asher demanded. 'Who's your girlfriend?'

'There's nobody here.'

'Becky's friend, Taylor, told me he'd seen you out a few times with the same pretty girl.'

'And that makes you assume I'm having an affair?' Hayden's voice was scathing. 'I do mentor several students.'

'You don't take them out in your car, though. And that's not all. You had the nerve to ask me to lend you money.'

'What does *that* prove?'

Imogen heard the crackle of paper.

'This just proves I bought a necklace,' Hayden said at last.

The cascade necklace. Imogen fingered the chain with the gorgeous icons dripping down.

'But Mum didn't get anything like this from you.'

'Did you ask her?' Hayden's voice verged on panic.

'Why would it bother you if I did?'

'Did it occur to you that I must've bought something I'm saving for a gift?'

'We both know Mum doesn't bother with jewellery. And what about this? This isn't a gift for Mum.'

'One of Becky's friends must've left it here.'

Imogen realised they must be talking about the lacy black cardigan she'd left draped over the back of a kitchen chair, just warm enough for the coolness of late summer nights. She pressed a hand to her mouth as bile surged.

'Nobody's come here for ages,' Asher pointed out. 'And you have plate settings for two, not to mention candles!' Crockery bounced as he pounded the table and began calling his father names that made Imogen's skin crawl. They kept pouring out of his mouth, like caustic poison burning her with their acid.

'You shut your vitriolic mouth!' Hayden's voice echoed off the walls. 'I'm not having an affair. I love your mother as much as ever, and you have no right to come barging in here unannounced, trying to stuff up my life. You can get the hell out of here, right now.'

'Too right I'm going. I spent long enough letting you stuff up mine. I've seen all I need to see, and I can't believe I wasted so much time trying to make you tell me I'm doing well. I don't care what you think any more.'

The front door slammed again. It seemed Asher was gone. Imogen waited until she heard his tyres rumbling away before sliding out, even though the dim light from the candles on the table stung her eyes.

Hayden stretched his hands, casting her a look filled with regret. 'I'm so sorry, Ginny. Let me explain.'

'Don't worry about it.' She'd overheard enough to have the whole picture. And now she knew she couldn't believe anything he said.

'I didn't know he was going to come.'

'That's obvious.' It might be the only truth he'd ever told her. Her eyes were still prickling. 'You were right. Asher is smart. He figured out what's happening and I didn't.'

'Ginny!' Hayden pulled her close and pressed her face into the front of his shirt as if he was trying to force her to stand still and listen. All she could do to show resistance was stiffen her body.

'I'm sorry I hurt you.' His voice boomed hollow above her.

Her eyes latched onto something that hadn't been on the floor before. An iPod with cords and ear phones. Asher must've let it fall while he was tearing through the cabin.

'I didn't mean to,' Hayden was saying.

She felt heartache rise inside. She mustn't let it erupt, or it'd make him want to comfort her more and she couldn't let herself be touched by him like that again.

'You know that day at your school? I only wanted to say hello. Why'd you have to tell me those lies, take me places and bring me here?'

She felt the movement of his throat swallowing. 'I just let my feelings run away with me.'

'I want to leave. Would you drive me into town?'

'If it'll make you feel better.' His voice was ragged. 'But please, listen to me first.' Hayden sank onto the chair he'd been sitting on over dinner. She looked the remnants of their meal on the empty plates—bones from the barbequed spare ribs and vanilla bean pods in their dessert bowls—and almost groaned when she considered how hard he must have worked to prepare them.

Hayden stooped to pick up the iPod and twirled the cords around his fingers. 'He left this behind. It fell down while he was yelling at me. At least I got something back on him.' Hayden tried to force a laugh but it was empty. He seemed to realise that he couldn't make things normal again. Sighing instead, he sank his face into his hands.

Imogen felt a wave of pity for him but it turned into a shudder when she considered what he'd done.

He looked up at her with red-rimmed, tired eyes. 'I just wanted to have a break from looking after Marian for a couple of weeks.' He opened the palms of his hands on the table top. 'I wanted to feel like a normal man again. I'm sorry. I've upset you, and ruined things with Asher too.' His strong shoulders caved over. 'I suppose it's probably what I deserve.'

Asher remembered to look out for the slippery bottom steps back at the cabin, the ones with moss growing in their dips. They always turned to slick seaweed in wet weather. He was surprised rational thought was still possible when his world had turned on him like a horrible, sick joke.

He hoped Mum and Imogen had gone to bed.

'Asher, can't we talk?'

Her soft voice made him jump. It seemed Imogen had been sitting up in the window seat waiting for him.

'Nothing to say yet.' Taking care to keep his voice low made it come out in a rasp.

'Please just let me say one thing. I didn't know anything about your father's intentions. I wasn't going to have an affair with him. That's ridiculous. He started frightening me a bit just before you got there. And I left straight after you did.'

He knew the woman couldn't have disappeared. 'Where were you, then?'

She studied him for a moment. 'Down in there.' She pointed to the longest, lowest storage cupboard in the cabin, only about a foot from ground level. To his recollection, Mum and Dad had only ever kept long, skinny things like canoe oars and tent pegs in there. That was the sort of cupboard it was, for things they only needed occasionally and didn't want to keep crouching down to retrieve.

'What?' A rough laugh slipped out of him. All that time he'd been storming through the cabin, yelling at Dad and looking behind doors and beneath furniture. It was like the game of hide-and-seek from hell. 'Well, I lost. I'll bet he was laughing when I left.'

She shook her head. 'He wasn't.' Imogen's eyes were filling with tears. 'I made him give me a lift into Victor Harbor to stay the night at a motel. The next morning, I caught a Greyhound bus back to Adelaide. That was probably just before he went down to the rocks.'

'So you're saying it was my fault he was killed?' He drew a ragged breath.

'No, Asher. Not at all.' A pulse in her throat was racing. 'I just want to talk to you.' A tear streaked down her cheek.

'Well, you could've talked to me before. How about five years ago? You must've heard that he'd died. You must have guessed how guilty I've felt all those years, for tearing strips off him just before he went off and got himself killed. I spent so long wondering whether I might have got the whole thing completely wrong. You could've at least told me I'd been right, that he had been seeing someone.' He marched to the bedroom he'd always shared with Seth when they were children and closed the door behind him.

Imogen sank down by his closed door and rested her face in her hands. Although he hadn't slammed it as he'd slammed all the doors that other long-ago night, it felt as terrible. The click was soft, cold and final. She kept her rising sobs quiet, making her heart ache. If they were loud enough for him to hear and then he still didn't come out to talk, his hatred would be clear and she couldn't bear it.

Besides, she wanted to hear what he was doing, as that was the nearest she could get to him. Just hours ago, he had held her in his arms and spun her off her feet, igniting emotions she could never extinguish. As far as he was concerned, it seemed that might never have happened. The opening and closing of cupboards and general shuffling around his room soon gave way to silence.

Asher, please come out and talk to me.

It was like the hush following a holocaust. The world as she knew it had imploded in on her, just as she feared it would if anyone found out what she'd done. It was worse than she'd imagined because, on the surface, everything looked the same. The shabby old holiday furniture seemed to mock her with its homeliness, the tips of the trees still swayed outside in the wind, the wall clock still ticked, marking time, yet beneath the shell of all that, her heart was broken.

She'd been carrying around an emotional bomb that had just been detonated. Would Asher reach out in the wreckage? No, because it had blown up his heart too. All the invisible things that mattered were shattered, torn and bleeding. And it was all her fault.

Why should he ever talk to her again? If it wasn't for her, his mother would be totally healthy and his father would still be alive. She should've stayed and talked to Hayden—told him she understood and forgave him, as he'd clearly wanted her to. She couldn't forget the sadness in every line of his profile as he'd given in to her demand and driven her to Victor Harbor. He'd stopped talking and just looked at her, his eyes brimming with sorrow. And she'd just seized her duffle bag from the back seat, slammed his car door and watched him drive away. She'd been hurt, but was that a good enough excuse? She'd surely been the last person to see him alive.

Asher had a perfect right to resent her with all his heart. Because of her, his father was dead before they had a chance to talk and repair their relationship. If she'd stayed around to talk to Hayden at the crucial time, he wouldn't have climbed down the rocks, further than he was supposed to. If it wasn't for her, that talented man would still be alive, loving his family and doing all that he did best.

It was enough. Imogen scrambled to her feet. Although the bomb had left everything still standing, the shell was surely fragile. If she stuck around, Asher might lose what control he'd mustered and tell her exactly how he felt. Neither of them could bear that. She went to Marian's bedroom and quietly tapped the door.

It opened instantly. It seemed nobody could sleep that night.

'I think it'll be best if I go,' Imogen told her. 'Would you please drive me into Victor Harbor?' Her words were almost identical to those she'd spoken five years earlier to Hayden. Imogen steeled herself in case Marian reacted suddenly by doing something like slapping her face.

Marian just stood blinking at her. 'Running away never helps.'

'Well, you did the same thing earlier today. Ran away here, I mean.' Imogen flinched again. She'd meant her words to be appealing but instead, they might sound accusatory. *I'd better just shut up.* If Asher was still talking to her, he'd remark that she'd been around him for too long. Then she just wanted to cry.

Marian grasped Imogen's hand to pull her into the bedroom. 'You're right. I know I ran away too.'

How can she touch me, after what she found out tonight?

'I shouldn't have done it, but for me, it worked out well,' Marian went on. 'Not only was I saved from what I thought would be certain death on that slippery platform, but now I know neither you nor Asher did the things I thought you did. He didn't kill his father. And you were innocent of wanting to hurt me.'

Imogen felt her own shell beginning to crack. She dared a quick look at Marian.

'I've grown very fond of you. I couldn't bear it when I was talking to Ross Fletcher this afternoon and realised that girl with Hayden was you. But you didn't know what he was up to. I don't mind hearing about his lies as much as I would've hated thinking you were party to his deception. He didn't intend to hurt me. I know how his mind must have worked.'

The understanding that flowed from Marian's brown eyes was a welcome balm. They were like Seth's eyes. Asher was more like Hayden. That thought caused another chink in whatever was holding her together.

'Marian, I really don't want to be around here any more.' The aunt appellation would have to go.

Marian reached out and smoothed back a strand of Imogen's hair – a motherly gesture making Imogen think of the way her own mother treated the foster girls at home. Marian seemed as good as Mom at mothering girls who weren't hers.

'Let's have a talk,' Marian said, 'and work everything out.'

Chapter 22

Dawn had barely broken, and Asher was afraid Chris wasn't going to answer his door so early. While he considered turning away, he heard the sound of footsteps and humming from within. The old man stood on the threshold in his dressing gown and slippers.

'Hey Asher, come in.' Chris' wide, toothy smile turned to concern as he squinted at his face. 'What's the matter, son?'

'Sorry if I got you out of bed. I didn't consider the time. Selfish, I know.' Asher hadn't even been home. He'd crept out of the cabin while it was still dark, long before the others were up. Imogen would have to get a lift back home with Mum. He still didn't feel ready to talk to her.

'That's fine, it was almost time to get up and set the fire. No time is too early for you, anyway. Now, what's wrong?'

Where should he begin? 'Something that's really bothered me for years has just got worse.'

'You're not talking about a physical problem, are you?'

Asher wearily shook his head. 'Not this time.'

'Well, come into the kitchen. I'll set a fire, but can't offer you a slice of cheesecake yet.'

'That's all right. I'm not hungry, anyway.'

'Now, tell me all about it,' Chris said.

Asher wondered how much he should reveal. 'For years, I've been upset that a person who was close to me let me down. Now I've found out that it involved somebody else I thought I knew really well.' He had to run a hand across his stinging eyes. 'And it's stupid to care this much because neither of them were even giving me a thought while they were doing it.'

'I'm totally confused.' Chris was watching him with his head tilted to one side. 'I hope you don't mind explaining. You came here to talk, didn't you?'

Asher nodded. He'd barely opened his mouth since he'd found out about Imogen, with a deep dread that talking would, as usual, prove the wrong thing to do. He'd decided to bother Chris so early because he was the only person he felt he could safely unburden himself to.

'Okay, it's this. Imogen was going around having a … thing with my dad.' He hardly knew what to call it. After all, it wasn't an affair, despite his father's dubious intentions. Weird relationship, fling, liaison, fixation? 'I'd figured out that he was seeing someone. That was why I went to confront him—but I didn't know he was going to rush off and get himself drowned.' He squeezed his eyes shut until he was certain they were dry again. 'I thought he was cheating on Mum. I never saw the woman he was with but I hated her. And now she turns out to have been Imogen.'

Shock showed up differently on Chris' face to most people's. His eyes widened and turned slightly more luminous. He shaped his mouth into a matching 'O', and blew out a long breath. 'She must have a story of her own. I guess she's been through a terrible time.'

Asher suddenly wished he could have reacted as calmly. He'd thought clamming up was the best course of action, but his silence was filled with as much fury as his word explosions had ever been. He sank his face into his hands. *I don't even need to use words to stuff things up.*

'Let me tell you more. I'll start from the time I figured out what Dad was up to, when I was nineteen. And I'll tell you what Imogen told us tonight.' He peered out at the clear, early sunshine. 'Last night, I mean.'

At the end of his story, Chris rested a hand on Asher's shoulder. Seeing it coming, Asher steeled himself in anticipation of the weight, but it didn't hurt.

'To me, it sounds like the normal way a lonely girl, not all that long out of school, might have reacted to the attention of someone as charismatic as your father. She didn't love him in a romantic way. She just liked to think she had the approval of an older man she used to admire. Why were you so angry with Imogen once she told you how it was?'

'Well, it's just that she didn't see through his corny pick-up lines and tell him where to go. And because she didn't tell me any of this before. She let me tell her lots of stuff about me.' He sank back against his cushion. Perhaps Chris wouldn't understand. He couldn't describe why

Imogen's secrecy had cut him so deeply and why he felt betrayed by her holding back.

'Maybe she didn't tell you because she feels such a lot for you and knows you have enough on your plate without being upset by something from the past.'

'But that's just mad. If she'd told me before, like when she first came back here, I wouldn't have acted the way I'm acting now. I'm sure I wouldn't. She should've told us when she first came. She shouldn't have waited until I fell …'

He snapped his mouth shut and looked at Chris to see if he guessed what he'd been about to say. Chris was nodding as if he wasn't at all surprised by the thing Asher hadn't said. Yet Asher's heart was thumping hard, filling his ears with the torrential sound of his own amazement.

Mum's car was back beneath the carport. He steeled himself for a moment before going inside to face Imogen. When he turned the handle, it seemed someone had barricaded the front door. He had to push aside a heavy cardboard box to squeeze inside and saw two more piled near it.

'Asher, is that you?' Mum shuffled out of the kitchen. 'Thank God. You left the cabin so quietly this morning. Are you really angry with me?'

For a moment, he wondered what she was talking about. Then he remembered in a rush. He'd been so upset about Imogen's bombshell he'd relegated his mother's assumption to the back of his mind. 'Yeah, I am. You should've known that if I'd pushed Dad over the rocks, I would've owned up to it.'

'I'm sorry. I knew you wouldn't have killed your father on purpose. I thought it was an accident. It's just that he had your iPod. And when I woke you up for work that morning, I know you had it with you. I knew from the very fact that it had changed hands that you must have been with him. Yet when you were asked, you said you hadn't been near the cabin. I jumped to the wrong conclusion.'

'I didn't say anything because I didn't want you to find out why I'd been there.' The whole thing had been an even bigger mess than he'd thought for five years.

Looking behind her up the empty passage, she lowered her voice. 'Because he was seeing another woman?'

All Asher could do was nod.

'I'd suspected that already,' Marian said.

He nodded again. He knew that now. She'd said so at the cabin.

'I'm grateful to know that you cared so much about my feelings,' she went on, 'but when somebody you've been married to for twenty-five years turns strange on you, there's no way you can miss it. I had no idea you'd figured out what he was up to, too. You should've spoken to me.'

'But you know me. Whenever I spoke I'd say the wrong thing. Now it turns out that whenever I don't speak, that's the wrong thing too.' He felt exhausted.

She reached out to clasp his shoulder. 'Do you know you're so much like your father?'

He snapped his head up. He'd probably take that as an insult from anyone else, but from her, it might be meant as a compliment in spite of everything. 'What are you talking about? Both Seth and Becky are far more like him.'

She shook her head. 'Not as much as you. Can't you see, you always had his way of shining among people, of coming up with spontaneous things to say and being an individual?'

'But Dad couldn't understand me or relate to me.' His eyes were burning. 'You know that's true. I heard him tell people often enough.'

Marian heaved a deep sigh. 'I think that's the biggest proof that you were like him. When he said those things, he didn't realise it was because facing you was a bit like looking into a mirror. He couldn't understand or relate to himself.'

'Mum, it's too late to tell me this now.' Years ago, being compared to his father might have made him feel flattered and happy but not any more.

'I can understand why you were disillusioned with him but he was only human. I've had five years to come to terms with all this. His one big mistake doesn't negate all his wonderful qualities.'

'Where's Imogen?' Asher tried to sound casual, but the question caught in his throat.

'She didn't come home with me.'

'What?' He felt as if he was standing in an elevator that suddenly plummeted. Mum must've packed up and left, assuming that Imogen had returned with him, the same way she'd come. Leaving without telling anybody turned out to be the most callous thing he'd ever done. 'We have to go back for her.'

'She doesn't want to leave yet. She didn't feel like facing anybody, so I offered to let her stay on by herself at the cabin for as long as she needs to.'

'Oh.' He didn't know whether to be relieved or deflated. By 'anybody', Mum probably meant him. 'Well, what is she going to do?' Fear took its grip around his heart. He could tell by the jerky way it was beating. Since Dad's death, he hated to think of anybody brooding alone at that cabin, let alone Imogen.

'I don't know. She said she knows we need some time to process things too. But I'm sure she's not going to do anything silly.' It was as if Mum read his thoughts.

'Did she say when she's coming back?'

'Not yet. I'll be speaking to her tonight. I told her I'd like to touch base every evening.'

His heart seemed to be swelling against his ribs, making each breath ache. 'Shall I speak to her too?'

Marian shook her head. 'It might be best not to yet.'

Asher had missed his chance and wanted to kick himself. His mind had been filled with hurt and everything he had held back from saying. Now it was too late, he'd give anything to hear whatever she would have said to him. If he was to phone her mobile phone to ask, 'What did you want to tell me before?' she'd have every right to hang up on him.

But I had a right to be upset too, didn't I? Just because he found out he loved her didn't change how gutted he felt when he found out what she'd done, or more accurately, who she'd been.

He heard grunting from the passage. Becky came through backwards, lugging another heavy box behind her.

'Hey, what's in all those?' Asher didn't really care. Like old times, his mouth was shooting off just for the sake of it.

'They're full of magazines.' She paused to mop her forehead. 'Props for my play and there are three more. I'm taking them to the studio.'

'Do you need a hand?'

Placing her hands behind her hips, she arched her back. 'Are you well enough?'

'I feel fine.' He ignored the stab of annoyance her question elicited.

'Well, would you be happy to come to the studio and help me set up the stage? It'll just be putting things where I tell you to. I volunteered, but

I have no idea how I'm going to get it all done in time for tonight's dress rehearsal.'

It was the last thing he wanted to do, but he needed to do something while he was wondering what to do about Imogen. He'd have to either think about her or try not to and he couldn't decide which.

'I might as well. Are these boxes going out to your car?' When she nodded, he heaved one into his arms.

Mum gasped and Becky asked, 'How can you be doing that?'

'Huh? They're strong storage boxes. They're not going to break.'

'I meant with your shoulder.'

'Oh, yeah.' With all that had been churning around in his mind, he'd forgotten all about that. Now, he glanced down at his left arm. 'It seems to be okay.' If he hadn't had his mind full of Imogen, he might have found himself growing a little excited.

Imogen was the only customer in the outdoor area of the Granite Island kiosk. She'd walked the six kilometres along the beach from Port Elliot to Victor Harbor, wrapping her coat around her shoulders. She had been in Australia for long enough to begin thinking in kilometres instead of miles.

How different the South Australian seasons were, not only from what she'd been used to at home but from each other. She remembered being at that beach in scorching Christmas heat with Seth and the twins, watching sunscreen dissolve into her hot skin while the sun blazed down and the sky was a brighter blue than the sea. Today, the ocean was deep green and the sky a swirling grey. Black-edged clouds taunted her with the threat of rain for her walk back. Waves slammed into the rocks along the Causeway with a foamy smash, covering her with briny mist even at a distance, and making her throat ache as she thought of Uncle Hayden. The wind that drove the waves whipped the hair around her face and froze the tips of her ears.

Now she'd reached her destination, there was nothing to do but drink the hot chocolate she'd bought. It was in a cardboard cup with rippled sides to prevent scalds—not the sort which would warm her fingers when they wrapped around it. The clouds banked up heavier and darker as she leaned over the railing. She'd have to walk back through heavy rain. She had no other choice.

Something landed in her cup, making a ripple. It was not a raindrop but a tear. Was her time in Australia over?

I guess I've done what I came to do. Aunt Marian assured her that she now felt peaceful and even happy because she finally knew the truth about what happened that night.

What's more, Imogen had done something good. She never imagined she'd be able to help save Aunt Marian's life, but she had. Marian was convinced that her ordeal up on the platform in the storm would have ended in disaster if Imogen and Asher hadn't turned up. Was it God's way of allowing them to redeem themselves after their role in Aunt Marian's horrible accident?

Maybe he's letting me know there's been closure. Am I supposed to go home now that I've done what I came to do? Was she meant to feel relieved like Marian? If she was, she just felt wretched. How could she help it when Asher wouldn't talk to her?

She'd heard him creeping around the cabin before daybreak. Imogen hadn't been able to sleep. She'd been listening near her door, on high alert for any sound from him. At last she held her door slightly ajar, watching his dim outline while her heart pounded. When he'd finally emerged from his room, she hadn't dared obey the impulse to rush straight out to plead with him to listen. It was important not to push things. *If he wants to talk to me, he'll come and knock.*

She had thought of pretending to walk out to the kitchen for a glass of water and feigning surprise when she found him there. Then, at least he'd be forced to greet her, wouldn't he? But what if he snapped at her to go away? While Imogen was trying to make up her mind, Asher went outside and closed the front door behind him. She heard him start up his car.

She didn't care how she would look then. She raced outside with bare feet, waving her arms, but it was too late. She could only imagine whether or not he would have looked back through his rear vision mirror. Were his retreating tail lights the last she'd ever see of Asher?

It was like revisiting five years earlier, when she stood there with Hayden watching the back of Asher's car get further away. Now that she was in the cabin with Marian instead, was it a sign that her time with the Dorazio family had come full circle and it was time to leave?

Imogen threw the remainder of her drink in the bin. She couldn't take another gulp because it hurt going down. The signs were clear. It must be over.

Chapter 23

Asher had spent half an hour helping arrange the stage how Becky told him to. After a while, others began to enter the auditorium.

'Hey everyone, this is Asher, my twin.'

While he shook hands with her theatre friends, a frizzy mass of canary yellow hair caught his eye. It used to make his heart leap whenever he saw it, but this time his chest stayed calm, even though she was coming in his direction.

'Hi, Kaitlyn.' He resisted the urge to fiddle with his hands.

'Hey, Ash.' She was looking him up and down. 'Wow, you're looking pretty good.'

'Thanks. I'm feeling pretty good.' He'd dreamed of having this conversation with her, but now he wondered why his heart wasn't racing.

Her eyes widened. Had she increased the amount of blue eye-shadow she wore? No, he'd simply got used to having a new friend with sweet, nutmeg-coloured eyes who used very little make-up.

'Are you for real? I thought by now, you might be …'

'Closer to death,' he finished for her. 'That's okay. You'd be forgiven for thinking so.'

'Let's grab a drink after this rehearsal.'

'Maybe.' The prospect of talking about his health with Kaitlyn sounded like hard work.

She gestured to somebody at the foot of the stage. 'Hey, D-Man, come over here.' As Kaitlyn swung around, the hem of her full skirt swirled.

A tall man approached, with a heavy, black fringe and an aristocratic profile. He looked vaguely familiar.

'This is Darius, our stage manager.'

Asher stiffened. That guy. He made sure to give him a bone-crunching handshake.

'And this is Asher, my boyfriend.'

'Is that so?' Darius' grey eyes narrowed.

'Hold on, no, I'm not.' It slipped out before he could wonder if he sounded rude.

Her eyebrows drew together. 'Asher!' She shot him some sort of imploring look. Although he used to be clued up on her battery of expressions, he wasn't sure what she wanted him to do. He didn't want to be part of any game she was playing with this bloke.

'I used to be her boyfriend,' he corrected himself.

Darius' thin lips curved. 'You and many others, probably.'

Beneath her make-up, Kaitlyn turned chalky white. 'Darius, there's no need to be mean. Excuse us for a second.' She tugged Asher's wrist. 'Come here.'

He saw no reason to resist as she dragged him to an empty corner of the auditorium, where a door stood open, letting in a breeze.

'Why did you tell him that?' Kaitlyn stopped just short of stepping outside.

'Tell him what? That I'm not your boyfriend any more? It's true, isn't it?'

She rolled her eyes and pouted. 'You could have just gone along with me. It doesn't have to be true for always, anyway.'

'What do you mean? You broke up with me.'

'That wasn't necessarily a total break-up. Just a break.'

'It sounded like a total break-up. You stood there in my bedroom and told me you'd prayed long and hard and decided to stop seeing me. You said you felt certain God wanted you to. That he'd planned a different direction for your life.'

'Why do you have to take everything I say so literally?'

'Well, you sounded very convincing.'

Her curls rippled as she shook her head. 'You guys make things so complicated. You don't understand a woman's emotions. I needed to take a step back but it wasn't necessarily meant to be forever. I just couldn't cope with your cancer.'

'So it's only supposed to be a break-up if I get sicker? If I start improving, or if things don't work out with Darius, there's a chance it could be on again?'

'Asher, why are you being so mean?'

'I'm not being mean. I'm just figuring out where I stand.' He directed his mind away from the beautiful, pensive face of the girl who had been his staunchest ally for the last several weeks. 'What's gone wrong with Darius anyway?'

'Who told you about me and him? It was Becky, I suppose.'

'Does it matter? Was it supposed to be a secret?'

'Listen, I just needed to take a step back from my relationship with you to think. I was so upset for you, Asher. I needed to do something.'

'Well, dumping me and going out with someone else is a pretty weird way of showing you're upset for me.' His heart started to accelerate, but he was surprised by how calm he felt. It seemed his heartache level had already been filled to the top by Imogen.

Kaitlyn stood blinking at him. 'Okay, what do you want me to do to make things right again? Are you having a go at me? I just told him that you're my boyfriend. What more can I do?' Somehow, her clear face looked all wrong without the scattering of fine, dusty freckles he'd become used to seeing on somebody else.

He met her gaze. 'You haven't asked me what's been happening in my life.'

'What are you talking about?'

'It doesn't matter.'

A shadow flitted across her face. 'Come on, Asher, tell me. What could possibly have been happening? You've been staying home, sick with cancer.'

'That doesn't mean the world stands still.'

'Well, I have a life too. If you think yours has been full, you wouldn't believe how horrendous mine has been. Just because you've been sick, you're not the only one who's been suffering. I went out with Darius because I needed some personal attention from someone whose life didn't revolve around medicine and treatments and feeling sick. That's not a crime. My tank felt empty. Instead of criticising me, you should try to understand me and build me up.'

'I do understand.' He felt quite strange, as if she were part of his past he'd grown out of. She even looked like some kind of kids' storybook

187

character, in her billowing pink skirt and bright make-up.

'Hello.' Somebody was standing on the threshold just behind them. Asher turned to see a delivery man holding a huge flower arrangement.

'I'm glad there are people here now. The place was empty when I tried to drop this off about an hour ago.'

As Asher was closest, he took the heavy load, noticing again how strong his left shoulder felt.

'Thanks.' Kaitlyn reached to take them.

He looked at the tag. 'Hold on, they aren't for you.' As he pulled them back, a couple of yellow roses bobbed beneath his nose.

She shot him an incredulous squint. 'Huh? But they're normally for me. I mean …'

She didn't finish but he guessed what she'd been going to say. She had the starring role in the play.

Shaking his head, he raised his voice to catch his sister's attention on stage. 'Hey, Becky, flowers for you.'

Her look of curiosity when she saw him standing close to Kaitlyn changed to bewilderment. He relished Becky's expression of dawning joy as she leaped off the stage and hurried over to them. He'd seen similar pleasure several times on Kaitlyn's face over the months he'd known her, but never on Becky's.

'I really am okay. I'm just having a break.' Imogen was talking to Jodie, who'd called to find out why she was spending time alone at the cabin. Imogen had to tread carefully, trying to figure out what, if anything, Marian had told Jodie, Seth and Becky about her absence. It seemed to be nothing at all. She wondered whether to even mention Asher's name. Even though he filled every corner of her mind, she didn't want that fact to be obvious. 'How are you going?'

Jodie's growl came across the line. 'Okay, apart from the fact that Becky thinks Asher might be trying to warm things up with Kaitlyn.'

'Is he?' How could she expect to sound offhand while her throat was swelling tight and her stomach churning?

'Yeah, he went to help Becky set up for a dress rehearsal and Kaitlyn zoomed over to him the moment she saw him.'

'But … she'd left him.' Imogen hoped any strangeness in her voice could be attributed to a bad phone line. At least faking nonchalance would have to be easier over the phone than in person.

'Yeah, of course she did. You were right in the house when she did it. We all know she left him to start chasing that Darius guy. You should hear the stories Becky was telling us. Kaitlyn threw herself at Darius, kissing and cuddling him every chance she could. But now he's brushed her off and started going around with another girl.'

'Is she somebody else in their theatre group?'

'Yes, a make-up artist. I wonder how Kaitlyn felt about that, being the leading lady.'

Imogen didn't have the heart to join in Jodie's chuckle.

Jodie turned sober again. 'Now that Darius has turned out to be such a philanderer, I'm relieved Becky didn't go out with him after all. She was interested in him. But I hope Asher's not going to be silly enough to fall for Kaitlyn's feminine wiles again, after the way she treated him. Becky said she wished she hadn't asked him to go along to the studio with her.'

So do I. Yet Imogen suspected his reunion with Kaitlyn was bound to happen anyway.

'She's sure Kaitlyn decided to chat Asher up on the spur of the moment to annoy Darius. But Asher seemed to be swallowing whatever line she was feeding him.'

Imogen needed to clear her aching throat but Jodie seemed to be waiting for a response.

'Time will tell, I suppose.'

'What is it about men and their intelligence?' Jodie asked. 'How can someone smart enough to earn Asher's salary not understand a woman like Kaitlyn?'

'Maybe he doesn't want to understand her. What does Seth think?' Hopefully Jodie's answer would be lengthy enough to give her time to compose herself.

'He doesn't like the way she's been twisting Christianity to suit herself. It's making Becky even more cynical than before, and that makes Seth so sad.'

'How does he mean?'

'Well, Kaitlyn first told Asher she was breaking up with him because God told her to. And now that she wants to make Darius jealous, or whatever selfish reason she has, it seems he's conveniently told her that it's okay to start seeing Asher again. She's dragging up God's name to suit her plans. I don't understand how Asher can just go along with her. Becky said they were standing near the door, talking for quite a long time. If I were him, I wouldn't give her the time of day.' Jodie heaved a deep sigh. 'I wish Becky had never introduced him to her in the first place.'

So do I. She left him. She doesn't deserve him. I'm sure she doesn't even understand him properly. 'But it was Asher's plan all along to get back together with Kaitlyn.' A sick weight sank low in Imogen's stomach, settling in the pit. It was true. His motive for getting well had always been to win Kaitlyn back. He'd been open about that with Imogen, and never led her to believe anything different. He'd never treated her like anything other than a good friend. Imogen had been the one foolish enough to fall in love with him anyway.

'But I don't think he really knows her,' Jodie said. 'He only knows the part of her that she wants him to know. Seth and I are really worried about him. Becky's sure Kaitlyn still has a thing for Darius. She could easily hurt Asher again and it's so important for him not to get too badly upset while he's fighting cancer and having chemotherapy. If she sets him back again, I'll kill her.'

Imogen heard a brisk tapping sound come over the phone line. She could easily imagine Jodie taking angry strides across her polished floorboards. Imogen's heartbeats were hard and sore. *Jodie, you should kill me, too.* Nobody had hurt Asher the way she had. Her onset of shivering had nothing to do with the biting cold, although she was huddled near the window in a thin blanket that smelled musty like the interior of the cabin. The only heating was a slow combustion stove and there was no wood to set it.

'Whoops. Bubby just gave me the strongest kick ever.' Jodie let out a laugh.

'So you haven't had any more trouble?'

'No, and I'd say by the way he's squirming, he must be very healthy.'

'I'm really going to miss not being around to see him grow up.'

'What? You're not going home to America yet, are you?'

Imogen's teeth began chattering. 'You know I have to go home eventually.'

'But I thought you were going to stay for longer. At least until I've had my baby.'

'I would've liked to have stayed for longer, but something's changed.

I need to go home.' Tears were dripping down her face and onto her jacket. She'd have to find a way to tell Jodie her departure date would be soon. If she hung around and went back to Marian's house, Asher wouldn't be able to bear looking at her. He might leave the room whenever she entered, and her heart would be broken. Of course, the others would notice and want to know why. Then when they found out, instead of urging her to stay for longer, Jodie would be demanding that she return to America.

The whole sordid story would come out, and finding out the truth about their beloved father would grieve Seth and Becky. She had to fly home for everyone's good.

What would Jodie think if she knew she was talking to the one person who'd just broken Asher's heart more than anyone? Imogen would never forget the look on his face—the hurt in his wonderful green eyes. She'd always remember that one last look of intense disappointment he'd cast her. Writing to him to explain how she felt about him was the last thing she should do. He'd never been interested in her. Not that way.

God, please don't let me set him back on his healing path. If being with Kaitlyn would boost him and give him the happiness he needed to get over what she'd done, she'd have to force herself to wish them all the best. Imogen buried her face in the crook of her elbow so Jodie wouldn't hear her muffled cries, and ended the call before she completely broke down.

Asher leaned across to pull open the doctor's surgery door for an elderly lady with a walking frame.

'Thank you.' She gave him a gummy smile.

'Thank you,' he responded. That must have sounded weird to anyone who didn't know his story. Such a short time ago, the mere thought of opening a heavy door with his left arm would have made him wince, but now it was easy. He clenched and reclenched his fist over and over, just to prove that no residual pain would shoot to his shoulder.

I've been healed. The more he repeated that to himself, the more the wonder of it burst over him. His next chemotherapy session was looming up. That was what convinced him to consult a doctor. There was no way he wanted to go through that ordeal if he didn't have to. To subject himself to a body-battering while he felt fit and healthy would surely be even dumber than going to the doctor claiming that he felt healed.

He didn't look too bad, with a cap jammed over what was left of his hair. This visit was to a different surgery, one that didn't know him and that didn't have any bad memories. That might have been dumb but he had to face the fact that he was a moron anyway. The way he'd treated Imogen was crazy and stupid. Every time he thought about it, he wanted to bury his face in his palms and never look up again.

He'd thought that pulling back from her and refusing to talk had been the right thing to do, that he'd come across as restrained. It turned out he'd been just as hostile and horrible as he would have been if he'd blasted strips off her with his tongue and maybe even worse. The message had been the same—rejection and pain. *Idiot.*

He'd just ruined things with the very best friend he'd ever had. The more he thought about it, the clearer it was that he'd had no right to be angry with her at all, because she'd done nothing wrong. It was his dad who'd been the one stringing her along, treating her as special, while hiding the fact that he was still married. Dad had been the one giving Imogen the time and affection she deserved. He'd been captured by her beauty and deep sweetness. Asher understood how it must have been because he was captivated too, but it was too late for him to make amends. Imogen deserved an official apology on Dad's behalf, not cold-shoulder treatment and shame.

He was foolish all through for not figuring out how he felt about her until it was too late. Seeing Kaitlyn again reinforced his feelings for Imogen. He wanted to hear her voice, see her warm smile and the way she tilted her head before saying something droll, intended to make him laugh. Most of all, he wanted to tell her, 'My shoulder feels really strong. Come here and I'll prove it.' Then, he wanted to lift her off her feet and spin her around again, just as he'd done in the storm at the bottom of the ladder. But he'd forfeited the right to do anything like that again because of his own stupidity.

His phone began to ring, and he twisted his right arm to pull it out of his back pocket. For so long he'd been nursing his left arm and playing it safe, he kept forgetting he could use it again like any normal limb.

'Hey, Ash. Seth here.'

'G'day, bro.' He waited for the point of the call. There was a tentative note in Seth's voice, as if he had something he wanted to launch into. He was probably still treading lightly after his last attempt.

'Jodie and I are wondering if you'd like to come and join us for dinner tonight.'

'What's the occasion?' Asher wondered why he was still feeling wary.

'I don't need an ulterior motive to see my brother, do I?'

Something certainly seemed fishy. Seth was the one who mentioned ulterior motives. Asher hadn't put the words in his mouth. 'I guess not. Okay, I'll come around six then.'

'Great.'

'Great,' Asher echoed.

'Hey, Ash, can you please come on your own, though?'

Huh? 'Well… yeah, why would I bring anyone else to your place?'

'We just thought you might be inclined to bring … a partner, but we have a few things to talk to you about first.'

It dawned on him what this was all about. Becky must have been in Jodie's ear. 'So Kaitlyn can't come?' He felt like stringing Seth along a bit.

'Not this time, mate. She wouldn't be interested in what we have to talk to you about.'

I'll bet she wouldn't. 'I was thinking she and I might like to help with the meal because Jodie should still be resting at the moment.' He grinned, wondering if he was pushing it too far, because they all knew Kaitlyn wasn't the sort to offer help. She never noticed things that needed doing. That was just Kaitlyn.

'We'd honestly find it more helpful without her. Besides, I'm taking Jodie for a few days of rest to the cabin next week.'

'Imogen's still down there at the moment.'

'I know, but probably not for much longer. Imogen told Jodie she's thinking of flying back home to America.'

'What?' All Asher's muscles suddenly clamped tight. 'When?' His eardrums pounded so loud, he could barely hear Seth's voice over the line.

'Pretty soon, by the sound of it. Jodie doesn't know what's come over her. A sudden bout of homesickness or something.'

'I know what's come over her. She can't go.'

'What are you talking about?'

'I don't want her to go.'

'You don't want Imogen to go?'

'No! If she goes home, it'll be all my fault.' He wanted Seth to be his big brother again and advise him what to do, but he couldn't possibly

193

tell him the whole twisted tale over the phone while he sat in the doctor's waiting room. Imogen might not want him to, anyway. If only he had some reliable gauge warning him when he should speak up and when he should shut up.

'I don't know what this is all about, but I know you and Imogen are good friends. If you don't want her to go, you'll have to tell her you want her to stay.'

'I wouldn't know what to say.'

'Of course you would. Talking has always been one of your strengths.'

Asher managed a gruff laugh. 'That's not what you used to call it.'

A youngish doctor poked his head out of one of the consulting rooms and called, 'Asher Doratso.' It was such a straightforward surname but people so often got it wrong.

'I've got to go.'

He wished he wasn't there now. It would have to be a very quick doctor's visit, because all he longed to do was find Imogen and speak to her.

Chapter 24

Asher spotted her straight away, standing near the water's edge at Horseshoe Bay, wearing the same coat she'd worn the night they'd driven down in the storm. It whipped around in the wind, blending with her beautiful flowing hair. Imogen tugged the coat closer around her and hunched her shoulders to face the wind. The sadness in her pose made him long to rush down and wrap his arms around her, but for some reason, he hesitated. Was it because she looked so much like an exquisite seabird, he was afraid she might fly away?

She sat on the sand, curling herself up in a ball and facing the sunset. He could see her profile as she rested her chin on her hands. She was gorgeous.

If only it were possible for Dad to come and sit on the foreshore beside him. They had a lot to talk about. Never had Asher communicated properly with his father. He'd moved from one ineffectual extreme to another without exploring the middle ground. Now it was too late.

As a child he would chatter a stream of whatever was in his head without processing it. Hayden used to indulge him for a while, then shush him long before he felt he'd finished whatever he'd wanted to say. During his teenage years, he used to clam up and hardly say anything to his dad in case it was the wrong thing. Those years of censoring himself had ended with that great eruption on his father's last night alive.

Now was the time he could've spoken up with more confidence. If Dad could sit beside him, what would he say? *I really love Imogen, but now I've ruined everything. Why would she want to see me again after I was so mean to her? Is there anything you think I could do to fix things up with her?* He would have liked to have had proper talks with his father, as he knew Seth often had.

The other day, Chris had asked him, 'Have you ever forgiven your father?'

Asher attempted to say yes, but the word caught in his throat. *Have I?* He'd admitted that he loved and missed Dad, but had he forgiven him? It was not only the hurtful spoken words between them. Had he forgiven his father for the reason he'd worn his tyres to shreds to confront him at the holiday cabin? The thing Dad had done was far worse than anything he'd ever upbraided Asher, Becky or Seth for. Had he forgiven Dad for his hypocrisy? Had he forgiven him for the thing that was so horrible that Seth had refused to believe him? Had he forgiven Dad for loading a ton of guilt on his shoulders by going off and getting himself killed?

'I've been working on it for years. I want to forgive him. I know I need to forgive him.' Then other things filtered into Asher's memory, like the way Dad would rock Mum in his arms and hum her favourite songs to distract her from the pain, while his own eyes pooled with grief. And the times he'd bring them all impromptu gifts and keep his eyes fixed on their faces to gauge their reactions. Then, of course, he'd never forget how Dad's eyes had glowed with pride when he told him about the scholarship to work at Lewis and Thorne. He let out a deep sigh. 'Yes, I want to forgive him. I do forgive him.' He couldn't hold onto it any more. The breath he drew seemed to fill his lung cavity deeper, as if pressure he didn't realise he carried had been lifted.

Although he couldn't talk to Dad now, he remembered what Chris had said. 'Imogen is a beautiful girl, inside and out. Your father took a chance with her that he shouldn't have, but with you, it's a totally different case.'

Lurking on the grassy foreshore, spying on her, was wasting time. He should just go down there. What would she do if he took the chance to intrude on her time alone? Maybe she was thinking about forgiving him. He wouldn't want to interrupt that train of thought, and cause her to change her mind. On the other hand, if rushing to her would distract her from plans to return to America, he'd do it. He'd plead, kneel in the sand and cling to her hands, if it would make her reconsider and stay.

But how can I ask her not to go home when I know I must be the reason she wants to? He might have been wiser to ask Seth and Jodie to come and plead with her. Sure, she'd told him she wanted to talk, but a few days of reflection could have changed everything.

He was up on his feet. If she rebuked him for the way he'd treated her, it was no more than he deserved, and he needed to take it like a man. But what if the sight of him hurt her, after the way he'd behaved? That was the last thing he wanted to do.

He walked back toward his car instead. *This is crazy, now that I've come all this way to see her.* He pulled his mobile phone out of his pocket. Even though it seemed a cowardly option, she might prefer him to contact her that way. He wasn't normally so insecure, but Imogen wasn't like any other girl. And if she didn't want to see him, he ought to respect her wishes and honour that. After busily writing, the beep and tick on the phone's screen told him his text message had been sent. His heart was thumping fast, as if pressing his thumb was the same as running a marathon.

She didn't hear it. She made no move to extract her phone from her pocket or from the fabric bag on the sand beside her. Maybe she didn't have it with her. He shook his head with a groan. So much for that good idea. There was only one thing he could think of to do. His hand shook as he twisted the key to start the ignition. The cabin wasn't all that far away, and at least he was certain she would be returning there.

Imogen thought she heard the tune of her cell phone from deep in her bag but it might have been her imagination. It was probably only her mother, asking more about her plans to return home. She didn't want to pull her eyes away from the glorious South Australian sunset for that. It would keep until she returned to the cabin.

Maybe it would be different if she was looking forward to going home, but she didn't relish the lonely trip and all the arrangements ahead of her. She especially didn't know how to say goodbye to the Dorazio family.

The sun soon set, making her shiver in the winter darkness. Standing up and slinging the strap of her bag over her shoulder, she tightened her fingers around the key in her pocket and headed back toward the cabin.

There was a white piece of notepaper poking out beneath the door. Stooping, her heart skipped a beat when she discerned the shape of the handwriting in the moonlight. She groped for the inside light while her breath caught in her throat.

Dear Imogen,

Her windswept hair fell across the paper and her fingers tangled around it in her haste to flick it back.

Is it too late for us to talk? I won't bother you if you'd rather not. I'll come past the cabin at about 8.30. If you don't mind seeing me, leave a light up in the window of the loft. If you'd prefer I just go, leave it dark and I'll drive on.

Love, Asher

PS I'm really sorry.

She could hardly breathe. Eight-thirty? How long had she lingered on the beach? She rushed into the kitchen, chewing her nails, to look at the clock. Five past eight.

She whipped her cell phone out of her bag. What if that message on the beach hadn't been from her mother?

Hey, do you still want to talk? If you do, I'm right behind you.

With a gasp, she instinctively spun around. *Stupid, stupid me! He meant an hour ago, not now. He was near me on the beach. I should've read it!*

Well, she wasn't going to make any more silly mistakes.

What did he mean by '*Love* Asher'? Didn't he usually sign his letters with a more casual 'Cheers'?

Asher stared when he cruised along the pebbly driveway toward the cabin. The loft window was clearly visible. Not only was the interior light on, but several tiny tongues of flame flickered on the window ledge. It must be her sign that she did have words to say to him, and he hoped a display that looked like Christmas lights suggested that they might be friendly words.

With a thumping heart, he leaped the few steps to the front door and knocked. The sound of her quick footsteps from within made him giddy. There she stood, with the shy smile he now knew how much he loved. For a chronic talker, all his dry mouth would allow him to say was, 'Hi.'

'Hi.' Her smile widened.

'What you've done up there in the window … that's like … Wow.' It wasn't just his mouth in trouble. His brain was failing him too.

'You saw them?'

'Yeah, what are they?'

She turned around and beckoned. 'Come and see.'

He followed her up the short flight of steps to the loft. When he saw the chunky wax squares in the window, memories swept over him. 'Hey, we made those candles, didn't we? With milk carton moulds.'

Imogen nodded, eyes sparkling. 'They were one of the activities your mother brought along for us to do over the holidays here. The three of us spent a whole day making them.'

Asher stepped closer to the window to look down into the flickering flames. 'Didn't Seth tell us the weather forecast predicted blackouts right across the coast?'

'Yes, that's what inspired us to get to work, and later he said he was just joking. We sat there in the kitchen eating our tea and feeling let down because the power was still on.'

'That smart alec Seth thought he was so clever for tricking us.'

'And Becky got cross because she was proud of herself for making the most candles, and then it all came to nothing.'

'So, do you remember much about those days?' he asked. So far they were putting out feelers, re-establishing friendly footing.

Imogen nodded again. 'I've been thinking about them for weeks. I have loads of memories I'd change if I could. Like how we used to run away when we saw you coming with your chemistry set and didn't want you to show us any science experiments.'

'Hey, that old chemistry set might be up here somewhere.' Several of the toys and games they'd outgrown had been cleared out of the house and relegated to the cupboard in the cabin loft. Sure enough, after a quick search, he laid his hands on the box. 'Would you like to see some now?' He was still stalling for time, hoping the perfect move would dawn on him suddenly.

She grinned. 'Sure.'

Asher hadn't expected to sit, face to face, on the loft floor, with the chemistry set between him and Imogen while flames cast flickering shadows. Feeling a bit like an alchemist in a fantasy novel, he ran his fingers over everything in the box. Many substances in the plastic tubs had long since dried up, but he was able to show her a few tricks with the prank deck of cards.

'So you see it's all based on things not being as they seem.'

199

'That's awesome, Asher.' Her eyelashes cast the most wonderful, dancing shadows over her face.

'Please don't go home to America.'

Now, she raised her eyes to stare at him.

'That's what I came here to say tonight. Seth told me you're going home, and I know it's my fault. I had no right to treat you so badly these last few days. Coming down here to tell you this has made me petrified, but there you have it. And I can't think of one more thing to say except, "Please don't go."'

'I'm sorry,' she breathed.

Asher felt his heart sink. His worst case scenario was coming true. He had to hold himself together and be a man, but how he would miss her. 'That's okay. I just wanted to tell you.' He aimlessly began shuffling cards. 'I wish all the best for you back over there ... hope you have a fantastic life. You deserve it. I wouldn't have got through all this without you. You stood in the gap and prayed for me. You never gave up. You've helped save my life.' His vocal chords were constricting. 'But I'm not trying to blackmail you, to make you stay.'

'Hold on.' Her lips parted and those gorgeous lashes flickered again. 'What do you think I'm saying sorry for?'

Hope stirred. 'Not because you're going anyway, whether or not I want you to?'

'No. I meant that I'm sorry to think you felt petrified, and for letting you keep talking without butting in sooner. I wanted to soak in your words.' She lowered her eyes. 'And when I remembered how mean I used to be about the chemistry set ... and other things, I promised myself to never say, "Keep quiet, Asher," again.'

He felt hope rise in his heart. 'That's a promise you might regret making.'

A vein in her throat was racing hard. 'If I stay, will things change or be the same as before?'

She looked so anxious, he had to tread carefully. 'Which would you prefer?'

'What's happening with Kaitlyn?' she asked softly.

Shuffling the cards again, he heaved a sigh. 'Nothing. I saw her a few days ago at the studio. That was enough to show me. It's all over, Imogen. I can't stir it up again. I found out I don't want to.'

'Are you sure?' Her light brown eyes were fixed on him. 'Becky and Jodie were certain that you wanted to start seeing her again.'

'Have they been bashing your ear with that nonsense too?' If he'd realised the silly assumption had spread further than just Seth, he would have been even more nervous about approaching Imogen.

'Well, Becky said she saw you trying to chat her up in the studio.' Looking at his face, Imogen gave a wan smile. His expression must have been gobsmacked.

'That takes jumping to conclusions to a whole new level. I only spoke to Kaitlyn for a few minutes. And she didn't like what I had to say. Is that crazy Becky trying to ruin my life or something? Since when does passing the time of day with someone mean you're making a move on them?'

He couldn't keep his eyes off her. 'Imogen, I need to tell you something.' He had to rely on his words now. He felt them welling up and they were all he had to make her understand. 'Things have changed for me since you came. I was wondering whether I fell out of love with Kaitlyn, but it's not that. I've just realised my feelings for her aren't what I always thought they were. When I saw her the other day, I knew I still felt affection for her. I always liked that pretty, loud-mouthed personality of hers. But I was wrong when I thought it was love. I've learned the difference.'

He watched her mouth fall open and hurried on, 'Everything about you gets to me. Your smartness. Your stubborn way of pressing in to your faith and refusing to let go. Your sweet face, your cute freckles, the way you tease me when I'm off guard, challenging me to think of a quick response.' He drew a deep breath. 'Your brave heart, your loyalty ... well, the whole package has caught my heart completely. You enthuse me and excite me and stimulate me. I reckon you complete me, because when you weren't around these last few days, I felt as if something vital had been ripped out.'

A tear streaked down her face. He couldn't tell whether he'd pleased or upset her. That was part of the mystery about girls in general and Imogen in particular.

'I can't believe you're here, saying these things to me. I'm glad you are ... because it helps me to know what to tell you. I had no idea before, but now I do.' She was trembling.

'Go on, then.'

'My story is pretty similar. I did love your dad. I loved him since I was a little girl. But definitely not that way. I don't know what I would've done here that night if you hadn't come. I'm so glad you came. You might have saved me.' She glanced over to the candles. 'I didn't understand real love, either. I just knew that wasn't it.' She cleared her throat. 'But now I know what it's like.'

'Come here, then?' He shoved the chemistry set aside and held his arms open. She moved straight into them.

Pulling her close, he kissed her hair. Having done it once, he found it hard to stop. He'd never touched her before, and now it wasn't enough to do it with just his hands. He had to experience the soft warmth of her hair and cheeks with his lips too. Another tear slid down her cheek, and he gently rubbed it away with his thumb. Then he pressed his lips where it had been.

'Imogen, don't be sad any more. I've found out what I want to do with my life. For every tear you've shed over me and my family, I want to give you a reason to smile.'

Her smile was instant and wobbly. 'That was a happy tear.' She buried her face into his shirt with a sound that seemed to fit somewhere between a laugh and a snuffle.

'Are those ones happy too?'

He felt her nod.

'Then keep 'em coming. Hopefully, you'll soon be ecstatic.'

She nodded even harder. 'You don't know how easy it is to make me happy.'

'Do you mean me personally, or was that a general statement?'

She raised her face to look up at him. 'What do you think?'

The first thing he did was cup her face between his palms and next he had to kiss all those freckles he'd admired. He kissed her temple, her cheek, her chin, and then leaned back to look at her. 'Hey, there's something I've often wondered. Are you supposed to ask a girl if you can kiss her properly, or do you just lean in and hope she'll get the message?'

Imogen's laugh was music to his ears. 'Give it a try and see what'll happen.' She wriggled onto her knees, wrapped her hands around his neck and pulled his face back down to hers. Every nerve impulse was electric but he was too busy kissing her to ask if it was the same for her. The way her arms tightened around him was a good sign.

At last they drew apart.

'I'm going to have to break that promise to myself.' Imogen's eyes were sparkling. 'I said I'd never say, "Be quiet, Asher," again, but I might have to.'

'Why's that?' He kept hold of her hands.

'Because you can't kiss and talk at the same time.'

He felt a laugh bubble up. 'Shall I shut up again now then?'

She grabbed his hand and pressed a kiss in the palm. 'Only for a moment. You've got to do both. Kiss me. Then keep talking to me. Then kiss me again.'

Chapter 25

'Look at this.' Asher had driven off for ten minutes and returned with a large plastic bag full of firewood from the service station. He lifted it high above his head with one arm. Imogen didn't comprehend the significance of his gesture until she saw the expectant smile on his face. When it dawned on her, she could hardly draw a breath.

'Hey, are you holding that up with your left arm?'

Smiling wider, he nodded. 'It feels just like the right side—as if it never even got hurt. I don't remember it ever being this good even before I got sick.'

'When did it stop hurting?'

He pondered. 'I'm sure it was ever since we helped my mum down from the platform.'

'Wow! That's a few days.'

His quick smile made her heart flip. 'That's what I love about you. Others might say, "It's only been a few days, so don't get your hopes up," but you say, "It's a few days. That's awesome."' He knelt down to set the fire. 'I've missed having you around.'

Imogen settled on the floor to watch him work. She'd never tire of hearing him say that.

When Asher had a fire blazing in the stove, they settled on the couch. He rubbed his thumb across the back of her hand in a way that made joy swoop through her all over again. When he raised it to his lips, her insides flared hot along with the fire. How the atmosphere of the cabin had changed so dramatically with one visitor. All traces of coldness and misery had fled.

She spread her other hand close to the stove to feel the radiant heat.

'I've dreamed of this for so long.'

'Do you mean having a fire or having me?'

'Which do you think?'

'Well, I'm curious. I thought there was a chance you might tell me where to go. You've no idea how nervous I was to drive here to find you. So how long have you felt anything for me?'

'Maybe it started when you had your first chemotherapy session and you were so brave that night when you got sick.'

'Bzzzt.' He made the computerised sound of an "error" response. 'Nope, that's the wrong answer.'

Imogen felt a laugh rising. 'But they're my feelings. How can you tell me it's wrong?'

'Because it was pathetic, sad and not at all manly. Try again.'

She could drown in the saucy sheen of his green eyes. 'Maybe it was seeing you struggle with tears that first day we visited Chris, when you told him about your sickness.'

Asher buried his face in his palm and groaned. 'Imogen, you're no good at this.'

'Why don't you tell me when I first fell in love with you, then?'

'Challenge accepted. It was a couple of months ago, when you first stepped into our house with all your luggage. You took one look at me and thought, "What a stunning specimen of a bronzed Aussie. I wish we had blokes like him at home."'

Turning her giggle into a cough, she tried to match his matter-of-fact tone. 'Thanks for letting me know.'

'Actually, it was way before then. It was when we were kids and I used to amaze you with my sports prowess, my super knowledge and how fast I could run.'

Suddenly she had to turn away before he saw her tears. 'I wish it was then.'

It was too late.

'Hey, I'm sorry.' He pulled her into his arms. 'I was just being silly. You know me. It doesn't matter what the catalyst was, as long as you love me.'

She cleared her throat. 'I was just thinking about the sad history we have together. First your mum's accident, then your dad's.'

Asher smoothed back her hair. 'That history's over. Things have changed. I've been grappling with those memories too, and there's one thing I've come to accept.' He paused to make sure he had her attention. 'We've both spent too long blaming ourselves because neither of those times were our fault. Neither of us had any intention to hurt either one of them. Have you got that too?'

She nodded.

He brushed a kiss against her cheek. 'I think figuring that out helped me fight this cancer. And I'm sorry for the way I acted. You can talk to me about them… about him, any time you like.'

She had to tell him something important. 'Asher, I'm sure your dad really loved you. Back when I was seeing him, he told me he was proud of you.'

He rested his chin on the top of her head and she felt him swallow hard. 'I ended up doing the same thing I always scoffed at Seth and Becky for. I spent years trying to impress him. At least they were doing it openly. I was doing it in some woeful, twisted, unconscious way, according to Chris.'

She rested her head on his shoulder, trusting that it wouldn't hurt him at all now. 'Hey, stop being so hard on yourself. There's no shame in being a clever computer software engineer.'

'Huh? Are you talking about me?'

'Are you going to make me argue? Just accept compliments as true.'

His affectionate gaze lingered over her. 'You know, I suffered in those few days without you.'

She felt her pulse racing. 'I didn't do much.'

'Hey, you can take your own advice and accept a compliment.'

She admitted, 'I honestly felt like a jinx, especially where your family is concerned. It was a terrible feeling, and I didn't know what I could do.'

He shook his head. 'I can't think of anyone less jinx-like than you. I think of you as the angel God sent me, the most precious blessing and I can't believe I was about to lose you. I could never have got through these last several weeks if not for you. You're the best thing that's ever happened to me.'

She felt her face crumple again. 'Sorry, I've never been so happy but wanted to cry so much at the same time.' Tucking her arm through his, she squeezed his hand. 'I don't know if either one of us knows how to accept compliments. Maybe we both need the practice.'

'Well, prepare yourself for a lot of practice then, because you'll be a pro in no time. Giving you compliments and spoiling you will be the easiest thing in the world for me.'

She turned her head slightly to press her lips against the side of his neck. 'I've seen your thank you notes. I'll be looking forward to some pretty creative compliments.'

Dear Asher/Me/Self/Yours Truly or whatever,

I was surprised I hadn't thought to write a thank you note to myself, I mean to you, before. Imogen challenged me to do this so here goes.

Thanks for being such an idiot and going completely bonkers for a few days. I really mean it. Because now I believe that Imogen really must love me in spite of it all. There can't be any other explanation for her being willing to see me, let alone lighting all those candles. She's the most ravishing, awesome, beautiful and loving person I've ever known. She had the opportunity to tell me where to go and didn't take it. And now her face keeps lighting up whenever I walk into a room where she is. I keep feeling like going out again just so I can come back. You must be an okay bloke, if she feels this way. Keep doing your best to make her happy, mate, because you know she deserves it.

You know who it's from.

Dear Me Again,

Imogen found that last letter and read it. She says I copped out and she wants me to write another thank you note to myself because, according to her, I didn't mention enough good things about myself. I don't think I'm really good at that sort of thing. Although it all sounds wonderful coming from her, it sounds pretty bad coming from me but I'll give it a go.

Come on, just go for the obvious things first. Gorgeous green eyes, heartbreaking smile, generous heart, wonderful courage, quick wits, intelligence, determination.

Hey, this letter has been sabotaged. I didn't write all that. Oh well, if this is the sort of sabotage I can expect, I have nothing to complain about. Now she reckons she could fill a book the size of Shakespeare's plays with my good points, but I don't think I'm totally convinced. I'll have to ask her to convince me more.

Cheers, Ash

Dear Asher's Thank You Notes,

Thanks so much for the wonderful things you've helped achieve in both of us. You made us smile, helped lighten the mood during those dark times when he was so sick, but you've been so much more. You've helped him to find his voice and realise what a funny, remarkable person he is. And you helped me fall in love with him. Let me rephrase that. You helped me realise I love him, because when I think about it, he was right—I did start to fall in love with him the moment I first stepped into his house. Even Chris loves the thank you notes he's seen, and says he'd like to show others who might benefit from writing them too. Before Asher panics, I'll assure him that we won't show all of them, just the ones he wouldn't mind people seeing.

Keep coming because I look forward to you,
Love, Imogen

Chapter 26

Asher found his stomach churning while the doctor read his case notes on the computer screen. Even though his shoulder wasn't sore, it was tense, like the rest of him.

'It all looks fine.' The young Dr Sparks looked up with a smile. 'You're disgustingly healthy.'

'But how about the blood tests?' Asher's heart was racing.

'All completely normal.' The doctor must have noticed something unusual in his expression because a crease appeared above his brow. 'Were you expecting something different?'

Asher drew a ragged breath. Although it was more than he'd dared hoped for, his senses were trying to take in the news. He felt himself trembling deep in his core, and wondered whether the shakes were making it to his outside where they could be seen. He was too keyed up to figure out if his hands were moving or whether his quivering insides just made it look as if they were.

'Is there anything specific you wanted to talk about?'

He might as well come clean. 'A few months ago, I was told at another surgery that I had cancer that had spread to my lymph nodes. They said I probably only had a few years to live, even with chemotherapy.'

Dr Sparks' startled expression made him want to laugh.

He stepped out into the waiting room, planning the right words to tell Imogen. The news was far too significant to just blurt out. As it happened, he didn't have to speak a word. She stood and took the few steps toward him, holding out her hands.

'It's gone, hasn't it?' Imogen's chest rose and fell.

'How do you know? I haven't said a thing.'

'You don't need to.' Her trembling was plain for him to see. 'I can tell by your face. You're glowing. It's true, isn't it?'

Asher nodded and grasped her hands. 'All the blood tests were clear. I'm disgustingly healthy. Those are the words he used.'

Her face crumpled and she threw herself into his arms. Although crying had been the last thing on Asher's mind, something swelled in his throat which might have been related to tears. Even though they hadn't stepped outside the waiting room, he lifted her off her feet and spun her around. When he set her down, neither of them made a move to release the other. He lowered his head so his forehead touched hers.

'Why don't you tell us all the good news, son?' The booming voice belonged to a large man in a tank top and sandals who leaned back, grinning at them.

'He had cancer and now it's gone!' Imogen told them.

The waiting room erupted into cheers. Even the children who sat amid the toys on the floor joined the clapping.

'Give 'er a kiss,' a skinny lady demanded. 'Go on, love.'

Asher was happy to oblige. He tilted Imogen's firm chin, then kissed her softly and lovingly. On the spur of the moment, he swept her into his arms.

'The cancer started in my shoulder,' he explained to everyone. 'I wouldn't have been able to do this before.' He carried her outside, followed by more applause, and shut the sliding door with his foot. With a wonderful beam on her face, Imogen wrapped her arms around him and rested her cheek against his. It was such a short distance to the car, Asher wished he'd parked further away so he could carry her for longer.

'What is your first impression of this patient?'

Asher had returned for more blood tests, scans and examinations. He knew he didn't need them but the medical staff wanted to carry them out for their peace of mind. Now, Dr Sparks had called in a more experienced colleague, Dr Morton, who sat looking at the computer screen.

'He presents as a fit young man, and the results of these tests verify that. Why have you called me in?'

'Look at these.' Dr Sparks produced the original files which had been transferred from Asher's normal clinic. As Dr Morton perused them, his brows rose.

'I have to say I'm very surprised.'

'Surprised.' the younger doctor echoed. 'It's a miracle. It's impossible that this sort of thing can happen.'

'Are you suggesting their initial diagnosis wasn't accurate?'

'It was,' Asher put in. 'I felt every symptom. Bruising, crashing tiredness, tender glands, shortness of breath. I know I had it all.'

'Then it appears that your two sessions of chemotherapy were enough to knock this right on the head. Very unusual.'

Asher shook his head. 'I was still experiencing the symptoms long after I had them.' He knew in his heart that it wasn't the chemotherapy. And he suspected by the way Dr Sparks was leaning back, almost imperceptibly shaking his head, that he didn't buy it either.

'We'll have to put it down to one of those strange aberrations that sometimes happens,' Dr Morton said.

'What aberrations?'

'Sometimes spontaneous remissions occur that baffle everyone and have no reasonable explanation. An AIDS or hepatitis virus may inexplicably rid itself from a patient's body. In your case, it seems the cancer has gone into remission.'

'So I'm helping make medical history?'

Dr Morton appeared a tad uneasy. 'I suppose you could say that.'

'So now you can cite my case to give other people hope?'

'Er ... in a limited way.' Morton seemed to be looking to Sparks for support.

'Why limited?'

Morton seemed to wait for his younger colleague to reply.

'Cases like yours are so rare, we can't give people false hope,' Sparks said. 'They aren't called aberrations for nothing. Those cases are still far outweighed by the usual case scenario, when patients succumb to the disease and live out the predicted life expectancy.'

Asher folded his arms in front of him. 'I don't mean to sound rude, but wouldn't it make sense to follow those cases up and try to figure out if they have any common factors?' In the past, he might have launched straight into his own story whether or not they asked for it, but he had learned his lesson. 'Do you want to hear what I'm certain cured me?'

'Go ahead.' Dr Morton sounded a little wary.

He moistened his lips, wondering where to start. 'It sounded too simple for me to accept at first, but I'd been given a death sentence. I knew I had nothing to lose. I found out that there's a big difference between being simple and being easy. I thought that merely trusting in God didn't sound complex enough. That's what made it hard for me to start with, but that's what worked.'

Asher drew a breath. 'When you accept something as the truth, it doesn't do you any good if it's just theoretical. You need to let that truth shape every thought you have until you automatically reject anything different. That's how it ended up, for me.'

His words were bubbling up as they used to and alarm bells rang in his head. *Be quiet, Asher, you're talking too much.* He'd trained himself to heed that voice but this time, he chose to ignore it and spoke on as he would have done as a young boy. Both Chris and Imogen had been right. When he had something important to say, he needed to talk.

He spoke about all that happened to him, including his visits to Chris, his prayers, thank you notes, conscious turn-around of attitude and deep trust in God's good intentions for him.

'Well, it isn't everyone's cup of tea,' Dr Morton said at last, 'but all that faith business has obviously been working for you, so keep it up.'

'Maybe if I start sharing my story with other sick people, it might encourage them to take the first steps in changing their attitudes to get better too.'

'You're healthy again, and that's excellent, but there's no way of proving that your recovery was caused by all that faith stuff. We need something measurable.'

Asher longed to make his point clearer. He wanted people to grasp what he'd come to understand—that a rock solid base of truth gripped onto by unwavering faith made the building blocks for an unshakeable reality. He was only just beginning to tap into it himself.

'I'm not going to criticise the medical profession. I just want people to know that sawing up flesh and bones and pumping chemicals into us isn't necessarily the full picture.' He looked from one to the other.

'If all our patients were as strong-minded and focused as you, Asher, our work might be much easier, but they're not.' Doctor Morton's voice was firm.

Asher smiled, knowing that if Imogen was there, she'd be pleased to see him accepting the compliment. He wanted to talk to her, begin planning something new. She would help, he was sure of it. He wanted Chris on board too. He wanted to see their reactions to his thoughts. Somehow, he could explain his experience and the theory behind it to suffering people, to help usher in a world of change in which recovering from cancer and other serious illnesses was commonplace. Although there was a long road ahead of him, light shone in Asher's heart and he began to see part of what his future held unfolding before him. Ironically, it would involve a lot of talking.

Imogen and Chris would have to help convince him that his mouth was a gift and not a hindrance.

Epilogue

'He's so gorgeous.' Imogen sat with the Dorazio family around Jodie's hospital bed, gazing down at his soft, peaceful face. She'd been given the new baby to hold. His eyes were closed behind the tiniest fair eyelashes. Enchanted by the rising and falling of his breath, she didn't want to pass him on any time soon.

'I know.' Jodie looked tired, but lovelier and more luminous than ever.

'Isn't it interesting, how the world works,' Marian commented. 'Just as one person moves on to heaven, another is born to begin a new life.'

'Who's moved on to heaven?' Asher asked.

'A student from Seth's school. It's very sad.'

Asher looked up. 'Do you mean Robbie? The boy I lent those books to?'

Nodding, Seth pulled a folded piece of paper from his wallet. 'Read this. He dictated it to his mother just a day before his death. It mentions you.'

Asher took the letter and came closer to Imogen so she could read it too.

Dear Mr Dorazio,

Thank you for all you've done for me. I want you to know you were my favourite staff member at school. I looked forward to your sessions because you were different from all the teachers. I could tell that you really cared for us as people. Even though we used to joke about you, everyone likes you. I enjoyed your stories and role playing games. You had more imagination than anyone else and knew how to get us thinking the right thoughts.

Imogen glanced up at Seth. He nodded, while his throat rippled. 'It's the nicest thing a student has ever said to me.'

She went on reading.

> *Thanks for taking me to meet your brother. I hope he makes it. He looked pretty fit to me, so I think he might. Tell him thanks for the books. I was aiming to get through them all but don't think I'll make it now. I've got two and a half left. I'm disappointed not to read to the end of the series but I think I can guess what might have happened.*

She heard Asher shuffling and clearing his throat beside her. 'No, there was a big twist in the last book. I think he would've been surprised.'

> *Anyway, I hope you keep your job at our school for many, many years because you're the best. And I hope you have a great life.*
>
> Robbie Davis

As Asher carefully refolded the letter, nobody spoke.

He handed it back to Seth. 'People who've been told they're going to die always tell the truth. I've learned that through experience. There's no point lying about anything. You must be a great chaplain. He wouldn't bother dictating this letter if you didn't make a big impression.'

Seth began pacing the room. 'I wish he hadn't passed away before I received this. I could've told him that his words helped me more than he'll ever know. I was wondering whether I was in the right place. I guess I am, after all.'

'You're doing a wonderful job,' Jodie spoke up from the bed.

'Well, I guess it's my way of trying to bring a bit of light wherever I go, including the education system. We really are God's hands and feet. And I'm very aware that it's the same system new babies like Hayden here will be growing into. I want to do my bit.'

'Are you calling him Hayden?' Imogen hadn't heard the baby's name before.

Seth nodded. 'Hayden Asher Dorazio. We were intending to call him Asher these last few months but now that we know Ash here is going to live, we can't have two of 'em running around.' His voice crackled as he gave his brother a playful punch. 'Our little guy would have far too much to live up to.'

Asher pulled a face back at him.

'And the more I thought about it, the more I wanted to honour Dad's memory,' Seth added.

Asher stroked his nephew's velvety head with the back of his finger. 'Hayden's a good name.'

'We were hoping that putting the two names together might be a reconciliatory gesture.'

Asher squinted up at him. 'How do you mean?'

Seth seated himself again beside Jodie. 'Well, I know you and Dad weren't always on the best of terms. You were sad when he died, like we all were, but you never spoke about it much. That was unusual for you. You might not know this, but I think that from a few things Dad said to me, he admired you a lot.'

Asher bowed his head. 'Thanks, man. I think I stuffed it up with Dad, so maybe I'll be able to make amends with this new Hayden.'

Imogen sensed it was a good time to hand the precious baby on to him. 'Here, hold out your arms. I'm passing the parcel.'

Asher's smile lit her all through. 'Okay, young fellow. Come to your uncle.'

Jodie clasped Seth's hand and said, 'Why don't you ask Asher that other question you had?'

He shook his head. 'I'm not sure if this is the right time or place.'

Jodie smiled up at her husband, a mischievous look on her face. 'If I left it to you, I'm wondering if you'd ever find the right time or place.'

He sunk his head into his hands. 'You ask him, then.'

Jodie looked across at her brother-in-law. 'Seth was wondering whether your attitude isn't a slap in the face for Robbie's family, insinuating that his faith or his love for them wasn't strong enough to keep him alive. Isn't that a heavy load to lay on the shoulders of a terminal patient who already has enough to bear?'

Seth let out a sigh. 'You could have said we were wondering.'

'But I wasn't wondering, until you put the idea in my head.'

Gazing down at baby Hayden's face, Asher shook his head. 'There's no more shame in it than getting struck by a random bullet. Satan and sickness are formidable enemies that people have been succumbing to for years. We're not blaming people for not overcoming.' He scanned Imogen's face for her tacit agreement. 'We don't criticise tennis stars for losing a hard-fought, gallant game. Patients and their families should know that just because they've lost the battle, they're not being criticised or condemned. But I reckon we shouldn't be so cautious about not loading suffering folk with false guilt that we rip hope away from others and send them to early graves. A bad diagnosis isn't necessarily a death sentence.'

Seth was staring at him. 'You've thought long and hard about this.'

'I've had time on my hands.'

'Okay, I've got to say something.' Seth rubbed his hands through his hair. 'It's hard for me to ask questions of my younger brother. I always felt I was the one who was supposed to tell him the way things are, not seek his advice or opinions. But I suppose that's just pride on my part. Ash, after all you've been through this year, maybe I should listen to you more often.'

Asher was grinning. 'Now that I feel clueless, you want to listen to me, but you never did in the days when I thought I had all the answers. Basically, it's one of those paradoxes when what seems hard is really simple. If you decide his word is all-powerful, you take it on board, no matter what else is happening on the game board around you.' He rubbed baby Hayden's cheek. 'Maybe it's what's meant by becoming like a little child.'

His brother was still staring at him. 'I want to be more like you.'

'Hey, what?' Asher was staring at him.

'You've changed such a lot.'

Marian, who sat closest to the door of Jodie's private room, said, 'Here comes Becky. She's been very cheerful lately.'

Jodie smiled. 'Well, I suppose she has good reason. If you have a new nephew and your twin brother has just been healed of cancer...'

'There might be more to it.' Marian lowered her voice. 'I think she's met somebody.'

'You mean a guy?' Seth's voice carried enough for Becky to hear and she crinkled her nose at him as she stepped into Jodie's room.

'Are you talking about me? What's so surprising about me seeing someone?'

'Are you seeing someone, then? When can we meet him?'

'I haven't even met him yet.' She turned to her twin. 'Hey, Ash, do

217

you remember the day you were helping set up stage and those flowers came for me?' She leaned down to take baby Hayden from him. 'They were from a really nice fellow. We've spoken over the phone a few times, and on the weekend, we're going to meet for coffee.'

'Well, I hope you're sure he's okay.' Worry creases lined Seth's forehead.

Becky looked up from the baby to glare at him. 'Don't do your big brother thing on me. Why wouldn't he be?'

'Because you've never met him.'

'So? Once upon a time, you hadn't met Jodie either. What other reason do you have to think there might be something wrong with him?'

'Maybe it's because he sent flowers to you,' Asher teased.

Becky's brows pulled together. 'You're back to your usual form, aren't you?'

'Sorry.' He winked at Imogen.

'Is it definitely safe for me to respond the way I used to?'

Asher looked wary. 'Before I answer that, what are you going to…?'

Becky directed a playful kick at his shin. 'I've seen your doctor's report. It says you're fine.'

'Hey, look out for the baby,' their mother cried.

With a contented sigh, Asher wrapped his arm around Imogen's shoulders. 'This is just the way it should be. You're worried about the baby instead of being worried about me.'

Imogen didn't want the day to end. As she left the hospital, hand in hand with Asher, she looked up at him anxiously. 'We haven't told Seth, Becky or Jodie any of those things that happened five years ago with your dad. They don't know what we had to do with his death. I've been wondering if we should tell them.'

Asher shook his head. 'I dunno. Maybe we should tell 'em some day, but for now, I think they're far happier not knowing. It's not a cop-out, Imogen. I'm thinking of them. Seth didn't want to contemplate the idea of Dad being less than perfect that night when I went to tell him my suspicions. He kicked me out of his house. He wouldn't want to know how Dad behaved with you. Neither would Becky. She was always Dad's special princess. It'd just make them all upset for no purpose. Let Seth enjoy little Hayden, and let Becky get to know this new man in peace.

Don't you think? It's not as if we're keeping secrets to spite them. Maybe one day, we can change our minds.'

She felt as if he'd lifted a burden from her back. 'Yes, that makes a lot of sense.'

'Now, how about you and I head off for a hike in a really good place?'

'Where did you have in mind?'

'Waterfall Gully. It has the most awesome views.'

Imogen smiled to herself. She had another secret but kept quiet. *I'm taking his own advice. He'll be happier if I keep it to myself.* So far, Asher had taken her to all the same places she had visited with his father during those few weeks before Hayden's death, while he was showing her his favourite spots. They turned out to be Asher's too, and knowing him as well as she did, he might be aghast to realise that was the case. He liked to think he was an individual, nothing like his dad.

Imogen might have assumed she'd feel strange about it too, but to her surprise, returning to the same places with Asher turned out to be a beautiful, symbolic thing – a gracious sign of closure. With every step they took, she was stomping over the painful, regretful memories and replacing them with something new and wonderfully special.

'Sounds great.'

About Paula

Paula Vince's youth was brightened by great fiction and she's on a mission to pay it forward. Her first novel, Picking up the Pieces, was republished after being out of print for ten years and went on to win first prize in the International Book Awards. A wife and homeschooling mother, she loves to highlight the beauty of her own country in her stories.Paula's books are a skillful blend of drama and romance. Together with elements of mystery and suspense, you will keep turning pages.

Best Forgotten

Winner of the 2011 CALEB Prize. A young accident victim wakes up in hospital with no idea who he is. Why does he despise the person he used to be? Why has his best friend disappeared without a trace?

Picking up the Pieces was the winner of the International Book Awards, 2011. Dramatic and engaging.

The Risky Way Home is a heart-warming story of sheer suspense as dark family secrets are revealed.

A Design of Gold

Please visit Paula's blog,
www.justoccurred.blogspot.com

The Greenfield Legacy

Co-written with other Australian authors, Meredith Resce, Rose Dee and Amanda Vince, this is a sweeping drama across different timeframes exploring four family members whose lives are intertwined, by an unexpected event.